Barking	8724 13...		
Fanshawe	8270 4244		
Marks Gate	8270 4165	Wantz	82...
Markyate	8270 4137	Robert Jeyes	8270 4305
Rectory	8270 6233	Castle Green	8270 4166
Rush Green	8270 4304		

OVER THE SEA TO SKYE

Recent Titles by Sally Stewart from Severn House

APPOINTMENT IN VENICE
CASTLES IN SPAIN
CURLEW ISLAND
THE DAISY CHAIN
FLOODTIDE
LOST AND FOUND
MOOD INDIGO
POSTCARDS FROM A STRANGER
PROSPERO'S DAUGHTERS
A RARE BEAUTY
ROMAN SPRING
A TIME TO DANCE
TRAVELLING GIRL

OVER THE SEA TO SKYE

Sally Stewart

severn House

This first world edition published in Great Britain 2007 by
SEVERN HOUSE PUBLISHERS LTD of
9–15 High Street, Sutton, Surrey SM1 1DF.
This first world edition published in the USA 2007 by
SEVERN HOUSE PUBLISHERS INC of
595 Madison Avenue, New York, N.Y. 10022.

British Library Cataloguing in Publication Data

Stewart, Sally, 1930-
    Over the sea to Skye
    1. Skye, Island of (Scotland) - Fiction
    2. Love stories
    I. Title
    823.9'14 [F]

    ISBN-13: 978-0-7278-6469-7

Typeset by Palimpsest Book Production Ltd.,
Grangemouth, Stirlingshire, Scotland.
Printed and bound in Great Brita
MPG Books Ltd., Bodmin, Corn

One

Ottawa at the tag end of winter was just as he remembered it, and so was this room he was being shown into. The arrangement of the heavy furniture was as it had always been, and the air still smelled of leather, polish and the cigarettes that Tom Macrae had continued to smoke against his doctor's orders. The only alteration was in the man who sat behind the handsome desk; it was James Hollister now who got up from the senior partner's chair to shake his visitor's hand and stare at him longer than civility decreed.

'It's good to see you back again, Iain. How long is it since you were here – two years, more maybe?' James sat down again, still flustered by the gauntness of the brown face opposite him. He knew Iain Macrae's age, but if he'd been asked to guess, he would have said ten years older. 'We missed you at your father's funeral, but I think it was just as he'd have wanted it – simple, sincere and attended by all his friends; he had a lot of friends.'

Iain Macrae nodded. 'I heard about it from my stepmother. She was kind enough to insist it didn't matter that I hadn't got back in time.' His deep voice laid no emphasis on what he'd just said. The man facing him could make of it a woman's wish to give comfort, if he chose. James, familiar with Katherine Macrae, heard the sweet malice that would have been intended instead, and abandoned the subject of the funeral.

'You know about Tom's will, of course. There are some papers to sign, but everything's very simply arranged if you're anxious to be on your way soon.' James hesitated

for a moment, then went on: 'I don't know what you've
got in mind, but forgive an old friend for saying that you
don't look fit enough to go back to Africa. Can't someone
else struggle with its hungry millions for a while?'

His visitor smiled briefly. 'Malaria,' he admitted. '*Not*
rejuvenating! I'm getting over that, but it's harder to forget
the misery that's out there. The natural disasters are bad
enough; add to them what human beings do to each other
and you wonder why God Almighty bothered to make
Africa at all.' He wiped a hand across his face, then pushed
it into his jacket pocket in case his fingers still shook
slightly. 'I've been told to take a year off. It seems like a
good idea.'

James fiddled with the papers in front of him. 'I expect
Katherine's told you she plans to sell the house – she
wants to go back to New York. It's understandable, I
suppose. Living here for twenty years hasn't made her a
Canadian.' He abandoned the papers and looked at his
visitor instead. 'What will *you* do, Iain?'

The quiet question did no more than hint at concern for
a man whose life seemed to be remarkably empty of normal
ties and fixtures. It was all the more extraordinary in
someone who'd long been wealthy, having inherited from
his mother's family, but as far as he knew Iain Macrae
had no close companion and apparently owned nothing at
all; with his father's house sold, there wouldn't even be
a family home to link him to the city he'd been born in.
'You've got a year to fill – what will you do?' he asked
again. 'You could do worse than stay here among friends.'

His guest stood up and walked over to the window to
stare out at the street. It was a handsome view in James
Hollister's opinion; he was proud of Canada's capital city,
and couldn't imagine wanting to live anywhere else.

'Too many people, too many cars, and too many buildings shutting out the sky,' Iain finally answered, then turned
to look at his host. 'I thought of going up to the north –
the far north. I read about it in a book called *Sick Heart
River* by John Buchan, as he was then – must have gone

there himself to have written about it so well. Perhaps it's changed, but it'll still be as different as I can get from the chaotic turmoil that is Africa.'

He smiled briefly as if to say that the year ahead had been sufficiently described. 'What about those papers you wanted me to sign? I can come back at any time.'

'Come to dinner tomorrow evening and sign them then,' James suggested. 'It'll give me time to look at the atlas and discover where Sick Heart River is.' And by then, he hoped, his inventive wife would have been able to suggest a more suitable convalescence for the withdrawn and self-sufficient misfit that his old friend's son seemed to have become.

'You won't find it on any map,' Iain pointed out. 'It's an imaginary place that Buchan thought you had to go looking for.' Then his rare smile reappeared. 'The narrator of the story was a lawyer, as it happens, but I can see the idea doesn't appeal to you!' He walked towards the door, then halted there. 'I must get back to the house. I'm not staying there, but I've been given first choice of my father's books and papers.'

'Not over-generous of Katherine,' James felt obliged to say, 'if that's all she's offered you.'

'Generous enough; there's nothing else I wanted. The rest of it is what she chose herself.'

The lawyer nodded, knowing it to be true, and knowing the extent of the damage she'd done, intentionally or not, in eradicating all trace of his old friend's first wife. But fairness insisted on what he said next. 'Iain, she was good for Tom, if not for you. Her family's legal connections certainly did this firm no harm, but they weren't the reason he married her. He needed a wife again, and Katherine was elegant and clever, as well as being a born hostess. She's still all those things.'

'I'm sure she'll be a great success back in New York,' her stepson agreed gently. Then, with a wave of one thin, brown hand, he opened the door and went away.

* * *

By late afternoon the following day, he was ready to leave for the last time a house that had ceased to feel like home to him from the age of fifteen. It had mattered very much then – he could still see in his mind's eye the desperate boy who'd gone from room to room trying to pin down some remaining memory of the lovely, gentle woman who had been his mother. The truth was that the house had died with her, but he'd refused to admit it; his father's remarriage two years later had been easier to blame instead. Now, with Tom Macrae dead as well, he need never come back to it again. Unexpectedly, the thought made him feel rootless and lonely.

Katherine was in the drawing room when he went in to say goodbye. For once she seemed content to be idle, which was not her usual habit at all, and she was even lost enough in some train of thought not to notice him walk into the room. There was time to register the fact that she was still beautiful, and that the conventional mourning black she wore accentuated the fact. She'd be aware of it, of course, but for the moment her face looked sad and it suddenly seemed possible to think after all that she was more than conventionally regretting the loss of a husband much older than herself. Then, aware of being no longer alone, she lifted her head and looked at him.

'I've packed up everything I'd like to take,' he said quietly. 'There must be libraries here that would be glad to have what's left. I could see to that if you'd like me to.'

'Kind of you, but James will send someone round.' She leaned forward to poke a slipping log back into the fire, and he thought for a moment that he'd been dismissed and was being told that he was free to go. Then she found something else to say. 'When I spoke to James this morning he said that you were off the leash for a while – not before time, if I may say so; you look unwell. Some lazing in the flesh-pots would be good for you but I gather that's not your idea at all.'

Iain hesitated, tempted to simply agree with what she'd

said. But he was more curious to know how aware she was of something he'd only just discovered himself. 'I'm not sure *what* my idea is,' he finally admitted. 'Like thousands of other Canadians, I have a Scottish-sounding name and ancestors who arrived here long ago from across the ocean, but I thought that was the extent of the Macrae connection. Skimming through some of my father's papers this afternoon, I'm no longer quite so sure.'

Katherine's shoulders lifted in a little shrug. 'I suppose you saw the letter he'd received from someone in . . . in Edinburgh, I think it was. He mentioned it, but only en passant, not because it was important.'

'There were several letters,' Iain corrected her, 'one of them inviting him to go and meet the man who'd written them. His name is Thomas Hepburn. It seems that when the Macraes were thrown off Skye a hundred and fifty years ago *his* great-grandfather went no further than Edinburgh while my father's ancestors set sail for Nova Scotia.'

'Does it really matter now where they went?' Katherine enquired. 'Tom can't have had the slightest intention of accepting the invitation; he didn't even speak of it.' She sounded bored rather than irritated by the subject of his Scottish antecedents, and that in itself made him persevere.

'There was something else among the papers, a rather battered diary that had belonged to his father – William Macrae, killed in Normandy in 1944. God knows how the diary survived when he didn't, but there it still is, testifying to the fact that William was sent to train in Scotland before he landed in France. All I've read of it so far is his description of Edinburgh – which seems to have made a great impression on him – but he also traced some relatives while he was there, and made contact with them.'

Katherine suddenly remembered how the conversation had begun. 'Don't tell me you're going to make a pilgrimage of your own, with William's diary in hand?' He didn't answer for a moment, and she went on herself.

'Well, I suppose it can't be any worse than our own frozen north . . . but then again it might! We were once talked into going to a Burns Night dinner at the Caledonian Club – pseudo-tartan drapes, things called haggis and neeps to eat, and a piper making noise enough to awaken every soul in hell. I imagined that it must all be harmless make-believe, but perhaps you should consider that it might be what Scotland's really like!'

'I think I may just go and find out,' he said, surprising himself as well as her. Until that moment he hadn't known the idea was in his mind.

Now there was the problem of how to say goodbye to her, without acknowledging that they might never meet again. She'd been his father's wife for twenty years, but school and college and work abroad had meant that he needed never to try to get to know her. He'd probably been determined not to, he realized, and now in any case it was too late. While he hesitated over what to say, she – the perfect social animal, as James Hollister had said – knew just how to deal with the problem.

'At least we haven't pretended all these years, have we, Iain, so we won't begin now. I shall miss your father very much, but Ottawa not at all – New Yorkers never really change their spots! *You* don't seem to need to belong anywhere; but that's your good fortune – attachments get uncomfortably in the way sometimes. No doubt we'll keep in touch through James Hollister, but wish each other well and go our separate ways.'

As farewells went it was meagre but honest, he thought, and he couldn't 'daub it further' any more than she could. 'Enjoy being back in New York,' he said merely. 'My father would have wanted that.'

'I think so too,' she agreed, and turned away, leaving him free to leave the room.

He drove back to his club, carried in the boxes he'd filled, showered and changed for his dinner engagement with the Hollisters. He was aware of the weakness that his body still had to fight against and tried to blame it for a state of mind that seemed to hover between indifference to the rest of humanity and total despair. He spoke, as needed, to other people, probably even smiled at them because they smiled back, but all the time his mind replayed what Katherine Macrae had said; he'd become a man without attachments, even though all his adult strength and intelligence had been devoted to staving off the misery of other human beings in various parts of the world. He had colleagues around the globe, and some of them would have called themselves his friends, but that damnable word drummed in his head again – attachments were what he didn't have. His stepmother had counted it a blessing, but he knew that was wrong; it was an affliction of some kind not to need other people, not to want to care about some other human soul. It brought to mind again the sick and disenchanted hero of Buchan's book who'd found an unlikely contentment in the frozen solitude of the Canadian Arctic, and that memory wiped away the odd idea that he should go and find out what his father's correspondence had been about. That had been a momentary impulse born of Katherine's amused contempt for all things Scottish.

Later that evening, with dinner over, and their legal business settled, James Hollister realized that one object of the evening hadn't been achieved. Their guest had quietly taken charge of the conversation and somehow defeated every attempt they'd made to talk about the future. All that was left was a direct question that he might simply refuse to answer.

'Your northern trip sounds arduous, Iain, as well as lonely. Are you really well enough for it? Jean and I are worried about you – that's the truth of it. We haven't seen much of you in recent years, but that doesn't make you any less one of the family.' He sounded sincerely anxious to include the man opposite him among the numerous children and grandchildren who contributed to the Hollister tribe, and Iain acknowledged the kindness with a smile.

'It's kind of you both, but there's no need to be concerned. My stepmother rightly pointed out this afternoon that I'm a solitary animal, happiest alone!' He took a sip of the whisky James had poured for him, thinking he was about to insist that his northern journey was already neatly planned. What he heard himself mention next was the very thing he'd decided wasn't in his mind.

'I spent the afternoon looking through some of my father's papers, and discovered that he was in touch with a very distant relative in Scotland; not only that, *his* father had been there during the war and made contact with the family.'

'But Tom never knew his father,' James Hollister pointed out. 'William was killed before his child was even born.'

'I know, but William kept a diary that somehow found its way back to my grandmother. She must have given it to my father, who simply kept it with some other family records.'

'You've read it?' James asked.

'Not all of it yet, but I know that William visited Edinburgh before he was killed, and there made contact with a man called Hepburn. Presumably, somewhere along the way a marriage had joined the two families, because William seemed certain that he and the man were distant cousins.'

'Interesting, but what has it to do with you?' James asked thoughtfully. 'It happened sixty years ago.' Then he corrected himself. 'No, there's something more recent than that if Tom was involved with someone there.'

Iain nodded. 'There are several letters from a Thomas Hepburn, presumably the son of the man William met. They suggest that my father ought to go over to Edinburgh . . . that there's some family matter he should be concerned with.'

James Hollister studied his guest's face for a moment. 'And now, with Tom dead, you think you should do something about it yourself?'

Iain's answering smile was wry. 'You sound as astonished as my stepmother was – I'm the cat who likes to walk by himself! I guess I'm curious, that's all, and God knows I've nothing more urgent to do.' He was silent for a moment, then suddenly spoke again. 'It's not quite all. The truth is that I was angry for years – with my mother for dying when I loved her so much, with my father for marrying again, and with Katherine most of all. Such pointless rage it now seems, but I left it too late to tell my father so. Now, just in case he *did* plan to visit Edinburgh, I think I'll go instead.'

'Shall you tell Mr Hepburn you're coming?'

Iain gave a faint smile. 'I'll just turn up on his doorstep . . . I can always change my mind if I don't commit myself beforehand, but I'll go soon, I think.'

But even that decision had to be changed because by the following morning a bout of fever that had been threatening to return got the upper hand again. With nothing to do for a week but rest, he re-read William's diary and struggled to make head and tail of Scotland's bloody, turbulent history before he could begin to set within it the story of his own family. It made tragic reading, and taught him what he hadn't properly known before: the extent to which Scotland had fought and been damaged by its larger, southern neighbour. England clearly emerged as the villain of the piece.

At last, thinner still but now himself again, he boarded an eastbound flight – for London, not Edinburgh. It seemed right to approach Scotland by way of its old enemy, and cross the land border as English soldiers had so often done in the past.

Two

He stayed two days in London, but was glad to leave it. The city could look splendid on a fine May morning – he knew that; but under the lash of rain and bitter March winds even the parks seemed hostile.

Still clinging to the idea of the gradual approach he'd settled on before leaving Canada, he caught a morning train to Edinburgh, and found a window seat from which to inspect the depressing inner suburbs of north London. The carriage was full, except for the three seats that remained vacant in his small section, but just as the train gathered speed a young woman towed two small children along the aisle towards him. Oh God – hours ahead of their bored fretfulness, and probably incessant demands for food, and frequent visits to the lavatory. Why, in heaven's name, hadn't he taken a flight to Edinburgh?

The small girl – he guessed her to be four or five – fixed an unblinking, blue-eyed gaze on his face, presumably wondering why it looked brown when no one else's did. The boy, who looked a little older, ignored him and simply watched the unappetizing view outside with unhappy, almost adult, concentration. The woman with them glanced at him and then offered the children books to keep them amused, but the boy shook his head and the girl preferred to watch her strange fellow-passenger. Aware of the onset of yet another headache, Iain gave up trying to outstare her and closed his eyes instead.

He awoke an hour later to find the seats beside him empty. The only sign that they'd been occupied was a soft, pink scarf that had fallen on the floor. He picked it up, feeling faintly regretful – the child would probably be upset at having lost it – but there was something else bothering him too: the misery in the boy's set face. What small tragedy had overtaken him that would seem at that age not to be trivial at all? It was harder to call their mother to mind; he only remembered that her voice had been quiet when she spoke to the children, and that she'd registered his own dismayed reaction to their arrival; her glance had clearly said that only an inhuman swine failed to love anybody else's offspring.

To put the sad little trio out of his mind he concentrated on his book, and the sickening history of the Highland Clearances, in which the Macraes, like many others, had suffered so cruelly, but as the slow hours went by he gave up reading and watched the changing landscape instead. They were among the hills and valleys that had been invaded and counter-invaded innumerable times over centuries of Border warfare. Ruined abbeys and abandoned, half-demolished keeps told the story of the past vividly enough, however green and peacefully beautiful the countryside now looked. He found the hills on his map – Cheviot, Lammermuir, Moorfoot and Lowther – and the very names made up a Border ballad in themselves.

The people around him were beginning to stir, putting belongings together, getting ready for their arrival in Edinburgh, but he stayed in his seat, seeing no need to hurry. He was still there when the young woman who had been his neighbour suddenly reappeared, and when he held up the pink scarf she edged her way towards him through the crowd waiting to get off.

'It had fallen on the floor,' he explained briefly when she reached him. But something else needed to be said as well. 'I hope you didn't change your seats because of me.'

'Not at all – we decided to spend most of the journey sitting in the guard's van; the children preferred that.' There was nothing in her face to say whether she was serious or not; all he *could* see was that she was tired, and younger than he'd thought.

'Can you manage when we get into the station?' he suddenly heard himself ask. 'I could lend a hand.'

She looked surprised for a moment – the small civility hadn't been expected, he realized – then shook her head.

'It's kind of you but we're being met.' Her accent was English, so she didn't belong in Edinburgh, and her refusal was definite. 'Thanks, anyway.' Then she gave him a little nod and worked her way back through the crowd.

With the carriage emptying, he could retrieve his own luggage and head for the door. Reassembling it on the platform, he caught one more glimpse of her and the children, walking towards the station exit; but now the boy struggled to hold a large, excited dog on a lead, and it seemed to explain the journey in the guard's van. At least he could now feel a little better about that.

Not encumbered with luggage, he could have walked easily enough from Waverley Station to his hotel, but a taxi took him there in a few minutes and he discovered that his stepmother had been unduly pessimistic; the North British Hotel looked what it was – long-established and comfortable, but not oppressively Scottish. The weather was also a pleasant surprise; it was cold, which he'd come prepared for, but dry and bright; no pall of London rain, and even no sign of the dreaded 'haar', the dank sea mist that his guidebook admitted too often seeped into the city from the Forth and the North Sea.

He put aside the thought of his father's correspondent for a few hours; just for the time being he'd be any North American tourist rubbernecking his way around, getting to know what had so enchanted the young soldier who'd been his grandfather. With William's diary in his coat pocket, he set off towards the ridge that made a stunning backdrop to the city – the castle on its spiny hill, there since the beginning of time, it seemed, and looking set to remain so for ever more. From the wide esplanade in front of the castle he could look down the Royal Mile to the Palace of Holyroodhouse and the new Scottish Parliament building at its foot. He could see the glint of the sea to the north beyond the ordered pattern of the new town; and southward even glimpse, because the afternoon was so clear, the hills he'd crossed that morning. He thought he could understand what the new parliament building meant to the Scots – for bitter centuries they'd been a nation yoked to their larger neighbour, denied the right to rule themselves. They'd fought in England's wars and helped substantially to build her empire, but the laws that governed them had come from Westminster. How could they not have rebelled against that?

Surprised and faintly amused by his own indignation, Iain acknowledged to himself that William's enthusiasm for the city seemed to be catching. But inspection of the medieval wynds and alleys of the old town, and the elegant squares and crescents that lay north of Princes Street would have to wait. He was beginning to shiver in the biting wind, and the walk back to the hotel would exhaust his day's small store of energy.

But two mornings later, now confidently navigating his way about, he knocked at an elegantly transomed door in St Andrews Square and asked for his card to be given to Mr Thomas Hepburn.

'I can call again whenever he's free to see me,' he suggested to the small, grey-haired lady who inspected him for a moment, then adjusted her spectacles to read the name on the card again.

'No . . . no, step inside, Mr Macrae; I think Mr Thomas will want you not to go away; he'll be free in a wee while.'

She sounded pleasant but firm, and Iain thought it likely that Mr Thomas usually wanted whatever it occurred to her to suggest. He accepted the instruction to remove his thick jacket, and waited to be told what would happen next.

'I shall bring you a nice cup of tea,' she announced. 'You're cold – not used to our weather, I'm thinking.'

He managed not to say that Ottawa wasn't noted for its mild winters, nor that he didn't normally drink tea. In fact, when it arrived, and she'd made sure he drank it, he was glad of it and said so with a smile that she thought much improved his bony face; he was 'gey thin' and 'drumlie-looking'. Five minutes later she led him along the passage to the head of the firm.

He was greeted by a man of nearly his own height, but with a fringe of white hair surrounding a bald pate – perhaps a little older than his own father would have been? Iain wasn't sure, but Thomas Hepburn's handshake was still brisk and firm.

'I wrote to *Tom* Macrae,' he pointed out at once. 'Am I right in thinking you're his son?'

'My father died four weeks ago. I'm here in his place, although I can't tell you whether he'd have come or not; I wasn't back from Africa in time to speak to him.'

'My condolences on your loss,' the lawyer said gently. 'I'm so sorry for you . . . and a little for myself; I enjoyed the correspondence I had with your father.'

Iain's brief nod accepted the comment before he went on. 'Going through his papers of course I found your letters – did I imagine some urgent reason for wanting to see him?'

'You didn't imagine it,' Thomas confirmed, 'but I don't know where to begin. How familiar are you with the family history?'

'Until a week ago I knew very little,' Iain admitted, 'but since I couldn't set off immediately, I did some home-work. I won't pretend I've got a real grip on Scotland's history even now – it's so bloody and so damn compli-cated – but at least I know the broad outline. I also know that a hundred and fifty years ago, when my great-great-grandfather and his wife sailed for Nova Scotia, her brother – your great-grandfather – came here. And my only other fact is that when William Macrae was posted here during the war before he was killed, he somehow made contact with your father.'

'Quite right,' Thomas Hepburn said, sounding relieved at this much knowledge in his guest. 'The miracle is, of course, that your ancestors survived at all. The ships that took the emigrants to Canada and Australia were disease-ridden, leaking hulks, and the loss of life aboard them was very considerable.' He mourned the terrible past in silence for a moment, then put it aside.

'Now I must come back to the present – that's what I wrote to your father about. The story is complicated, and I must start at the end of it and work back, I'm afraid. It concerns my lifelong friend, Andrew Maitland, a school-master at the Royal High School here until he retired two years ago. Before that happened his son, Angus, married my daughter, Ailsa. She was very young – twenty at the time – but they were ideally happy together, running a sheep farm in the Cheviot Hills. It was our wedding present to them, Andrew's and mine. He said he didn't need what capital he had; his pension would more than cover the rent of a house in Skye, which is where he now lives with his spinster sister.'

Thomas halted for a moment, marshalling what to say next, while his visitor wondered if the point of a story that scarcely concerned him would ever be reached. The lawyer sensed his impatience and smiled apologetically.

'I'm coming to the crux of the matter! Andrew's croft belongs to the Church of Scotland; he and Janet live in the manse, because a minister only goes out from Broadford to conduct a service once a month. He retires quite soon and, with no chance of any replacement, the little church next door will be closed for good, but the glebe land surrounding it – that is to say, also church property – has become very valuable in real estate terms. Already a devel-oper here is preparing to bid for it, and Andrew and Janet face the prospect of being homeless.'

Iain tried to look suitably regretful. 'Worrying for them,' he agreed, 'but is *that* why you wrote to my father?'

'You see no connection, of course, but there is one. The land Andrew rents at present, and much more besides, was precisely where your ancestors and mine once lived before the evictions began. In fact your great-great grandfather was the minister who chose to leave with his flock – many

of them didn't, I'm afraid. That land should still by rights
belong to the Macraes and the Mackinnons. I hoped that
your father might agree – William Macrae certainly seemed
to share that view, according to my father.'

Iain smiled at the suggestion but thought it needed
demolishing. 'Forgive me for saying so, but William was
an impressionable young man living in emotionally-
charged times. He'd just discovered his Scottish roots and
gone slightly overboard about them.'

'Nevertheless, *your* father was interested when I wrote
to him and not, I think, just because he was too courteous a man to brush me aside,' Thomas insisted gently.
'I realize, of course, that his sad death changes things.
It was more than good of you to come yourself, but I
understand very well what you are trying not to say –
family history has no claim on *you* and why should it
indeed? I shall have to try to find some other solution
to Andrew's predicament.'

'The developer you spoke of,' Iain said, 'is it likely that
his bid will be accepted?'

'Almost certain, I should guess. The Church needs
money to keep old buildings repaired and to pension off
its old ministers; they are in no position to let sentiment
stand in the way of sound business sense.'

When had any church ever done so, Iain was tempted
to ask, but he'd no wish to offend a man who probably
paid a regular Sabbath visit to the kirk of his choice. It
was time to make a different suggestion instead. 'Your
daughter and son-in-law ought to be able to help. Is life
on a hill farm in the Cheviots so different from crofting
on Skye that your friend and his sister can't be trans-
planted?'

It seemed a reasonable enough question, but Thomas
Hepburn's face suddenly changed; the veneer of professional calmness cracked and now heartbreaking grief lay
exposed instead to the man who sat watching him.

'Of course Angus would have gone,' he managed to say,
'even though it was his dream to retire to Skye as a Gaelic

scholar, not as a crofter. But that's of no importance now –
Angus's farm is being sold and the proceeds must be put
in trust for his children, because he and Ailsa were killed
in a dreadful car accident in France three months ago. I
still can't . . . can't . . .' His voice cracked and faded into
a silence that Iain chose not to break, but at last the lawyer
spoke again himself.

'The children weren't with them – Angus and Ailsa had
only gone to look at some animals they wanted to buy.
Since then the children have been looked after by a grandmother in London, because my own wife is very unwell,
but the arrangement couldn't last. Cooped up in a small
flat and grieving for his parents, the boy especially was
like a wild bird going mad in a cage; something had to
be done. Taking him to his other grandfather in Skye
seemed to be the only hope of repairing some of the
damage, but now it's a respite he isn't likely to have for
very long.'

Iain still found nothing to say. It seemed impertinent to
even try to sympathize when a man's family had been torn
apart by tragedy to this extent. But the image in his mind
of a desolate child reminded him of someone else – the
small boy in the train, also locked in some unhappy world
of his own. He found himself wanting that child at least
to have allowed his mother to soothe whatever distress he
struggled with.

'It's not your problem, Mr Macrae,' the lawyer finally
broke the silence to say. 'We must deal with it ourselves
as best we can.' He managed a faint smile, and a polite
interest in a man who'd bothered at least to come and
explain his father's absence.

'I can see that you've been in a hotter climate than ours
recently – shall I make a guess at oil wells in the Middle
East, or military peacekeeping in some dangerous trouble
spot?'

'Nothing so exciting, I'm afraid. I work for the United
Nations agency that tries to keep Third World countries
from starving. For the past couple of years I've been in

Ethiopia and the Sudan, where things are bad enough but
would probably be a great deal worse if we weren't there;
but I'm on sick leave at the moment, which is why I was
free to come. Now that I'm here, perhaps I should take a
look at Scotland. It won't make me feel any less the Canadian
that I am, but at least I am beginning to understand Scottish
hostility to England, and sympathize with it.'

The lawyer's returning smile was rueful. 'That's kind
of you, of course, but you mustn't give us more sympathy
than we deserve! King James VI was more than happy to
go south to become James I of England, and the Scots
themselves voted for the Act of Union that moved our
parliament to London. Forbye, we haven't done altogether
badly out of the alliance, although that isn't a point of
view that any of our politicians would admit to!'

'You're more even-handed than most of the authors
I've read,' Iain commented, thinking that the lawyer was
both honest and fair. 'Are you also going to tell me
that the Highland Clearances can't be laid at England's
door?'

'English troops helped to enforce them,' Thomas Hepburn
conceded, 'and nothing excuses the brutality of what
followed Charles Edward Stewart's defeat at Culloden. But
don't underestimate the greed and cruelty of the Highland
chiefs themselves who drove their own people from the
land they wanted to fill with sheep.' Then, as the telephone
on his desk pinged, and Iain made to get up and leave, he
waved him back again and listened to what was being said
at the other end of the line. When he replaced the receiver,
he was looking so troubled again that Iain felt bound to
acknowledge that he'd noticed the fact.

'Something's bothering you, I think, so I'll apologize
for not having been any help with your other problem,
and then leave you to deal with it.'

'It's the same problem,' Thomas Hepburn decided to
admit. 'Miss Morrison has just taken a call from Louise
Maitland, the children's aunt; it's she who brought them
up from London. They should have got safely to Skye by

now except that Louise thought it best to break the journey at Fort William because wee Fiona was feeling carsick. But by this morning Jamie had disappeared with his dog, and now Louise has got the town police searching for him. They'll find him . . . of course they will . . .' the cracked voice trembled, then went on, 'but that poor girl sounded so tired and anxious, Miss Morrison said. It's difficult to leave my wife, but I think I should drive up there myself . . . just . . . just in case, you know . . .'

An unhappy boy and dog, plus a young woman and a small girl . . . surely they had to be the same sad little group that he'd seen on the train? Without stopping to think, Iain simply said the words that formed themselves in his mind.

'Look – why don't I go instead? There's a hired car waiting for me at the hotel – I need only go back and pay my bill. I've nothing else to do, and it's something I *can* help you with.'

The lawyer hesitated, thrown off balance by this fresh emergency, but half-tempted to believe that if this quiet, unknown Canadian promised to help, he could be trusted to be effective and reliable.

'I don't know . . .' he began uncertainly, 'I thought you were anxious *not* to be concerned. . . .'

There it was again, Iain realized – the impression he managed to give without even trying, of not being involved with the rest of the human race. This time he spoke more forcibly than before. 'Let me go, please – I promise I'll keep in touch. If it's a fool's errand and the child is found before I'm halfway there, so much the better all round. You can stop worrying and I'll be free to go on looking at Scotland. Now, shall we not waste any more time?'

Thomas Hepburn nodded, suddenly relieved to have made up his mind. 'Miss Morrison has the details of where Louise is in Fort William. She'll have them all ready.'

That turned out to be true, of course. His efficient handmaiden was waiting for them in her office with the information written out: Louise Maitland was at the Alexandra Hotel with Fiona, while the constabulary combed the town for a distraught boy and a large, excitable dog. Miss Morrison even had ready a map covering the route and looked faintly regretful, Iain thought, when her employer explained who it was that was going to set off; but she managed not to say that they'd have done better to send her, and smiled quite kindly at Iain when he thanked her for the map.

Half an hour later he was on the road, torn between concern for Jamie Maitland and astonishment at himself. He couldn't seriously believe that he was going to serve any useful purpose at all – either the child would be found unharmed if the Fates decided for once to be kind, or yet another tragedy would further damage an already anguished family. But it did occur to him that for the first time in his life he was involved, unprofessionally, in someone else's affairs, and that, stretching the idea about as far as it would go, he'd perhaps accepted some sort of family attachment at last.

Three

It was the first day of April, the *Scotsman*'s morning issue said; but for Louise Maitland, racked with anxiety and all too aware of the rain slashing against the hotel windows, the truth of it was sorely in doubt. Perhaps spring came late to Fort William, supposing that it came at all.

She laid the newspaper aside, and tried to smile at Fiona, sitting beside her with the hotel's large, tabby cat on her lap. Only the cat's contented purr kept her there, more or less quiescent, but after another moment or two she repeated the question she'd asked before, in a voice that now trembled on the edge of tears.

'I want Jamie to come back, Lou-Lou . . . why doesn't he?'

The urge to shout at Fiona had to be fought down, because she was already frightened enough, sensing something so wrong that even her aunt, in whose hands her care and dependence now solely lay, was frightened too. Louise forced her stiff mouth to smile again, but shook her head.

'Darling, I don't know. He'll have gone out because Macgregor wanted a walk, but I expect they're sheltering from the rain. I've asked some nice, kind men to go and look for them.'

The little girl's fingers went on stroking the cat, but she stubbornly repeated what she'd just said – as if, spoken often enough, the mantra in itself would bring her brother walking into the hotel. 'I want him to come *now*.'

Louise leaned across to kiss her flushed cheek. 'Sweetheart, so do I; but he'll be here soon.'

Dear God, she prayed silently, *please let it not be a lie . . . what bargain can I make, what promise to atone for every sin I've ever committed, if you'll only let my brother's desperate child be led back safe and sound?* But, occasional church-goer and faint believer that she was, why should her prayers be heard? The truth was that from the moment Angus and Ailsa had died three months ago, life, once so neatly under control, had become unmanageable. She was incompetent to take the place of the parents her niece and nephew had lost, and now it seemed that she couldn't even deliver them safely to a grandfather who might be able to take better care of them.

She looked at her watch for the twentieth time and decided that in another hour at the most she could wait no longer to share with her father on Skye the news that Jamie was missing. But for the moment there was nothing to do except wait and pray, and watch over Fiona who now, at least, after a disturbed night was losing her fight to stay awake. She'd just removed the cat, and lifted the child into a more comfortable position on the sofa when a maid came to call her to the telephone, promising to stay with the 'wee bairn' herself.

The policeman had little good news to report: the vicinity of the hotel, the railway and bus stations had all been searched; now his men were combing the roads leading out of the town. But they'd checked the hospitals and no child's accident had been reported – that at least was something, was it not? She agreed that it was, forced herself to thank him for ringing, and walked back to the lounge to find Fiona now being watched over by a strange man; no, not entirely strange because something familiar about him penetrated the fog of anxiety she was in.

'A maid was supposed to stay here,' she said in a low voice that nevertheless trembled with anger.

'She *was* here; I promised to take over.' The transatlantic accent chimed in Louise's memory, pinpointing for her a moment when she'd spoken to this man before.

'You had no right to do that—'

His lifted hand stopped her in mid-flight. 'Just listen, please. I was with Thomas Hepburn this morning when you spoke to Miss Morrison. He wanted to start out himself, in case you needed help, but I persuaded him to let me come instead. My name's Iain Macrae, by the way, and his people and mine meet – by various marriages, I guess – a long way back on the family tree; we had distant Mackinnon ancestors in common.'

Her pale, tired face didn't change, and for a moment he thought she was about to refuse his help – for the second time, because of course she *was* the woman he'd seen on the train. 'We've met before,' he reminded her. 'We briefly shared a compartment on the train from London.'

She nodded then, accepting what he said. 'You know about my nephew, Jamie . . . well, they haven't found him yet. The police are searching the roads now, but he could be anywhere . . .' Her voice wavered, then she got herself under control again. 'It's my fault he's run away. We stayed the night with the Hepburns, and he overheard someone there say that his great-aunt wouldn't let him keep Macgregor when we get to Skye. I don't think it's true, but my father's spinster sister does have a reputation for being very strict and fiercely house-proud. Jamie has almost given up talking since his parents died, but he was anxious enough to tell me why he didn't want to go to Skye. I thought I'd convinced him not to worry, but he remembers that his father told him they'd soon be back from France; and now he doesn't believe anything an adult says.'

'That isn't your fault,' Iain pointed out coolly. 'Where's the sense in blaming yourself?' It sounded even more dismissive than he meant it to, but he reckoned that sympathy would destroy her altogether; better to sting her into anger again than have her dissolve in tears.

'It's not *all* my fault,' she managed to agree, 'but the truth is that I'm out of my depth with these children. Some other woman – a mother, probably, though not mine – would have done better for them.'

'That's what I thought you were – their mother – when I saw you on the train.'

'You also thought we were a nuisance,' she remembered resentfully. 'What made you decide to come all this way now?'

It was a reasonable enough question; he'd asked it of himself several times during the long drive, and he still didn't know how to answer it.

'Let's say I was at a loose end,' he suggested carelessly enough to infuriate her all over again. 'Thomas Hepburn clearly wasn't, so I seemed to be the one to come.' He looked down at the still sleeping Fiona for a moment. 'You're bound to stay here, but I think I'll head for the police station; maybe they can find me something useful to do.' He lifted his hand in a casual salute and then went over to the reception desk, presumably to ask for directions to the police station.

Louise watched him go, aware that puzzlement was added to her dislike of Iain Macrae. The lack of warmth that she sensed in him was bad enough, but it was also disconcertingly at odds with what he actually did. He sounded indifferent, even downright bored, and yet he'd gone to considerable trouble for a man she supposed he scarcely knew. She was tempted to ring Thomas Hepburn and ask about him, but before Fiona began to stir there was another call that she knew she had to make instead.

With luck she'd hear her father's voice at the other end of the line – a conversation with Janet Maitland would be much more difficult. It was family knowledge that her aunt had disapproved of Andrew's marriage from the start, and time had proved her largely right. Drusilla Grant had been an enchanting English actress in a touring company at the Edinburgh Festival one year, and she'd made a sensible Scottish schoolmaster entirely lose his head; marrying her had been the only foolish thing Janet had known her brother do. Barely five years later Drusilla had fled back to London taking her infant daughter with her. She'd left four-year-old Angus in Edinburgh for his father and Janet Maitland to bring up – a division of labour that seemed only fair, she said.

Despite their parents' divorce the two children had got to know each other over the years, pleased to discover how little it mattered that one of them was as Scottish as the other was not . . . they were an Act of Union in themselves, they'd liked to claim. But brief duty visits to her father in Edinburgh hadn't really mended Louise's separation from *him*, and she was well aware that Janet Maitland would have preferred her not to go at all. Angus was the child who'd mattered, and now as far as she was concerned the wrong child was dead.

Louise forced herself to ring the Skye number and heard her father's voice, but it was still hard to explain that she was in Fort William instead of nearly on his doorstep, and even harder to explain why.

'The police will find him,' she insisted desperately, when Andrew Maitland found nothing to say at all. 'Please don't you or Aunt Janet despair; we'll have Jamie back again.'

'Maybe I should come,' Andrew suggested hoarsely. 'I could leave straightaway . . . be with you by nightfall, I think.'

'No, please stay with my aunt; she'll be upset enough as it is. The police here are doing everything they can, and a . . . a friend of the Hepburns has rushed over from Edinburgh; he's out with the police now. Stay there so that I know where to keep in touch with you.'

Her father slowly agreed, then put the question that it must have hurt him most to ask. 'Why did Jamie run away . . . do you know? He could *not* have thought that he and the bairn wouldn't be welcomed with open arms . . . Janet loves Angus's children as much as I do . . . in fact she thought they should come here as soon as . . . as they lost their parents.'

Louise heard clearly enough in this last muffled sentence what hadn't actually been said: his sister would have been quick to insist that her English sister-in-law was the last person to have the care of Angus's children, even if she hadn't lived in the den of iniquity that London was known to be.

'It's the dog, that's the problem,' Louise tried to explain. 'Jamie got it into his head that *Macgregor* wouldn't be welcome. I thought I'd convinced him that you – and . . . and Aunt Janet, too – wouldn't mind a large, exuberant mutt in the house, but he talks so little now that I didn't know what he was really thinking. What I'm sure of, though, is that he can't bear the thought of being parted from the only friend left to him.'

'Tell him . . . tell him when you find him,' Andrew corrected himself painfully, '. . . that Macgregor is expected here too; there's no question of parting them. Tell him that, Louise.'

'I will . . . I promise I will.' Then, having given him the telephone number of the hotel, she rang off, saying that Fiona was waking up and would be needing her tea, but although she agreed to drink some milk, the little girl turned her head away from buttered bread and honey. She'd even gone beyond asking questions now; with her blue eyes full of fear, she sat beside Louise, curled up in a ball, too distressed even to cry.

That was how they still were, being kept under compassionate but curious observation by members of the hotel staff, when the door opened on a gust of wind and rain and a small procession trooped in: the man she now knew as Iain Macrae, two policemen with the small figure of Jamie in his yellow sou'wester and oilskin between them, and a large bedraggled dog.

Unable to get up straightaway because her legs had turned to water, Louise sat where she was, just saying, 'Thank you, God . . . oh, thank you, thank you, *thank* you' while the strangely-assorted group walked across the hall to the sofa that she seemed to have been occupying now for at least half her life. Fiona recovered more quickly and hurled herself at the dog because, not flanked by large, strange men, he seemed more reachable than Jamie.

Louise managed to climb to her feet at last, removed

his hat, and bent down to kiss a cold, damp cheek. 'Nice to have you back,' she said unsteadily. 'It's been a long, sad day without you.' Tears now that the strain was over were ridiculous, she knew, but she had to smear them away before she could look at the policemen.

'I don't know how to thank you,' she mumbled. 'Will you tell all the officers involved that we're sorry to have been such a terrible nuisance?'

The man with a sergeant's stripes on his sleeve agreed that he would; then he bent down until he was nearly face to face with the small boy. 'We're very glad to have found you, Jamie lad, but you mustn't make a habit of running away. Our real job is to catch bad men, you know – miscreants, we call them. Will you remember that in future?'

Jamie's reddish head nodded, but the hand that clutched Macgregor's collar was trembling and, although she knew that he deserved the homily, Louise saw that he could bear no more.

'Will you let me take the children upstairs?' she asked the sergeant. 'I must ring their grandfather, and then a hot bath and bed are urgently needed, I think.' What else was required before the policemen went away she scarcely knew, and she glanced helplessly at Iain Macrae in case by any chance he knew.

His hand touched Jamie's head in a fleeting gesture surprising in itself, but even more so when Louise noticed that her nephew didn't seem to mind it. 'I'll deal with things here, and let Thomas Hepburn know as well while you see to these two,' he said calmly.

That he *could* deal with things, she didn't doubt; there was an air about him of someone used to taking charge. She wasn't in the habit of leaning on the nearest prop that offered itself, but at the moment she knew a prop was what she badly needed.

'Well, we'll say goodnight, and thank you again,' she said to the policeman, fearing that she sounded like an over-effusive guest taking leave of her hosts after a party she hadn't enjoyed. Then she looked again at Iain Macrae.

'Yes, please ring them in Edinburgh before you leave, and thank *you*, too. Crossing Scotland to help us was certainly going far beyond the call of distant family duty.'

Then she shepherded the children towards the stairs, remembering just in time that Macgregor would make an unseemly scene if invited to use the lift.

An hour later, with her call to Skye made and Fiona already fast asleep again, she went into the small adjoining room where Jamie, also in bed but still awake, was pretending to read about Mole and Badger in the Wild Wood. One hand rested on his dog's shaggy head, as if to insist on that much comfort.

'Time to turn out the light,' she said gently. 'You've had a long day. But before I say good night will you promise to tell me in future if something worries you enough to make you want to run away? Otherwise I have to try to guess what you're feeling, and I haven't had much practice at that.' He didn't answer, and she had to persist. 'You have to promise, Jamie.'

His head sketched a little nod, leaving her to hope that it was promise enough, because it was the most she could expect from him. Then, unexpectedly, he framed an accusing sentence. 'You won't be here to tell – you're going back to England.'

He named it as if it was a country immeasurably far away. His father's farm, though only just across the border, had been in England; he knew that well enough, so being taken to Skye seemed only to confirm that nothing was left of what he'd always known. Louise felt tears sting her eyes for the forlornness of a child asked to cope with adult tragedy, but she blinked them away to try to smile at him.

'I'm staying long enough to get you and Fiona settled in, and this chap, too,' she insisted, pointing at the dog. 'When I spoke to your grandfather again this afternoon he made me promise to tell you that Macgregor will be one of the family. Are you listening, Jamie love? The two of you and Fiona stay together.'

His dark eyes examined her face for a moment, then he gave another little nod, turned his head into the pillow, and suddenly went to sleep, worn out by an exhausting day.

She switched off the lamp and went back to the room next door, but her own tiredness had reached the point where, even if she got into bed herself, sleep wouldn't come. Food seemed something else she could now do without, even though she'd scarcely eaten all day. Grief for Angus and his young wife filled her heart, and anxiety for their children tormented her mind. They needed more than a gentle but absent-minded grandfather and a great-aunt whose stern puritan virtues didn't include loving kindness. Janet Maitland, not seen for two years, almost certainly hadn't changed with age. She'd take care of the children diligently enough; they'd be properly fed and freshly clothed, but what about the affection and laughter they also needed, and the comfort of being hugged and loved?

She was still wrestling with this anxiety when a tap sounded at the door. A young chambermaid stood there, come, she explained in her soft Highland voice, to ask if Miss Maitland would step downstairs for the dinner she must be needing. No need to worry about the bairns; it was arranged with the housekeeper that she was to stay with them herself.

Louise hesitated, inclined to insist that she wasn't hungry, but it seemed churlish to send the girl away, and food might combat her tiredness.

'They're all asleep – children *and* dog!' she said, smiling a little. 'But if you really can stay for half an hour I *will* go and get something to eat.'

The maid was settled in a comfortable chair, with some English magazines to look at, and then Louise quietly left the room.

The dining room was nearly full, but a waiter appeared at once to take her in tow, as if she'd been expected. The table he led her to was already occupied, and at the sight of the man getting to his feet she stopped in her tracks, reluctant to take the seat the waiter was now holding for her.

'I thought you'd left hours ago,' she said accusingly.

'But, as you see, I'm still here. Are you going to sit down or not?'

The calm enquiry sounded so indifferent either way that she was strongly tempted to refuse; even the smallest hint that her company might be welcome would have helped, but now – crowning insult – he was giving his attention to the menu instead.

He wasn't, she realized, like any other American she'd ever met – where in this sardonic, impenetrable man was the instant friendliness, the all-too-ready over friendliness, she was used to? Half-puzzled, half-resentful, she finally sat down, expecting that what he'd been hoping for was to see her walk away.

Four

S he took the menu she was being offered and decided to study it with care – the social duty of beginning a conversation she would leave to Mr Macrae.

Instead, he was now occupied in looking at her down-turned face. Marks of the day's strain and weariness were still visible, and she'd obviously gone to no pains to conceal them – vanity wasn't a high priority, it seemed. She could make no claim to beauty, he decided, because her features were too contradictory: a gentle mouth belied a very stubborn chin; wide-set eyes of a lovely and surprising grey merited more than a distinctly ordinary nose; soft well-cut hair, but a nondescript lightish-brown in colour. Yes . . . not beautiful; just so-so. Then he saw her smile at the elderly waiter as she ordered grilled salmon, and almost changed his mind.

'Children asleep?' he asked finally.

'Yes; being watched over, though, by a kind chambermaid. There wasn't time to ask this afternoon where Jamie was found.'

'He was sheltering from the rain in a byre about three miles out of town. Have you persuaded him that it's safe for the dog to be taken to Skye?'

'I think so, or at least he's prepared to give it a try,' Louise answered slowly. 'That's what we're doing by making them go there at all – giving the arrangement a try.'

'Is it really the best option those children have got – life with two elderly relatives?'

Her eyes met his squarely, with a spark of anger in them.

'Why not say what you mean . . . that I'm simply dumping responsibility for them on to other people?' He didn't deny the accusation, just waited until she went on. 'Jamie and Fiona have been in London with my mother, hating every minute of it. Leaving aside the fact that she's not accustomed to small children, and had no idea what to do with them, her elegant flat seemed like a prison to them; they're used to running wild on the Cheviot Hills. Jamie already knows more about wild animals and birds and wild flowers than I ever shall. At least on Skye with my father they won't feel shut in. It will take time, of course, but if they can only settle down at the manse their lives will at least feel secure again.'

Iain Macrae offered up silent thanks to whichever deity it was that had stopped him blurting out what she obviously didn't know. But how much longer would it be before she learned what was likely to happen to her father's home?

Louise accepted the wine that he poured for her, and, when their food had been put in front of them, decided that it was time to talk of something else. 'I thought you were going straight back to Edinburgh.'

'I've seen Edinburgh; now it's Fort William's turn,' he replied. 'I haven't decided what I'll look at next.'

'Scotland can do much better than this rain-soaked, rather miserable town,' she suggested. 'Go north before you return to America.'

'Canada,' he corrected her. 'Why do the English always assume that every North-American belongs south of the 49th Parallel?'

'I suppose because we can't tell your accents apart. But I should have guessed in your case – leaving here, your ancestors would have been more likely to settle in Nova Scotia than America.'

Now it was his turn to ask a question. 'You sound English and you live in London – why do you have connections up here?'

One fair eyebrow lifted at the blunt interrogation but she didn't refuse to answer. 'My mother *is* English; so, I like to think, am I. She and my father were divorced when I was three; I haven't lived in Scotland since then, and don't intend to do so again.'

'Very definite,' Iain Macrae commented. 'Let me guess the rest: you blame your father for the broken marriage, you dislike the Scots on principle, and think it only right and proper that they were ruled by the English for centuries, and to some extent still are.'

'While you, on the other hand, blame the English for everything that's been wrong with Scotland for centuries, and to some extent still is.' She was pleased with that, but her grey eyes sparked anger as she thought of something else. 'Don't feel too anguished on behalf of your ancestors – remember that Scots now make up a large proportion of our present cabinet – "time's whirligig" is giving them their revenge!'

He couldn't help smiling at the indignation in her voice, but risked another question that would probably provoke her still more. 'Don't bother to point out to me that it isn't my concern, but wouldn't your brother's children be better off with you . . . or can't your lifestyle be enlarged to take them in?'

The question was reasonable, he thought, but he regretted the way he'd phrased it. Her pale face looked stricken now, instead of angry, and her voice when she answered was unsteady.

'My lifestyle, as you call it, is a minute flat in central London, and a job that requires me to be out of it most of the time. Does that answer you?'

His nod agreed that it did, but, being a man who liked to be sure of his ground, all i's dotted and all t's crossed, he asked one more thing.

'What is the job? I can't guess, I'm afraid. Do you organize some important politician's life for him . . . design penthouses for the super-rich—'

'I cook,' she said flatly, interrupting him, and almost had to smile herself at the disbelieving astonishment in his face. 'I prepare food for other people to eat . . . very good food, I'm glad to say; my clients think highly of me.'

'I know what cooks do,' he pointed out. 'It just seems . . .'

'Not a very worthwhile occupation,' she finished for him. 'Well, I'm afraid we can't all be movers and shakers helping to make a not very enticing world go round.' She was damned if she'd explain to this sanctimonious Canadian that running company dining rooms for half her week enabled her to devote the other half to a dropouts' soup kitchen near Euston Station. Instead, feeling suddenly very tired, she wanted only to crawl upstairs and sleep away what remained of a dreadful, interminable day.

'I'm not going to wait for coffee,' she explained to the old waiter who now hovered beside her again, 'but the salmon was delicious – I enjoyed it very much.'

His grateful smile as he moved away thanked her for a courtesy that Iain suspected didn't often come his way; she had nice manners, did Louise Maitland. Then she got up to leave and he stood up himself as she offered him a brief handshake.

'If you *are* going to drive northward now, and it should ever stop raining, you'll see how beautiful Scotland can be . . . I'll give it that at least! Thank you again for helping this afternoon.'

And with that she walked away – a slender, elegant figure even in the sweater and trousers she'd been wearing all day. He registered the fact that some air of London sophistication still hadn't deserted her; she was out of place in a provincial Scottish hotel, and would be even more so in her father's manse on Skye.

It was tempting to think that she only wanted to hand the children over to her father and hightail it back to London. But the image that remained clearly in his mind of her controlled anguish that afternoon seemed to insist that she cared very much what happened to her brother's orphans. He remembered something else as well – the small, tear-stained face of a child under its yellow sou'wester, bleakly

accepting the fact that he couldn't put the broken pieces
of his young life together again, any more than he could
understand why the God his mother had taught him about
could have allowed it to happen.

The images were so vivid that Iain struggled to remind
himself of what was certain to be true: Hepburns and
Maitlands could work out their salvation without any help
from him. He was free now to forget about them and
become again the detached observer he'd always been.
Today's untypical interference in the affairs of strangers
was something he wouldn't repeat. Scotland, beautiful or
not, could be left unvisited; William Macrae's addiction
to Edinburgh hadn't rubbed off on him, even though he
might find it hard to forget that castle-crowned old city.
He'd fly back to Canada and admit to James Hollister that
his Caledonian journey had been brief but pointless.
Katherine Macrae had been right – a man as shrewd and
sensible as his father had been would never have contem-
plated coming at all.

The 'Eilean-a-Cheo' was living up to its name today –
such a pity, Andrew Maitland thought; he'd wanted the
misty island to be sunlit and welcoming for the children's
arrival. The only time their parents had brought them
across from England Fiona had still been a babe-in-arms,
and Jamie probably remembered almost nothing of the
visit either.

After a harsher winter than usual, snow was still lying
on the hilltops, and every wayside burn was brimful of
rushing, peat-coloured water. But spring *was* in the air.
There were rosettes of pale primroses under the hedgerows,
and every clump of ferns was hurrying to unfurl its vivid
new fronds, "Annihilating all that's made to a green thought
in a green shade". Andrew loved the imperilled Gaelic
language, but who could match the English poets when it
came to painting landscape in words?

The morning task of feeding the hens was completed
but he chose not to hurry back indoors; there was time to

stand and stare at the old grey house across the garden. It belonged there, its stone walls and slate roof speaking of a time when men used the local materials at hand instead of alien cement and garish orange tiles. Finding the manse empty and rentable, so conveniently close by the Gaelic college, Sabhal Mor Ostaig, had been a dream come true; now he had to face the threat of losing it, unable to believe that Thomas Hepburn's hint of a possible rescue plan would be enough to keep it safe. Leaving the manse would be bad enough, but his worse fear was that developers, so-called – was there ever such a misnomer as that? – would begin by knocking down what they had no use for, the simple, dignified church itself and the manse nearby.

But for the moment there were more urgent worries. He'd given Louise a promise yesterday that Jamie wouldn't be parted from his friend, and he must make good that promise, but he could foresee battles ahead. Even now Janet was indoors, polishing furniture that already shone with her incessant labours. No cushion would be out of place, no book left lying on the arm of his chair. The relentless neatness of the house no longer bothered him; he was used to it by now. But what would two children make of his sister's method of expressing love that she could show in no other way? And then there was the dog – large and exuberant, Louise had said yesterday on the telephone; how were they to fit him in?

He frowned over the memory of that conversation with her, wishing that she could stay and live with them as well. In the past he'd failed her, he knew, by allowing Janet's hostility to keep her away. Only yesterday his sister had blamed her for allowing Jamie to run away; what else was to be expected of Drusilla's probably feckless daughter! He'd chided Janet so sharply for saying it that this morning she was still looking hurt. He picked some wild daffodils – Lent lilies, she would call them – as a peace offering, and went into the house. She was in the dining room, replacing newly-washed china on the dresser shelves.

'Why not rest a wee while?' he suggested gently. 'You've been hard at work since you got up. Louise said not to expect them before late afternoon – Fiona gets carsick, so they have to keep stopping.'

'She'll not be wanting to stay long – Louise, I mean,' Janet suggested, not making a question of it. 'There's nothing here for a London-bred lassie to enjoy. Theatres and picture-houses are what she'll be used to. I doubt we'll even understand the half of what she says.'

'She speaks English, not a foreign language,' Andrew pointed out, 'and she can live without theatres if she has to. Angus used to say that she loved going to see them at the farm.'

He spoke his son's name deliberately, even though Janet now refused to mention Angus. It was even possible, he suspected, that she persuaded herself the car crash hadn't happened at all, and the children were simply coming for a visit while their parents waited for them at home. They'd lived together, he and she, all their lives except for the years of his brief marriage to Drusilla. But nothing in their upbringing had taught them to show affection to one another – kissing, clasping hands were the silly, soft habits of the southerners. The Catholics among them, those whom Janet most despised, even kissed statues and what they claimed were the relics of the saints. Unhealthy, blasphemous practices, she thought them. Hers was an unsentimental Old Testament God – judgmental and severe.

Andrew stared pityingly at her shuttered face, but forced himself to say what must be said. 'My dear, we both know that we may not be allowed to stay here, but at least we must try to be nearby, because of the school. Jamie is enrolled to start there after the Easter holiday. I've spoken to Elspeth Mackintosh, and she understands that, to begin with, he'll be needing some special care. Fiona's not quite five . . . it won't hurt to let her wait until the start of the new school year.'

He waited for Janet to answer, fearful that she might simply ask why any talk of school was needed when the

children were coming for a holiday. She adjusted the position of a plate on the dresser shelf, but her fingers were
trembling and she hid them in the pockets of her pinafore
before she turned to look at him with despair suddenly
written in her face.

'I try to pretend . . . that it's thirty years ago, and it's
Angus coming, not his orphaned children. But I know it
isn't true, and there's nothing we can do to change what's
happened. Now, instead of him it's Jamie and his sister
who'll need raising. Well, we must do the best we can for
them, and I'll not complain about the dog, Andrew. But
it will sleep in the back porch, not in the child's bedroom –
and that's my last word on the subject.' She picked up
another plate, then put it down again. 'I see you've gathered flowers that were better off left to grow in God's
earth; I'll put the poor things in water.'

She carried them out of the room, leaving him still
standing there. What difference would it have made, he
wondered, if they could have broken the habit of a life-
time and held each other and wept together for the loss
of Angus and his wife? He didn't know the answer to that,
but he'd made up his mind to two things: he would make
sure he hugged the children when they arrived, and he
would greet his English daughter with a kiss, even if Janet
was watching.

Five

Just at that moment, Louise was deciding that it was time to stop again. Fiona managed very well when the road was straight and level but, Highland travel being what it was, for much of their route it climbed and swooped and went round curves. Her pale face said that another respite was needed, with the car stationary and the window wound down to let in some cold fresh air. They'd been travelling beside a burn for some while, but soon ahead of them there waited an ideal stopping-place – a stretch of level green turf beside the road, at a point where the stream turned away to the left. Louise steered the car on to it, noticing rather anxiously that the ground felt spongier than she expected, but Fiona's face said that now wasn't the time to look for anywhere else. With the car door open Fiona began to recover, and ten minutes later Louise thought it was safe to continue their journey.

'Not very far now, we'll soon be there,' she said cheerfully to her small unhappy passengers, and turned the ignition key unaware of having tempted the gods too far.

The engine sprang into life but, instead of doing the same, the car refused to move. She tried again, and, even as she did so, knew what was happening – the spinning wheels were merely settling it further into its insidiously soft resting-place. What she'd assumed to be grass was treacherous bog instead, and they had no hope at all of moving without help. But where in the empty landscape around them was help to be found?

As calmly as she could, she explained the problem to Jamie, sitting in the back with Macgregor. He nodded as

if he'd already identified the problem too, and she remembered that cars needing to be towed out of mud slides and
snowdrifts must have been part of everyday farming life
in the Cheviot Hills. Neither child seemed greatly concerned, and that was something to be grateful for, but she
was painfully aware herself of their situation. These
were the empty Highlands, not a London street with a
garage every few hundred yards. At a busier time of the
year another passing motorist might have lent a hand, but
no other car had passed them while they'd been parked
there, and even if one came along, she was now ready to
believe that its driver would only be a frail octogenarian
lady quite unable to give them any help. She was about
to ring the hotel they'd left that morning to ask for advice
when Jamie, staring out of the rear mirror, suddenly burst
into unexpected speech.

'A car's stopped further back . . . a man's walking this
way.'

A man . . . a welcome godsend, Louise wondered, or a
fresh cause of anxiety; there was no certainty about it, and
she was there alone except for two small children for
whom she was responsible. But even as she thought about
that, Jamie's hoarse little voice sounded again and having
him speak voluntarily, without having words dragged out
of him, constituted a sort of miracle in itself.

'It's the yesterday man . . . you know, Louise.'

Yes, now seeing in her driving mirror who it was that
came towards them, indeed she *did* know. Her fear of a
moment ago could safely vanish, but there was equally no
doubt that the malicious gods above were determined to
amuse themselves at her expense.

She wound down her window as he reached the car,
and spoke first. 'No merry quip about women drivers,
please – I don't think I could bear it at the moment.'

His mouth twitched, but he answered in the detached,
almost indifferent way that she was now familiar with.
'Well, at least you didn't make matters worse by revving
the engine and spinning the wheels.'

A hint of concern, of sympathy, would have been nice, she thought, and it was tempting to tell him so, but she remembered that she must try to sound grateful instead. 'We're rather pleased to see you, of course, but how do you happen to be here?'

'Go north you said; that's what I did, but there wasn't a lot of choice. If there's another road to take in that direction, I didn't find it.'

It was a reasonable enough explanation given the scarcity of Highland roads, and he saw no point in telling her the whole truth yet – that he'd been following at a discreet distance from the moment she left the hotel in Fort William. Even now he couldn't have explained to anyone else why it had suddenly seemed necessary, watching them leave, not to let them go alone. He'd been meaning to drive straight back to Edinburgh; dammit, it had been clear in his mind . . . until he saw them walk out of the hotel and get into a not very reliable-looking car. Ready to leave himself, he'd simply waited until they were on the road and then fallen into line behind them.

Now, looking at the strained faces of the children, he supposed he knew why he was there. Jamie was a younger version of the boy he'd been himself and his own desolation still hadn't healed after more than twenty years. At least he could see these two safely to whatever comfort their grandfather could give them.

He shook the thought away at last, unaware of the long pause, but there'd been time for Louise to look more closely at him, and consider whether he should be helping them or not. Sunbrowned skin gave the illusion of health, but an illusion was surely all it was. The bones of his face were almost painfully prominent, and either he'd just recovered from some serious illness, or he wasn't even recovered yet. She was about to suggest that she should phone for help when Jamie – for the moment still released from silence by a technical problem he could understand – offered advice from the back.

'We need a rope . . . do you have one in your car?'

Iain Macrae's expression changed as he looked at the small boy, and a smile Louise hadn't seen before made his harsh face pleasant. 'As it happens, I do . . . experience has taught me never to set out on a journey without one. You'd better all stay where you are, you'll sink into the bog out here. I'll only be a moment or two.'

He walked back to his own car, and drove it past them, careful to park on the hard surface of the road. From the car's boot he took out a tow rope and a pair of boots – sensibly enough, Louise realized, remembering the soggy ground he would have to wade into. The rope was attached to the towing ring at back of his car, and he was unrolling it towards the ring in the front of hers when – sod's law, she thought, now that they needed no one else – another car finally appeared on the road. A Land Rover jolted to a sudden halt twenty yards ahead of them, and a large man jumped down, and then a fair-haired girl.

'G'day . . . d'you need any help? I can see the lady here's gone and got herself well and truly stuck!' The Australian accent and a broad grin that prompted an answering smile from Iain Macrae, combined to try Louise's overstretched nerves too far.

'Colonial old-home week?' she asked sweetly. 'No, let me guess, *your* great-granny was a Mackinnon too!'

She knew in the small uncomfortable silence that followed that an apology was required, but Iain Macrae answered for her before she could put it into words. 'The *lady's* not usually so rude, but it's been a trying day! Thanks for stopping, but we can manage very well.'

The Australian's blonde companion had now arrived as well, looking so relieved to hear a transatlantic accent she could understand that Louise made a guess at Glasgow as their Scottish landfall, where communication with its inhabitants would have been difficult bordering on the impossible.

'If you're touring Scotland I'm afraid you're a bit early to see it at its best,' she now suggested, ashamed of her previous rudeness, 'but at least the roads are emptier than they'll be in the summer.'

'We've been in Edinburgh,' the girl said, correcting Louise's guess. 'I wanted to stay – that's a really nice place. But Brett here –' she shot him a resentful look that spoke of some earlier disagreement – 'can't wait to get to Skye. His people came from there, but I tell him there'll be nothing to see except hills and sheep, and we see enough sheep at home.'

'Well, they'll figure in the scenery, certainly,' Louise had to agree, 'but you may not see much of *them* unless the weather improves! Still, you can't come all this way and not see Skye – it's a special place, not quite like anywhere else, even though the bridge does spoil things a bit.' If she could have been sure that Janet Maitland would be welcoming, she'd have asked them to call at the manse; as it was, aware that the time was passing, she glanced at the Canadian, to remind him that she still couldn't drive away.

He took the hint, shook hands with Brett and his companion, and in a firm but friendly way insisted that they must get on with their journey. Then, when the Land Rover had been driven off, he finished attaching the tow rope to Louise's car. Ten minutes later it was on terra firma again, and the success of the manoeuvre even brought a brief smile to Jamie's face. It was a man-thing not shared by her own sex, she supposed, this pleasure in mechanical achievement.

With the rope re-coiled and stowed away, he walked back to her car. 'We should be at the bridge in less than an hour,' he said. 'Would you rather lead or follow?'

She was about to query what he'd just asked, then realized how stupid that would be – where else could he go except to the bridge, when that was where their road went next? After that he'd strike off to the north while they crossed the narrow strait that separated the island from the mainland.

'You go first,' she answered. 'I might need to stop again, but at least I shall now know a bog when I see one.' She held out her hand, and smiled at him suddenly with genuine gratitude. 'Thanks for what you've done. Enjoy the rest of your journey, and if you end it back in Edinburgh and see Thomas Hepburn again, perhaps you could reassure him about us; he seemed anxious when we left.'

With reason, Iain thought, when he must be wondering how long it would be before Andrew Maitland had to transplant his sister and the children somewhere else. The rain had cleared away at last, and the soft afternoon light showed him the tiredness in her face. She was tiresomely opinionated and too sharp of tongue but he couldn't help an inward salute to her brave spirit. Her own life had been turned upside down, but he realized that he hadn't heard her complain. Beside her, Fiona clutched a shabby teddy bear for comfort and, in the back seat, Jamie gently stroked his dog's rough coat. The two of them, distressed and uprooted though they were, came nowhere near matching in hardship the droves of African children he'd had to try to save from starvation and death. They'd been enough to break anyone's heart, and only the protective skin of detachment that he and his colleagues had grown had made their job bearable at all. He'd have to recover that vital, saving approach to suffering . . . but not just yet. For the moment, *pace* Katherine Macrae, he'd found a small but real attachment – to these two children that Angus and Ailsa Maitland had had to leave behind.

Unaware of having kept Louise waiting for an answer, he finally spoke again. 'I shan't see Thomas Hepburn just yet – I'm still coming along with you; so on second thoughts you'd better lead – I don't know where your father lives.'

Her grey eyes examined his face before she spoke. 'If you're thinking of coming to Skye on *our* account, please don't. There's no need, unless of course you're intent on making me feel entirely incompetent.' She was angry, he thought, but heroically determined to remember that a moment ago she'd been grateful for his help.

His hand brushed her suggestion aside. 'Let's just say that I agree with what you told those two Australians – why come this far and not see where my ancestors hailed from? At the same time, I might as well escort the children to their grandfather's door.'

If he expected her to take instant exception to that as well, he was disappointed because fleeting amusement suddenly touched her face instead. 'Escort us that far if you must, but don't expect to get any further! My aunt is a very presbyterian spinster lady who is always deeply suspicious of the opposite sex, but you would have the added handicap of being thought an American! She disapproves of many things, but Coca-Cola, capitalism, and the entire output of the Hollywood film industry come pretty high on the list.'

'She needn't even know I'm there,' he promised. 'Now, we've been here quite long enough, I think. Shall we get started?'

His sudden desire to become acquainted with his family's long-ago starting-point was merely an excuse, she thought, to conceal his true reason for coming with them. He reckoned that she was a city-bred fool, unable to cope in the wilder places where life was real and life was earnest. It was irritating that, on present showing, she almost felt bound to agree with him.

'I don't know the island any more than you do,' she confessed resignedly. 'But once across the bridge, we take the road to Broadford, where we turn left and follow it all the way down towards Armadale. If the map doesn't lie there *is* only the one main road, so even I can't get lost.'

'It's a pity about the bridge,' he said unexpectedly, and then walked away to his own car.

She turned her attention back to the children – who'd listened to that conversation, she felt sure, but perhaps not understood much of it. 'Not much further now,' she promised cheerfully, 'but our kind friend Mr Macrae is going to make sure we get home safely.' Then she put the car in gear to set them moving forward again.

It was essential to concentrate on the job in hand – pride insisted that she make no more mistakes. But perhaps when

they'd reached the manse and the children were safely
installed, she might try to work out answers to the two
questions in her mind: why had this baffling, almost hostile,
Canadian insisted on involving himself in their disturbed
lives? He could have no understandable concern for two
unknown children, and he had certainly – she was experienced enough to be sure of this – no interest in herself.
Her second question was more trivial but even more
intriguing. He disapproved of the road bridge, and she
agreed with him about that . . . 'Speed bonny boat like a
bird on the wing, over the sea to Skye' *was* the only right
approach to the misty island. But did that mean that the
inhumanly detached and coldly helpful Iain Macrae wasn't
what he seemed, but a genuine romantic after all? Almost
certainly not, but she rather regretted that they would part
company without her solving the puzzle. She didn't like
the people she met, even the ones she found uncongenial,
to remain as inscrutable as the smile on the face of the
Sphinx.

Then, as she put the conundrum aside, still another question occurred to her: he hadn't even thought it worth
mentioning what had brought him to Scotland in the first
place. Presumably Thomas Hepburn at least knew the
answer to this; but it would have to wait until she was
able to drive back to Edinburgh and return the car he'd
arranged for her to borrow. She settled down now to driving
as well as she could, wryly aware from glances in her
mirror that Jamie, as doubtful about her as the Canadian
was, kept an eye on the car behind, to make sure that 'the
yesterday man' was indeed still following them.

Six

Careful study of the map before leaving Fort William had told Louise what to look out for. Even she couldn't miss the Five Sisters of Kintail – with shawls of snow about their shoulders still – towering over the road through Glen Shiel. Soon, now, they'd be at Dornie bridge, where the blue waters of Loch Duich merged with Loch Alsh – almost the end of their mainland journey. She'd found it something of an ordeal in the sort of weather conditions they'd had until now. Cloud-wrapped mountains, bare hills, and rain-lashed lochs had struck her as majestic but overpowering – what Dr Johnson on his tour of Scotland had pronounced 'a most dolorous country' – and she'd been made to feel woefully inadequate and out of place. In any case, London was her natural habitat, not this empty awe-inspiring land. But for the moment at least, sunlight, the magician, was painting it in colours no artist's palette could properly reproduce, and she wondered what Iain Macrae was making of it. Canada must offer magnitude and space that a small country couldn't match, but taken mile for mile could it be more beautiful than what they drove through now? Each loch a pool of sapphire blue, fringed with the bright young green of birch trees coming into leaf, and above them the cinnamon-brown hills still crowned with glistening caps of snow.

The pity of it was that the children scarcely looked out of the car windows now. She knew that they were tired of travelling, but it wouldn't help to insist that they were nearly home. Skye wouldn't be home to them any more than this breathtaking mountain land was. Unhappy as they'd been in London, Louise thought they'd choose to go back there at once if she suddenly offered them that option instead.

As they approached Dornie bridge she pointed out the famously romantic-looking castle of Eilean Donan on its spit of land by the loch-side, but they gazed at it without interest until Jamie spotted something that did seem worth a second glance.

'Look, Fee . . . the Land Rover's there that we saw this morning . . . when we got stuck in the bog.'

Fiona looked as bidden, but then went back to stroking her teddy bear's worn ears. The feel of his fur under her fingers was familiar; nothing else was except for Lou-Lou, sitting beside her, but Jamie had said that even she was soon going to go away and leave them behind.

Louise glanced down anxiously at her small niece. It wasn't imagination, she thought; unhappiness combined with fatigue and reluctance to eat seemed to have made Fiona physically shrink; she looked definitely smaller than when they'd started out. But by God's mercy, after hours of driving through an empty landscape, at least they'd arrived at a place that boasted an hotel.

'I think we'll stop here for some lunch,' she suggested gently. 'Breakfast was hours ago, and it'll be a while yet before we reach grandfather's house.'

The only response was Jamie's gruff little voice explaining to Macgregor that he could soon be let out of the car as well, so she took agreement for granted and turned off the road into the hamlet of Dornie. Five minutes later, disentangling children and dog from the car, she saw Iain Macrae pulling up beside them.

'You forgot to mention you were going to stop,' he commented. 'I can't believe you were trying to shake me off.'

She let that go, determined not to confess that the drive had in fact been easier for knowing that he was following behind.

'A break seemed to be needed,' she explained instead,

pointing to where Macgregor was happily relieving himself against the signpost pointing to the hotel entrance. 'But you mustn't let us keep you if you can't spare the time it will take for us to visit a loo and eat a sandwich.'

It was his turn to ignore a rhetorical question. He merely took out of her hand the leash she was holding, and spoke to Jamie. 'We'll wait for Macgregor shall we, and then find Fiona and your aunt inside the hotel?'

Louise saw the little nod that answered him, and realized that her own small hesitation about him wasn't shared by Jamie. At whatever level trust operated between a child and a scarcely known adult, something in Iain Macrae had found acceptance in her withdrawn and uncommunicative nephew. Perhaps it was simply male authority, painfully lost with the death of his father, but still familiar and recognized.

She led Fiona to the hotel cloakroom, and they emerged ten minutes later into the lounge to find that two more customers had arrived. Jamie had identified the Land Rover parked at the castle correctly because the newcomers were the Australians met earlier in the day. They introduced themselves – Ellie Moffat and Brett Macdonald, and Louise obligingly supplied the comment that Brett seemed to expect.

'It's a name to conjure with on Skye, if that *is* where you're going,' she suggested with a smile.

But his pleasant, blunt-featured face looked unexpectedly serious. 'Will I be run out of town? I've done some homework – I know what happened there; why should anyone like a Macdonald?'

'It was a long time ago; I think you'll be all right,' she said consideringly. 'Anyway the present Lord MacDonald still manages to live on the island, with his wife –' she shot a speaking glance at Iain Macrae – 'who happens to be a celebrated cook!'

'His Lordship's no relation as far as I know,' said Brett, 'though I suppose there might have been some sort of connection before my ancestors upped and went.'

Ellie, not interested in the past and proud in any case

to be a republican, thought it was time to change the subject of conversation. Smiling at Iain Macrae – and smiling she was very pretty indeed, Louise noticed – she pointed at Macgregor.

'Your dog's the funniest-looking animal I ever saw,' she said. 'What *is* it, for heaven's sake?'

For once Jamie was propelled by indignation into immediate speech. 'He's *my* dog,' he corrected her fiercely, 'and he's not funny at all . . . in fact he's very special . . . a crossbreed Border Collie.'

It had the merit of being true, Louise reflected, but it was also true that there *was* something comical about a dog whose nose was blunt when it should have been pointed, and whose coat suggested that his mother had mated with a large and very curly poodle. Still, the hurt in Jamie's face couldn't be smiled away, but even as she tried to think what to say, Iain Macrae came to the rescue.

'Jamie's right – you won't meet another dog like Macgregor; he's a very rare breed indeed.'

It was said gravely enough for Ellie to suspect that she was being teased. This treatment from an attractive man she was prepared not to mind; what she did object to was the frosty look from the woman he seemed to be travelling with. What's more, Louise Maitland's cool English manners were already being passed on to two unfriendly children. Not much interested in their dog, Ellie was much more concerned to know why they were travelling with the Canadian at all.

Louise was warned by the speculation in the Australian woman's face and spoke herself before it could be put into words. 'Excuse us if we head for the dining room; we need a quick sandwich before we get on the road again.'

As soon as she'd led the children away Ellie smiled at Iain Macrae, 'OK. . . OK . . . I said the wrong thing about . . . whatever his name is.'

'Love me, love my dog – it's an English thing,' Brett pointed out. 'You haven't got the hang of it yet; I keep telling you they're different from us.'

'Well, don't let it worry you,' Iain recommended. '*None* of the rest of us have got the hang of the English either. But I have got time to buy you both a drink – something non-alcoholic maybe while you're having to cope with Scottish roads?'

They opted for beer and lemonade mixed, and when he came back with it Brett got in first with the question he knew Ellie was now trying to frame in a way that might be considered tactful.

'We're just seeing Scotland, but we haven't figured out what the rest of you are doing here – none of our business, we know, but that's how Australians are: when they're curious, they ask!'

Iain took a sip from his glass while he decided how much information to give. 'Louise Maitland is delivering the children to Skye – to stay with their grandfather,' he explained. 'I'm only keeping an eye on them en route because a mutual friend in Edinburgh asked me to, and I could combine it with a visit to Skye where my distant ancestors came from.'

Ellie smiled, glad to know that her instincts had been right. She'd felt sure that there was nothing between him and the Maitland woman – no rapport, no chemistry; and she was never wrong about such things. But now, with the bridge across to Skye not far ahead of them, she reckoned that the English family could be left to look after themselves while she and Brett settled down to getting properly acquainted with the Canadian. He was very pleasant, and he was attractive in a haggard, worn sort of way that made him more interesting than the men she usually came across. Brett was better than most, and her very good mate besides, but where was the enticing mystery about someone you'd known since you were knee-high to a grasshopper?

They were comparing notes on Edinburgh when a waitress came towards them from the dining room to speak to Iain Macrae.

'The lady iss leaving by the other door, sir. She says

for you not to hurry away . . . she and the bairns can manage fine on their own now.'

He thanked the girl, but stood up as soon as she'd gone away. 'Never leave a job half-done, don't they say? But I'll have to catch Louise Maitland up because I don't know where she's making for on Skye.' He offered them a quick handshake and was gone, leaving Ellie staring at Brett.

'I still can't make them out,' she said resentfully. 'It's not as if the woman could even lose her way; there's only one road to follow when all's said and done.'

'No, but *something*'s wrong,' Brett insisted. 'You were too busy staring at Macrae to notice, but the children looked unhappy.'

'OK . . . so they don't like their grandfather maybe . . . in which case Louise Maitland would do better to take them home again. I suppose she's got some selfish reason of her own for dumping them up here.'

Brett didn't repeat his jibe about Iain Macrae; Ellie wasn't normally spiteful about other women, being sensible enough to know that it put men off more quickly than anything else. The fact was that she wasn't herself at the moment – half-missing her home after months away in Europe, but more than half-reluctant to go back. Once there, with the great escapade over, she'd be expected to settle down, and he knew that her bright, adventurous spirit could scarcely bear the thought of it. She loved the colour and variety and pace of life in big cities, but he'd come over himself as a reminder that it was time to go back to the monotony and isolation of an outback sheep station.

'Ellie love, you're cross with me, not Louise Maitland,' he said gently. 'You reckon we're wasting precious time up here. Maybe we are, but going to Skye is something I need to do, even though I can't properly tell you why.'

His face, too familiar to be exciting, was full of kindness as usual, but she'd begun to notice something different about him since they'd embarked on this drive across Scotland. He stared at the mountains mirrored in their

quiet blue lochs as if he recognized them . . . no, rediscovered them, as he'd rediscovered that castle they'd
walked around this morning. It was an uncomfortable idea
because it suddenly made him *not* familiar at all, and she
wasn't quite prepared for that.

'We'll see Skye,' she agreed finally, 'and you'll find
that it's just an ordinary itsy-bitsy little island . . . nothing
special about it to haunt your imagination, if that's what
it is doing. But first I'd like something to eat, please, if
you can wait that long – I'm starving!'

But he lingered for a moment looking at her intently.
'Still friends?'

She nodded, then smiled her quick, sweet smile, and he
reckoned that the path long since marked out for them
was the right one: they'd go home and marry and take
their place in the family procession, just as her people and
his expected them to. Nothing need interfere with a plan
that everybody agreed was exactly as it should be.

But first he was going to Skye.

After the brief stop at the hotel there seemed to Louise
now to be more traffic on the road. Instead of the familiar
dark blue car that had been shadowing them this morning
there were several other cars and even a lorry or two.
Disappointed in his new friend, Jamie gave up looking
out of the rear window and sat hunched up instead, the
picture of numb despair. Fiona, with less awareness of
apprehension than her brother, soon dozed off to sleep.

Not sure whether he was listening or not, but anxious
to keep talking to him, Louise spoke about the bridge that
now linked Skye to the mainland. 'Not long ago we'd
have had to drive the car on to a little ferry to cross the
strait,' she explained. 'More fun then, and the proper way
to approach an island, I can't help thinking; but it wasn't
always easy, because the tidal current is very strong. Pity
the poor cattle that used to be swum across at slack water
just a mile or two further south, roped together at the end
of a boat's line!'

In the driving mirror she watched his face reflect a slight interest for a moment or two.

'What happened to the beasts when they got to dry land?'

'They were driven a long way south to a great market called the Falkland Tryst, that took place every year, and then they probably went on to farms in England. The black cattle of Skye were greatly prized.'

But his little spark of interest died because now they were crossing the water themselves and his white face looked sullen with fear again. His small tense body was an eloquent but silent plea to wake up from the nightmare he was in, to find himself at home with his parents, loved and secure again.

'I need you to help me look out for things,' she said gently. 'On our way down the Sleat peninsular there'll be a little lighthouse on our left, at Isle Ornsay; then before we get to Grandpa's house we must pass a church – a kirk, it's called up here. First, we'll be on the road to Broadford, but we'll soon turn off to the left, and go south-wards to the manse where he and Aunt Janet live.'

'I thought Mr Macrae was coming,' Jamie suddenly decided to say. 'Why isn't he behind us any more?'

'He probably thought we could manage on our own; he didn't really intend to come to Skye at all,' she pointed out. She wasn't hurt that he'd taken her at her word, she told herself firmly, just surprised; she'd had him down as more stubborn than that.

They passed the lighthouse on its little spit of land that only became an island at high tide; they passed the sign-posted road that led to Kinloch Lodge, where the present Lord MacDonald now lived, and finally they passed the grey, dignified building that was Kilchrist Church. A hundred yards further on a sign on the grass verge pointing up a drive was marked simply 'The Manse'.

Louise turned the car in to it, and stopped for a moment – thankful to have arrived, but aware of feeling tired to the marrow of her bones and needing to recover for a moment or two before having to face whatever might come next.

Then she saw another car driving slowly past the entrance to the drive – a familiar dark blue car, whose driver gave a little wave and an ironic toot on the horn as he went by. Iain Macrae *had* been somewhere behind them after all, but apparently didn't reckon it worth the bother of stopping to say goodbye. He'd done exactly what he said he'd do – see them safely home – and he could report as much to Thomas Hepburn. But she was glad that Jamie hadn't noticed his friend drive straight past; that would have been one more hurt for him to bear.

Seven

The short drive led between tall banks of rhododendrons just coming into pale-mauve and crimson flower. Beneath them cream narcissi nodded in the breeze, not tidily planted but seeming to grow wherever they pleased, and the garden beyond had the same air of being only haphazardly cared for: the lawn was shaggy, and surrounded by shrubs that even to Louise's inexpert eye looked in serious need of pruning. But, such as it was, natural and not manicured, it seemed to suit the old grey house in front of her.

The manse door opened as she looked at it and her father walked down the steps. Not seen since their visits had coincided at Angus's farm two years earlier, she thought he looked older than she remembered, but his smile was full of sweetness for the children, and she could even believe that she was welcome, too.

'It's lovely to see you all,' he said simply as he opened the car door, 'and the sun is shining for you as I hoped it would.'

Louise urged the reluctant children out of the car to greet their grandfather but forgot in the confusion of the moment to warn Jamie to keep a tight hold of Macgregor. He leapt out, of course, delighted to be free again, and made unerringly for the far end of the lawn where Andrew Maitland's unsuspecting hens pottered in the sunshine.

As an arrival it was even worse than she had feared – Jamie mute, Fiona rebellious, and Macgregor joyfully on the way to savaging her father's livestock. Her call to the dog had no effect at all, but when she told Jamie to run after him, he shook his head.

'He won't hurt them – he knows not to; he's just . . . just herding them.'

At this pregnant moment Janet Maitland walked out of the house – all that was needed, her niece reckoned, to make the scene complete. But she lifted Fiona up to be given a peck on the cheek, got the same treatment herself, and then discovered that Jamie had finally gone to retrieve his dog.

They came back together, Macgregor prancing jauntily, pleased to have tidied the hens into a frightened huddle they didn't dare move away from. But even Jamie realized that something had to be said, and, bravely, he chose his great-aunt to say it to.

'Macgregor hasn't quite got out of being a puppy yet,' he suggested in bold but hopeless defence of an animal who already stood three feet high.

'He's very large for a puppy,' Janet Maitland pointed out unanswerably.

'Yes, but not growing any more . . . he's . . . he's just the right size now.' It was a plea for charity that even she couldn't resist.

'Well, we'll get used to each other, I dare say. Come in now . . . it's hours ago that we expected you.'

This, at least, Louise thought she could take the blame for. 'My fault, Aunt Janet. We're late because I parked the car on a bog this morning and someone else had to come along and tow us back on to the road again.'

She looked at her father, silently asking that the previous day's events shouldn't be mentioned at all. Gratefully, she saw him hold out his hands to the children.

'The hens have laid lovely brown eggs for your tea, but first we'll show you what's what indoors.' Then he glanced pointedly at his sister. 'Shall we go in by the back porch? Macgregor can investigate that while you take Louise and the children upstairs.'

It was a larger house than it appeared from the outside, and Louise commented on the fact when they were led up to the dormer-windowed attic floor. Three small rooms up there were even blessed with a tiny bathroom that didn't have to be shared with the two larger bedrooms on the floor below.

'The ministers a hundred years ago were expected to have large families,' Janet Maitland briefly explained. 'We asked permission to change one of the rooms into a bathroom . . .' Her voice tailed off, unable to say that it had been done for when Angus and Ailsa brought the children to stay, so she merely opened doors and announced where they were to sleep.

The rooms were simply furnished, bare of ornaments or any pictures on the walls, but Janet Maitland's effort for them had gone instead into the snowy bedlinen and counterpanes, and the dark gleam of beeswax on old wood. And bleakness was redeemed in any case by the view from the small windows. The house was positioned at an angle, looking down the shining stretch of water that was the Sound of Sleat. Facing them across it on the mainland were the majestic Knoydart Mountains, still snowcapped against a delicate blue spring sky.

'Lovely!' Louise exclaimed involuntarily '. . . what a view to wake up to.'

'It's well enough,' her aunt conceded, 'though sometimes a deal wilder than it's looking now. You'll be wanting to unpack the trunk that's waiting for you downstairs – the carter brought it yesterday.'

'The children's books and toys are in it,' Louise explained. 'I knew we couldn't manage everything on the train, or get it in the car Mr Hepburn was kind enough to lend me.' She looked at her aunt's face and saw there more than the plain features and severe expression that she remembered; Janet Maitland looked old and tired now, but perhaps it was with the effort required to conceal grief.

'We're making a lot of extra work for you,' Louise said gently. 'You must let me help while I'm here.'

The offer was a mistake, it seemed; her aunt's refusal came at once. 'You mean it kindly, I'm sure, but we're used to good, simple food here . . . not the sort of dishes you cook.'

Louise smiled faintly. 'Then I'll save my breath to cool my porridge, Aunt Janet! The trunk can wait until tomorrow, and I'll unpack our suitcases when the children have had their tea.' It wasn't clear whether she was expected to eat tea as well, but she was damned if she would, even though it meant going supperless to bed. 'We'll be down as soon as the children have washed their hands.'

Janet Maitland stared at her for a moment, then nodded and walked away, and it seemed to Louise a small but important victory. Nothing had changed, she still wasn't forgiven for being Drusilla's daughter; but at least, now, she met Janet Maitland on more equal terms than in the past.

Downstairs again, she registered that what her aunt *was* prepared to do she did with all her mind and heart. The table bore witness to that: delicious home-baked bread to go with eggs as speckled and brown as eggs should be, and tiny cakes iced in different colours. It wasn't an easy meal, because Jamie merely answered when spoken to, and Fiona as usual followed her brother's lead. But they ate the good food, and even that seemed a kind of progress.

Louise drank the tea she was offered and, since nothing else was, it seemed safe to assume that an evening meal – however 'simple' – would be shared with her father and aunt. With tea over, she suggested unpacking the luggage they'd brought with them, but Jamie was moved to insist that Macgregor first needed a walk. He didn't smile when Andrew Maitland offered to go too, but a nod of his small head at least accepted the arrangement. There would inevitably follow, of course, the vexed question of where Macgregor was to spend the night, but this turned out to be a needless worry. Jamie had already taken note of the basket and dog bowl in the back lobby, and made no fuss; there were some battles that couldn't be fought, and he was perfectly aware that his dog was only there at all on sufferance.

It took time to unpack their suitcases and transfer the

contents to drawers and cupboards – Fiona, especially, having strong but frequently changing views about how her clothes should be bestowed. By the time the job was complete and both children had been overseen to bath and bed, they were already half-asleep, and Louise herself would have been glad to forego the rest of the evening.

But, downstairs, she was agreeably surprised to see wine on the supper-table. Her aunt refused it – on principle, Louise suspected – and, once grace had been said, served the food in disapproving silence. The fish pie was perfectly edible but would have been improved by a few herbs, a hint of garlic, and a dash of cream – things she probably considered sinful luxuries, like the Chardonnay her brother and niece were sipping.

Clinging to the belief that conversation was also part of a civilized meal, Louise spoke of the brief stopover that she and the children had made in Edinburgh and it prompted her father to ask about Thomas Hepburn's friend who'd been so kind as to go all the way to Fort William for them.

'He's a Canadian by the name of Iain Macrae,' she had to explain. 'I didn't discover why he happened to be in Edinburgh, but there's some very distant family connection between them.'

'The connection will be the Mackinnons,' Janet Maitland put in unexpectedly. 'Four generations ago Jean Mackinnon married a Macrae and emigrated with him to Nova Scotia; her brother, James, went to Edinburgh and worked for the Hepburn family. His daughter married Alasdair Hepburn.' She glanced across the table at Louise. 'Iain Macrae will know of the connection, of course – to the Scots such things are still important.'

Louise struggled with herself not to point out that he'd seemed entirely Canadian and not recognizably Scottish at all, but was provoked instead into admitting something she hadn't intended to mention. 'It was Mr Macrae who towed us out of the bog when we got stuck this morning. He was following along . . . making a brief visit to Skye,

I think.' Then she returned firmly to the subject of Edinburgh, and it lasted them until the fish pie and the junket pudding had been dealt with.

What happened now, she wondered? Did Janet Maitland refuse offers of help and insist on toiling, Martha-like or martyr-like, in the kitchen alone? But, instead, she got up from the table, said a brief goodnight, and left the room.

'She rises early and retires early,' Andrew explained. 'She likes to read a chapter of the Bible in peace before she goes to sleep. I am allowed to do the washing-up!' But there was still some wine in his glass, and he poured more for Louise, as if to say that the dishes could wait.

'How is your mother?' he could safely ask now.

'Still hating widowhood, I think. She wasn't a brilliant mother – by her own admission! – but she gave me a very nice stepfather. He was kind to her and to me.'

Andrew Maitland thought about what he wanted to say next and finally put it into words. 'I was *not* kind, my dear . . . not even fair, I'm afraid, because I gave all the capital I had to Angus; some of it should have been yours. You should have gone on with your music, and it's my fault that you didn't. I've been wanting to admit it for years.'

Louise reached out to touch his hand where it rested on the table. 'There was no need, because it isn't true. It was talent that I lacked, not money. I could have gone on, but I didn't want to be merely an averagely good pianist . . . there are too many of those already. Better, I decided, to become a much more than average cook!' She smiled at him as she said it, suddenly reminding him of the English girl he'd married in the spring-time of his life – she wasn't as beautiful as Drusilla had been, but lovely enough, and kinder than her mother. That encouraged him to air his next anxiety.

'Is it going to work, bringing the children to us? We shall do our utmost for them – that goes without saying – but we can't bring their parents back, and that's all those poor bairns want.' He steadied his voice, and made himself

go on. 'Janet hasn't mentioned Angus since he was killed . . .
grief is locked up inside her. I haven't been able to help
her, so what can I hope to do for a desolate child like
Jamie?'

'I don't know whether it will work any more than you
do,' Louise answered slowly. 'It just seems to be the best
option we have. The London experiment with my mother
was a disaster all round and, apart from the fact that their
Hepburn grandmother is very frail, a home in Edinburgh
wouldn't be any better. The children are used to a free,
country life . . . at least they can have that here.' She
stopped for a moment, debated what else could safely be
said, and finally risked mentioning what might hurt the
gentle man in front of her. 'They're also used to being
loved . . . and for children that means being *shown* affection. Perhaps Aunt Janet could help herself as well as them
by learning how to do that.'

He couldn't bring himself to say how unlikely that was.
'Let us hope that other children will help,' he suggested
instead. 'When Jamie starts school here after Easter it may
be that he'll accept them even if he can't accept us adults.'

It reminded Louise of the off-hand, laconic Canadian –
the only adult she knew who, without trying at all, had
communicated with her nephew. But his casual departure
at the gate still rankled, and she refused to mention him
again.

'There's something else that might help. Jamie is very
aware of his surroundings – unusually so in a small boy.
It's very beautiful here. He'll notice that and be comforted
by it, I like to think.'

She'd hoped by saying that to encourage her father, but
he suddenly looked more careworn still. 'My dear, "here"
presents another problem. We rent the manse and some of
the glebe land; the rest of it has been used for grazing by
a local crofter although he's giving up now. But the worst
problem is that the present minister, who comes out from
Broadford, is due to retire. When he does, the church will
be closed and an Edinburgh-based developer is already

waiting for that to happen. My old friend Tom Hepburn is keeping a watching-brief for me.'

'And you can't afford to buy the manse because your cash went to Angus,' Louise said, not making a question of it. 'Well, that's what mortgage companies are for. My stepfather made me a gift when he died – we can use it as a deposit, and take out a mortgage.'

'My dear girl, you're kindness itself, but I couldn't allow you to do that,' he said unsteadily. 'In any case, it wouldn't be the developers' intention to let us buy this house – the chances are that they would want to knock it down, and probably the church as well. Some holiday complex is what they've got in mind, I believe.'

'And Thomas Hepburn knows about it,' Louise said with a calmness she was far from feeling. 'I realized that he was upset, but worry about the children and grief for Angus and Ailsa seemed cause enough. Oh God, how I hate greedy businessmen who don't care what they destroy as long as they make a profit.'

She stared at her father's sad face, thinking how strange it was that she should feel so involved in what concerned him, when he'd been almost entirely absent from her life until now. But at least she'd never been taught to hate him; Drusilla had played fair in blaming herself for a marriage that had always been going to fail.

'We can't give in without a fight,' she insisted. 'What can we do to stop the barbarians?'

A charming smile suddenly lit her father's face as he stood up. 'I don't know, but I feel better just for having you here . . . I was in danger of falling into despair! I'll speak to Tom again in the morning, but right now I think you should go to bed while I potter in the kitchen. I've done nothing worth the mention all day, and you've done a great deal.'

She thought it pleased him to let her off the washing-up, and the truth certainly was that she felt bone-tired. 'Then I'll say goodnight,' she agreed, getting to her feet. 'Will you make sure Macgregor's settled down . . . if he's spending the time chewing up everything in the porch we may never get Aunt Janet to agree to keep him.'

'He stays, whatever gets chewed up,' her father promised. 'And now, child, go to bed.'

She thanked him with an unexpected kiss on his cheek, and then walked out of the room to drag herself up the stairs to the attic floor. There, both children were deeply asleep – Fiona still clutching her moth-eaten teddy bear, and Jamie with tear-stains on his cheeks. She went back to her own room, to sit by the window and watch the last of the evening light glimmer on the Sound. She craved hours and hours of dreamless sleep but her tired mind went round and round a treadmill of worry instead: was it fair to leave the children here – fair either to them or to the two elderly people who would have to look after them? What would happen if the manse was sold over their heads? And last but not least, did any of them, remembering that her own life and living were seven hundred miles away in London, realize that she'd only come to deliver the children, not to stay?

She had no answer to any of these questions and, in despair, found herself slipping to her knees to seek the God that Janet Maitland, at least, believed in: 'Help us, please,' she whispered, 'we need help rather badly.'

Eight

At least the new day dawned bright with spring promise, although it was still cool out of doors, Andrew explained when they'd assembled in the kitchen for breakfast. The wind had shifted round to the north-east, bringing fine weather and the crystal-clear visibility that came with it. That was something to relish, because with the prevailing south-westerlies blowing, the mountains could be wrapped in mist or low cloud for days on end.

'It's a day for going over to Ord or Glen Brittle to see the Cuillin in all their splendour,' he suggested wistfully, 'but we'll leave them for another time. You must settle in here before we start exploring.'

The children scarcely took in what he said, being more concerned to watch their great-aunt ladling into bowls porridge the like of which they hadn't seen before: it was pale-brown in colour and had the look of very fine gravel that had been steeped in water. Rejection, writ large in Jamie's face, would be followed by Fiona, of course. Louise picked up her own spoon, took a mouthful and announced that it tasted good, but she added milk and sugar to the children's bowls.

'It's how they're used to eating it,' she explained to her aunt.

'Then it's an English habit they'd do better to grow out of,' Janet Maitland commented austerely. 'Good oatmeal isn't meant to be turned into milk pudding.'

But at least with Louise's pleading eye on him, Jamie picked up his spoon, and Fiona followed suit.

Breakfast finally over, they could be wrapped in jackets

and turned loose in the garden with Macgregor. Louise returned to the kitchen to find that her father had disappeared; Janet was there alone, watching the children from the window. Her desolate face spoke clearly enough of grief, but Louise knew better than to offer comfort that would certainly be refused.

'Don't mind, please,' she said instead, 'if they're not very approachable just now. They aren't sure of anything, don't know who to trust. Things will get better as they grow used to being here.'

'And what's the good of that, when we can't stay?' came the fierce question. 'Andrew says you know about that. I'd rather live in Edinburgh myself, but the poor man is happy here. God is punishing us very severely at the moment.' Her mouth trembled but she wouldn't allow herself to weep. 'We must bear it, I suppose.'

Louise resisted the temptation to agree, aware that the woman in front of her would be entitled to despise her for cowardice if she did. Fighting a biblical battle with Janet Maitland meant risking annihilation, but she must do her best.

'Aunt Janet, a tragic accident and children left orphaned as a result have nothing to do with punishment; and whether the manse is sold or not depends merely on the very human men who run Church affairs in Edinburgh. I think we should leave God out of it.'

There was silence for a moment while her aunt considered a frontal attack that had at least shocked her out of despair. When she spoke again it was in her usual definite tone of voice.

'You've grown very opinionated . . . I suppose that comes of the life you lead in London. Like all today's young people, you believe that the idea of punishment is old-fashioned enough to be merely comical.'

Louise shook her head. 'No, I don't, as it happens; but I can't believe you or my father have done anything that deserves such punishment, and in any case wasn't forgiveness earned for us on the cross?' She thought it a strange conversation to be having with her aunt, and hastily moved on to talk of something else. 'Don't let's assume you'll have to leave the manse. I think we should start, with Mr Hepburn's help, assembling the best case we can against the developers.'

'Very stubborn . . . very English,' her aunt commented resentfully. 'It's why they've won so many of their battles! The courage of Highlanders could never be matched at the charge, but if things began to go wrong they lost heart too quickly.'

At this point in the discussion, to Louise's relief, her father came back into the kitchen and suggested showing her round outside.

'You'll need a coat,' he said, smiling at her. 'The wind is coming over the mountains across the Sound, and you'll feel a touch of ice in it still.'

'It *is* cold,' she agreed when they left the house, 'but who cares when it means that we can have this view? I begin to understand why environmentalists get so worked up about pollution. I swear the air even tastes different up here.' She stooped to pick up Macgregor's ball that he obligingly dropped at her feet, and tossed it back to Jamie. 'It isn't what we breathe in London.'

Nearer at hand she stared now at the unkempt garden; a clever, modish, horticultural design it certainly didn't need, but some loving care and attention it *could* do with. Andrew Maitland read the thought in her face and smiled ruefully.

'I'm not a gardener, to state the obvious! Nor is Janet, but she has enough to do indoors. My only excuse is that lecturing at the Gaelic College three times a week involves quite a lot of work, but it's the greatest part of my pleasure in living here.' He led her round the side of the house to another part of the garden, where some work had been done but then seemingly, as Janet might have said, the gardener had lost heart too quickly.

'This was to be the kitchen garden,' Andrew explained, 'much needed because fresh vegetables are hard to come by. I found someone to rotavate the ground and plant all manner of seeds and then, in the way of people here, he drifted off somewhere else. As you can see, I'm fighting a losing battle with the weeds.'

Louise beckoned to the children, who'd abandoned their game for the time being to keep a watchful eye on what she was doing. 'Grandpa needs help, Jamie . . . what do you say?'

The small boy inspected the plot – on familiar ground at last, he didn't have to be prompted to speak. 'The carrots need weeding . . . and the peas want lots of little twigs . . . to climb up,' he added, seeing that his grandfather looked puzzled. 'It's all right – I know how to put them in.'

Louise smiled at her father. 'There you are – with my labour and Jamie's expertise you might get your kitchen garden after all.'

'Wonderful! Now there's one more thing to show you.' They followed him to a gate at the far end of the garden. It led to a path down through the overgrown hillside to a tiny beach left by the outgoing tide. Macgregor, of course, had come too, but a tentative sniff at the unfamiliar element of saltwater was enough to send him back to where Jamie and Fiona were already collecting shells.

'They can't come down here alone, ' Andrew said, 'so the gate must be kept locked. But perhaps we can have picnics in the summer . . . supposing that we're still at the manse by then.'

Back up the steep path and in the garden again, Louise mentioned that she needed to drive to the general stores; there were things they needed, most urgently food for Macgregor, who was running out of tins. Fiona immediately wanted to go too, but Jamie hesitated, not sure whether he could let them drive away without him. Then he suddenly made up his mind.

'I think I'll weed the carrots. Macgregor likes Caesar best.'

'Then Caesar he shall have,' Louise promised, content

to know that one small hurdle of fear in Jamie's mind had
just been bravely cleared. 'We shan't be long; then we'll
come and help you, won't we, Fee?'

The shop, some five miles away, was the only one in
view; what couldn't be found there required a visit to
Broadford. But crammed on its shelves were the tins
Macgregor favoured, and even a choice of wine to take
back as a gift to her father. He and Janet were frugal by
nature but also, she now suspected, by necessity as well.
The wine he'd offered her the previous evening had been
a welcoming treat; but she intended him to enjoy it at least
for as long as she was there.

They were back at the car and she was strapping Fiona
into her seat when a familiar voice spoke behind her.

'G'day . . . remember me? We met yesterday on the road.
My name's still Brett Macdonald.'

She turned to smile at him, and he saw her as she was;
not the tired, stressed, unfriendly woman that Ellie had
taken a dislike to.

'Of course I remember, and you're still in one piece
despite the Macdonald name! Is Miss Moffat not with
you?'

'No contest, I'm afraid, between the Clan Donald
Centre with me and a day's shopping in Portree with a
girl she's met at the hostel we're staying at. Seems a pity
to me – but she's only putting up with me being here,
not enjoying it. Me, I don't want to go home.' He smiled
as he said it, but some longing in his voice hinted that
it might be true.

'You aren't like any of the Australians I've met in
London,' she commented. 'They're all for living very richly
in the present, not delving into the past.'

'Ellie can't make me out either,' he admitted ruefully.
'Given the chance I'd enrol at that Gaelic College along
the road, but we can't stay long enough to make it worthwhile.'

'Well, you've got time to come and meet my father at
least – he lectures there, even though he was born in

Edinburgh and can't claim to be a Gael.' She opened the
rear door of the car, not regretting the invitation but
wondering what Janet Maitland would make of it. Did
Australians come above or below Americans on her list
of men she disapproved of?

Fiona peered round the edge of her seat to take a good
look at their passenger, and permitted herself a faint smile
because she remembered from the day before that his
voice had sounded different from those she was used to.
Louise pointed out the entrance to the college as they
passed, and five minutes later turned the car into the
manse drive.

'We left my father and Jamie weeding in the kitchen
garden,' she explained. 'Apart from them there's only my
aunt to meet. She's quite a formidable lady . . . don't take
it to heart if she should say something rude about
Australians.'

Brett Macdonald's pleasant grin reappeared. 'Sounds
familiar – just like my gran at home. She still puts the
fear of God into my father, and he's not afraid of anything
else that I know of!'

With Louise's basket of shopping deposited on the porch
steps, they walked round the side of the house, while Fiona
galloped ahead to be reunited with Macgregor and her
brother. Two rows of lacy-leaved carrot plants were now
beautifully free of weeds – testimony to Jamie's instructions to his grandfather about what should be removed
and what left to grow.

'Did you find Macgregor's food?' he only wanted to
know.

'Tins of it . . . and look who else I found – a friend from
yesterday.' Then she introduced Brett to her father,
explaining that he'd stopped to offer help when they were
stuck in the bog. 'Now he's investigating family history
in the Clan Donald Centre and yearning to learn Gaelic!
I'll take your place out here while you stop and talk to
him.'

But Brett could see that extra hands were needed, and

asked to be enrolled in the workforce provided there was anything to be done that required strength rather than horticultural know-how. He was given the job of breaking down rough ground that would be needed later, said Jamie, for transplanting. Seeing them usefully employed, Louise took Fiona indoors to start unpacking the trunk that still waited in the porch. She explained to her aunt who the stranger was in the garden, and left Janet Maitland to decide what to do about him when she went out to call the others indoors to lunch.

It was a small surprise to see Brett Macdonald brought in with them, to be told to wash his hands and then take a seat at the kitchen table. He complimented her on her lentil soup and home-baked bread – rightly, Louise thought, because both were very good – and even drew an approving smile from her when he explained that he'd been brought up on stories about the past handed down from his grandmother.

'The womenfolk were always the ones to keep family histories alive,' she pointed out.

'And they did a great deal more than that,' Andrew suggested. 'Opposition to the Clearances was most effective when the women led it, as they often did – with sticks, stones, any kind of weapon they had. Highland men were less inclined to challenge authority, even when it was clearly in the wrong – generations of obedience to the clan system had something to do with that, I'm afraid; the men were conditioned to accept whatever instructions were handed down from their chief.'

'The MacDonalds behaved badly here,' Brett said bluntly. 'I've been reading the archives in the museum and I can't help feeling involved in what happened, even though our very junior branch of the family set off early on for Australia. Dreadful things were done to people who had a right to go on living here.'

'A lot of them were done by the English, don't forget,' Janet Maitland insisted with sudden fierceness. 'That useless Stewart rebellion gave them the excuse they were looking for – The Disarming Act, they called it but it was meant to destroy the Gaelic way of life completely.'

Brett glanced at Louise, so English herself in looks and manner, wondering how much her aunt's open hostility troubled her. But it was Andrew Maitland who gently called his sister to order.

'You're right, my dear, but every coin has two sides. Yes, our masters at Westminster did outlaw the Gaelic language (their worst crime in my view); they certainly broke the clan system and turned clan chiefs into mere landowners; but they had a right to be tired of the lawlessness and treachery they found up here. The Clearances were brutal, inhuman even; but the crofting population had outgrown its ability to feed itself or to satisfy the greed of the very men who should have been its protectors.'

'Now I don't know whose side I'm on,' Brett said ruefully, and saw his host smile.

'You steer a course of majestic male impartiality, and leave the ladies – like my dear sister – to fight old battles all over again!'

It was beautifully done, Louise decided – harmony restored, but not at the cost of unfairness to anyone concerned. If this visit to the manse achieved nothing else it would at least give her a better and long overdue appreciation of her father.

They talked of Edinburgh then until the meal was over and Brett remembered that, hours ago, he'd been on his way to the Clan Donald Centre.

'You could come tomorrow – there's lots more to do,' Jamie pointed out when the visitor stood up to leave.

'I will if I can, but I don't promise . . . there's my friend Ellie to think of, you see.' Then he smiled at Janet Maitland. 'You wouldn't have to feed us both, Miss Maitland – we'd bring our own tucker!'

'You would do no such thing,' she said sharply. 'You're not in Australia now, remember.'

He answered this by bending down to kiss her cheek,

and for the first time in Andrew's knowledge of his sister reduced her to blushing, flustered astonishment.

'I'll walk you to the top of the drive,' Louise managed to recover enough to suggest. 'I forgot to empty the mailbox, as instructed.'

They were safely outside when Brett halted to stare out across the garden; the Sound lay quietly in the sunshine and the glistening mountains on the far shore were outlined against a sapphire sky.

'"Clothed in white samite, mystic, wonderful",' Louise quoted. Then smiled at Brett's look of puzzlement. 'Don't ask me what samite is – and I know Tennyson wasn't describing the Knoydart Mountains, but it's what seems to fit!'

He continued to watch her face, suddenly aware that she was part of the discoveries he was making. Nothing had prepared him for what he was caught up in now: the rich, violent history of a past that wasn't done with yet, the strangeness of this small island he was on, and its stunning beauty that kept taking his breath away. The grey-eyed, gentle-voiced girl beside him matched the place, seemed as if she ought to belong here.

'Why must you go back to London and leave your children here?' he suddenly wanted to know. But her expression changed, making him regret the question. 'Sorry . . . forget I asked.'

'I don't mind telling you, but it's a complicated story,' she finally replied. 'To begin with, Jamie and Fiona are my brother's children, not mine – he and his wife were killed in a car crash in France three months ago.'

'Jesus Christ,' Brett murmured, meaning no blasphemy. 'I suppose I guessed something was wrong . . . but never that.'

'To finish answering your question,' she went on, 'my job is in London, and that's where I live. We tried taking the children to my mother there but they hated it – they were used to life on a sheep farm in the Cheviot Hills. At least there's a chance that they'll settle down here.'

'One last question, please. Why is your aunt the way she is – so bitter about the English that she doesn't even seem to like you?'

'That's part of an older unhappiness. My father married an English actress. As Janet predicted, the marriage failed. She and my father brought up Angus in Edinburgh; my mother took me to London. I'm afraid we're a very dysfunctional family, not in good shape to cope with something as dreadful as Angus and Ailsa being killed.' She remembered what she'd come out for, and started to walk along the drive. 'Now it's my turn to ask a question, and it's a rather impertinent question, I'm afraid. You and Ellie are together obviously, but are you better matched at home than you seem to be here?' He took so long to reply that she answered the question herself. 'Of course you are; it was silly as well as impertinent.'

'Now *I'll* answer the question,' Brett said quietly. 'Ellie's younger than me by ten years; all of us, my family and hers, have been waiting for her to grow old enough to settle down – with me. She reckoned she was due a year of freedom first, seeing the world, and that's what she's been doing. I came out to remind her that it's nearly time to go home. It's true we make an odd pair here, but that's because this place means nothing to her and she's only here because I insisted on coming. At home there won't be anything to make us different.' He said the words as confidently as he could, unable to admit that he was no longer sure where home was.

'That's all right then,' she commented, smiling at him, and then stopped by the mailbox they'd now reached. 'You'd be very welcome to come again, but toiling among my father's vegetables isn't what you're here for. Don't let sympathy for a small boy get in the way of your and Ellie's plans.'

He stared at her upturned face for a moment, then, as the breeze blew a strand of light-brown hair across her mouth, gently brushed it away, and the touch of his fingers felt like a kiss. But he didn't say goodbye . . . just turned and walked off along the road, and she realized that she should have offered to drive him back to the museum. But she remembered at last to open the box and collect her father's mail before she went back to the house.

Nine

Iain Macrae would have liked Portree if he'd intended to be there at all; its cliff-edged harbour was attractive, filled with fishing boats and ringed with colourful-looking restaurants and guest-houses. But he was feeling thwarted and irritable, confirmed now in his opinion that for as long as he remained in Scotland every plan he made would be overset by someone else; this morning he could blame Thomas Hepburn.

After driving straight past the manse yesterday afternoon he'd turned and gone northwards to spend the night at the Sligachan Hotel. Every climber in the world knew of it, and he understood why when he got there. Anyone who wanted to see the Cuillin in all their changing, snow-capped, cloud-wrapped splendour went to the Sligachan. But there was more frustration than pleasure in being there, for a climber wanted to be *on* Sgurr Alasdair, not looking up at it from ground level. A climber who knew that he was out of practice and much less than fit knew equally that he must leave the Cuillin's jagged peaks alone. So in the morning he would drive straight back to the mainland, and then return to Canada – his odd Scottish escapade finally over.

But because courtesy seemed to insist that he speak to the man once more, if only to say goodbye, he'd made the mistake of telephoning Thomas Hepburn before he left the hotel. The lawyer had sounded very surprised to hear that he was on Skye at all, but then a note of hope had crept into his voice.

'I have no right to ask this, Mr Macrae – you've been

more than kind already – but I wonder if your departure could be delayed for a day or two, given that I'm correct in thinking you're your own master at the moment?'

'I've no immediate need to be anywhere else,' Iain Macrae said curtly, 'if that's what you mean.'

That had been his mistake, of course; he was trapped into listening to what came next.

'It's so very providential that you're on the spot,' the lawyer had bluntly pointed out. 'You see, since you were in Edinburgh my friend Andrew's situation has changed for the worse. The Kilchrist kirk will close sooner than we thought because the Broadford minister is in poor health. To make matters worse the crofter who has rented the rest of the glebe land adjoining his own holding is giving up, so the way is open for the developers to acquire an even more substantial piece of land than they originally thought.'

'So presumably the Church authorities won't hesitate to sell to them?'

There'd been a brief silence at the other end of the line before the lawyer spoke again. 'Not unless I can suggest that another prospective buyer might make them a more attractive offer!'

Feeling slightly winded, Iain had at least managed to ask a question. 'You don't have me in mind as the buyer, I hope?'

'Not seriously, of course . . . no, no; I just need someone to start making enquiries that will be reported back to Edinburgh. I could give you the name of the Church solicitor in Portree, and also the name of the crofter who is Andrew's neighbour.'

'Even if I were happy about the pretence, and I'm not, I don't understand what you'd be achieving,' Iain commented firmly. 'My enquiries wouldn't lead anywhere even if I could make them sound convincing.'

'They would suggest to the solicitor that the Church people shouldn't be in a hurry to accept the developers' offer, which in part they dislike anyway. They know that it will mean the destruction of the kirk and the manse – not something they could be happy about – but there is also growing unease about the extent to which tourism is already dominating the island's economy, at the expense of crofting as a traditional way of life. If I can buy Andrew some time, Mr Macrae, I might be able to build a case that the Church will listen to.'

The answer to that had seemed obvious but he pointed it out to the lawyer all the same: money would undoubtedly outweigh the Church's scruples, and the developers would win in the end.

Mr Hepburn hadn't been defeated even by this argument. 'Not if I can find someone to buy the land who would use it for its proper purpose . . . that is my ambition, you see – not only to help Andrew keep his home, but to restore what your ancestors and mine were driven from.'

It had brought them back, Iain realized, to their first conversation in Thomas Hepburn's office, and the reason for the lawyer's correspondence with his father. Now was the moment to finally refuse to help, and to say a firm goodbye. Instead, he'd found himself writing down the names of the people he was to contact; instead, he was sitting now outside the solicitor's office in Portree, plucking up the courage to begin the charade.

There was something similar the world over, he discovered a few minutes later, about the premises in which men of law conducted their affairs; being shown into Mr Carmichael's office was exactly like being ushered into what had been his father's room in Ottawa. And lawyers even had the same universal air of gravitas about them – 'only serious matters dealt with here' was always the unspoken message that clients were meant to receive.

'How can I help you? I understand you were given my name by Thomas Hepburn in Edinburgh,' said Edward Carmichael, 'but I don't know yours, I'm afraid.'

'He's a very distant relative of mine,' Iain explained to the portly, middle-aged man who sat facing him across the usual imposing desk. 'We spoke of shared ancestors on Skye and that led him to mention that the very part of the island they'd been forced to leave was soon going on the market. That interested me very much, but he seemed to think that someone else was ahead of me. If you're going to confirm that you're about to clap hands on a bargain with another buyer then I'm wasting my time in calling here, and my name doesn't matter.'

Instead of confirming anything at all, the solicitor asked a question of his own. 'May I know exactly what Mr Hepburn told you is involved?'

Iain counted off items on his fingers. 'To be exact: a church likely to be closed down, the manse and garden that go with it, currently occupied by a tenant, more land owned by the Church, and the possibility of still more adjoining land also becoming available.'

'You spoke of being interested . . . may I know why? Forgive me if I judge from your accent that you don't belong here.' The hint was slight, but nevertheless there, that a stranger's interest in the matter wasn't entirely welcome.

Iain was beginning to dislike the solicitor's manner, but he answered easily enough. 'I've done a lot of work in places where land is being desperately neglected or misused, but more often than not it can be made productive again. From what I've seen of this island so far it seems to me to fall into that category, and I rather like the idea of reclaiming some of it.'

The lawyer's smile was now gently regretful. 'My dear sir, much of Skye is little more than bare rock. Where crofting has been tried it has failed. If your intention were to try it again I doubt if such an ambition could be measured seriously against that of another bidder.'

His visitor now smiled back, beginning to enjoy the interview after all. 'The other bidder has a different purpose in mind, I take it. Wouldn't that require what is now agricultural land to be reclassified?'

Mr Carmichael's expression grew solemn. 'If your own

desire is to become a crofter, it's very laudable, of course, but it would have to be set against the general economic benefit to Skye as a whole of a different use of the land. This has been a depressed island for a long time, it needs imaginative, large-scale projects to bring it prosperity. I doubt if reclassification of the land would be a problem if any such project were being thought of.'

There was no doubt now in whose corner Mr Carmichael would be fighting, and some considerable doubt, in Iain's opinion, as to the rules he'd choose to fight by.

'You're right, of course, to think of the general good, but you know what it is when you get an idea in your head,' the troublesome visitor now suggested apologetically. 'I won't trouble you with it any more; I'll just ask Tom Hepburn to let the present owners of the land know that I'm interested. They're the ones who'll have to make up their minds . . . and weigh one sort of good against another'

Mr Carmichael still tried to smile. 'I shall inform them myself of course – that is my duty.' He even managed to infuse a little warmth into his voice. 'If you're wondering where to stay in the neighbourhood of the church, the Ardvasar Hotel is well spoken of. I assume, by the way, that you're also acquainted with the present occupant of its manse, Andrew Maitland – another distant relative perhaps?'

It was a nicely judged hit, and Iain was glad he could answer with convincing honesty.

'Never met him, I'm afraid . . . don't know Mr Maitland at all. But now that you've put the idea in my head, maybe I *should* call on him.' Then he stood up, received a reluctant handshake, and walked out of the room.

Edward Carmichael was left to think about the conversation for a moment or two; then he picked up the telephone.

Outside in the street the air smelt cold and fresh, with the tang of the sea in it . . . invigorating in itself, but there was now another stimulus as well. The fencing match with the solicitor hadn't only been enjoyable; for the first time in many months life seemed to have a purpose again. It was a negative ambition, Iain realized, to stop something happening, but even that was better than no objective at all. The charade his 'distant relative' in Edinburgh had persuaded him into was still that, but at least he now wanted it to work; it would be a pleasure to defeat Carmichael and the developers in whose pocket he sat. But first Tom Hepburn must be warned to float the idea of a phantom bidder in front of the Church authorities, since Carmichael almost certainly would not. He walked to the Royal Hotel, and made his telephone call to Edinburgh from there. Then, because it was already midday, he ordered coffee and a sandwich in the hotel bar.

He was studying a map spread out in front of him when a girl's voice spoke in his ear.

'Well, this *is* a surprise . . . you didn't say anything about coming to Skye.'

He looked up to see Ellie Moffat holding out her hand, with a mixture of pleasure and reproach in her smile.

'Sudden change of plan,' he explained. 'You know how it is when you're travelling rather aimlessly. Is Brett with you?'

Ellie's expression clouded over. 'I left him all set to spend an exciting day in the Clan Donald Centre, mulling over the history of his family – probably either bloody or boring, and in either case better left alone if you ask me!'

In his newly-discovered interest in what happened to other people, he found himself feeling sorry for her – she was clearly the child of wealthy parents, and free to roam the world, but she didn't seem to know what to do with her life. Destined for Brett Macdonald, she wasn't even sure about that, and hoped instead for a more exciting alternative.

'You're here alone, and I can't even invite you to lunch,' Iain apologized. 'I've just eaten a large ham sandwich!'

Ellie shook her head. 'I'm with a girl from the hostel

we're staying at. She's getting a broken tooth fixed; after that she'll come here. Apparently it's where Bonnie Prince Charlie said goodbye to Flora Macdonald . . . I'm surprised Brett could resist that.' She looked sadly at Iain. 'I didn't know anyone could fall in love with a place, but he's in love with Skye.'

'Temporarily,' Iain suggested. 'Propinquity does produce love affairs, and he happens to be here. When you go home the problem will disappear.'

He smiled ruefully, aware of the oddity of offering such comfort and she observed the change it made to his thin, brown face. Of course she'd realized straightaway that he was different from the men she knew – older and more experienced – but she hadn't met one before who kept so much of himself in reserve, as it were; whatever had happened had led him to stand back from the rest of them. Getting on terms with him wasn't difficult, but getting to know him might be, and the slight tingle along her nerves hinted that it would be dangerous as well. She'd have been warned by that as a rule, because she was a shrewd judge of what she could handle, but a challenge was just what she seemed to need when Brett was behaving so strangely.

She put out her hand to indicate where their hostel was on the map. 'Look – this is where we're staying, near Armadale Castle – the home of the MacDonalds before they let it fall into ruin. Brett can't get over the idea that they owned half this island, and a lot more besides, until they sold it off, bit by bit. Myself, I reckon one family should never have owned all that anyway; then there'd have been enough to go round.'

'Quite right,' Iain agreed, kindly not suggesting that her father probably owned a large piece of Australia. 'Down with the plutocrats and the idle rich, and the big fat cats of global capitalism!' He was laughing at her; she knew that, but she didn't mind. She thought he did it in a way that didn't hurt.

'You were looking at the map when I came in,' she remembered. 'If you don't know where to go next come and join us; the hostel might not be your scene, but you could stay at the Ardvasar Hotel instead.'

'Someone else recommended that to me this morning,' he admitted. 'I get the feeling that it's where I'm meant to go next.'

Her engaging smile reappeared. 'You make it sound like you're looking for clues in a treasure hunt!'

'It's rather how it feels,' he admitted, without explaining why. He glanced at his watch, then folded up the map. 'Will you think me rude if I don't wait to meet your friend? I've got a lot to do before I leave Portree.'

'Leave it for where?' Ellie wanted to know. 'Will you go and stay at the Ardvasar? We could come and have dinner with you if you do. That at least would be something to look forward to.'

He felt the twinge of unexpected pity again – she wasn't much more than a child, and for all her surface confidence she was puzzled and hurt by a change in Brett Macdonald that she couldn't understand.

'My plans are vague, Ellie,' he said gently. 'I'm not sure when I'll get down to Armadale.' Her disappointed face made him go on. 'Don't worry about Brett; you and he live in a big, new country where the past scarcely counts. That's not how it is here; every inch of this place holds a story, and because his ancestors were involved in what happened he feels involved too, for the time being.'

'But *you* aren't,' Ellie said seriously. 'Involved, I mean, and your ancestors were here as well.'

Iain shook his head. 'I'm a hardened case,' he insisted. 'I make it a rule *not* to get involved, with places or people. That isn't something to boast about – quite the contrary, I'm afraid, but it's how rolling stones are, not good material for impressions to sink into!'

He lifted his hand in a small farewell salute, and walked out of the bar wondering why, apart from at least making himself clear to Ellie, what he'd just said had sounded to his own ears such a thundering lie. The truth was that he'd simply been afraid of getting involved. He'd driven away from Louise Maitland without even stopping to say goodbye precisely because he'd been determined not to listen to the siren song of the past. He didn't want to know what his ancestors had been driven from, refused categorically to be moved by the sight of a clump of stones still standing that marked the hearth of a croft they might have lived in. In short, he didn't belong here. Now, thanks to Tom Hepburn and to a pompous solicitor he hadn't liked, he was going to the very part of the island he'd promised himself he'd stay away from, but there he would be able to prove to the ghosts of his forbears that his heart wasn't Highland and he, for one, did not 'in dreams behold the Hebrides'.

Ten

A ll in all it had been a good day, Louise reckoned –
thanks to the fine weather, a neglected garden, and
the cheerful presence of Brett Macdonald. Already the
children looked better for hours spent in the fresh air, and
the need to give advice to his team had begun to crack
the defensive wall that Jamie had built round himself.
Once or twice she'd even seen him grin at something their
Australian friend had said.

The only person he'd noticeably avoided was herself,
and she was still undecided about how to deal with that
by the time he'd had his bath and was about to climb into
bed. Then, somehow, the question suddenly spoke itself.

'Cross with me, Jamie? I can't do anything about it if
I don't know why it is.'

Jamie fiddled with a button on his pyjama jacket but
didn't answer, and she had to try again. 'Something is
wrong . . . tell me, please.'

He just shook his head, and when she knelt down and
put her hands on his thin shoulders, she could feel how
rigidly he held himself against any contact with her.

'I thought you enjoyed today, working outside with
Grandpa and Brett,' she suggested gently.

'I like Brett . . . he's nice,' Jamie's gruff voice suddenly
insisted, 'but he's going away, too, just like you.' Then
suddenly the truth came tumbling out. 'Aunt Janet frightens
Fee. We don't want to stay here with her.'

She knew she couldn't hug him unless he allowed her
to . . . couldn't talk about his parents until he was willing
to talk about them himself. It didn't leave much to offer

in the way of comfort except the one thing she wasn't
sure she could offer.

'Jamie love, listen, please. I'm only going back to
London because I work there, not because I don't want to
stay with you and Fee. Grandpa loves you very much and
so does Aunt Janet. If she speaks sharply sometimes it's
only because she gets tired and she's worried about you.
Can you remember that they are both sad too; they *need*
you here to help them.'

She couldn't even be sure he listened to what she said,
and when she leaned across to kiss him goodnight he
simply turned his face away and climbed into bed. He'd
cry himself to sleep again, not even able to stretch out his
hand and touch Macgregor's rough head.

She went downstairs tired, depressed, and so uncertain
about the future that she found little to say at the supper
table. Her father wasn't much more talkative and, for once,
it was Janet Maitland who calmly kept the conversation
going. Even so, it was a relief to both of them when she
said goodnight and retired to her room as usual. When
she'd gone Andrew leaned over and refilled his daughter's
wine glass.

'I feel like drowning sorrow tonight,' he explained with
a rueful smile, 'and my impression is that you do, too!'

'You first,' Louise suggested. 'Tell me your particular
sorrow.'

Her father considered the wine in his glass, not seeing
it, she felt sure. 'I heard officially from Edinburgh this
morning. The Church will definitely close at the end of
the summer; the land and this house will be sold. They
don't mention Donald Mackinnon's adjoining land, but
obviously that will go too, to the same buyer.'

'Do they say who the buyer is?'

'They don't, but when Tom Hepburn rang this morning
to warn me the letter was on its way, he told me. It's a
man called Sir James Guthrie . . . he's a rich entrepreneur,
I gather; a Lowland Scot, who's made a fortune out of
building holiday complexes on the mainland; now it's

Skye's turn. I believe a small luxury hotel and a mini golf course are what he has in mind, and because he offers to bring more tourists here he'll get all the licences and permissions he needs.'

'And it doesn't harm his prospects at all that he helps to fund the political party of his choice in Edinburgh,' Louise said bitterly, 'or that he's a particularly poisonous man!'

Andrew Maitland stared at her in astonishment. 'My dear, how can you know that – you aren't acquainted with him, surely?'

'Acquainted isn't the right word. I worked for him once – when I first started out as a professional cook. I went up to his mansion in the Highlands to cook for a shooting party there. He thought his fee entitled him to the cook's services in his bedroom as well. In a rather theatrical gesture I tore up his cheque and stalked out – only regretting that I'd already done all the cooking. I pray he doesn't remember my name – if he scented a connection he'd be all the happier to evict you.' She was silent for a moment, then asked another question. 'Have we lost the battle before we begin?'

'I suspect so, my dear,' Andrew Maitland said sadly, 'though Tom Hepburn still insists that he's got a secret weapon up his sleeve – some pretend bidder who will at least hold things up while he hunts for a bona fide prospect. He's the best of friends, but I don't really expect him to be able to work a miracle.' Andrew sipped some wine, then smiled at his daughter. 'Don't grieve over it too much; having to find another house will be very sad but not the tragedy that losing Angus and Ailsa was. Now tell me what else worries *you*.'

'Going back to London,' Louise said baldly. 'I'm not sure that I can do it. Jamie refuses to see it as anything but the most cruel desertion, and the dear Lord knows that they've had more than enough to bear already. I can't even try to make him understand, because he simply won't listen.' She hesitated about whether or not to mention Janet

Maitland and decided that she couldn't bring herself to repeat what Jamie had said.

'We're too old for them, Janet and I; of course we are,' Andrew agreed simply. 'But *could* you stay? What about your life and work in London?' The note of hope in his voice was there, despite all his efforts to conceal it, and she realized that not only the children had been dreading her departure.

She thought for a moment about what to say next, knowing that whatever she committed herself to now would alter her life completely.

'It's true that I want to go back to London,' she admitted finally, 'that's where my home and my friends are, but it's more than that. I'm city-bred and I'm not sure I can cope with life up here – even the mountains overwhelm me. But I think I must, because I can't walk away leaving Jamie as he is now, and if *he's* unhappy so will Fiona be.' She hesitated, but made herself go on. 'There's someone else to think of, though. This is Aunt Janet's home too, and for her I might be the straw that breaks the camel's back! She's putting up with me at the moment because she thinks it's only a brief visit, but I know she doesn't want me here. If I could, I'd buy a small croft and take the children there, but that would use up all the money I've got, and I should have nothing to live on unless I could get a small job of some kind.'

Andrew Maitland stared at her across the table, trying to see in her the beautiful, wilful creature he'd fallen in love with long ago. Occasionally he saw a brief glimpse of Drusilla in this girl's smile and in her bright spirit, but 'steel-true, blade-straight' his wife hadn't been, and he knew with joy and thankfulness that his daughter was. He put out his hand to touch hers where it rested on the table.

'We'll stay together, my dear, whatever happens . . . if not here, then somewhere else. Janet will understand how it must be – I'll make her; and I pray that she'll learn to love you as she loved Angus. She can't fail in the end.'

Louise expected neutrality at best, and more probably an armed truce, but there was no point in saying so. 'I shall give my mother some work to do,' she commented instead. 'She's very competent at things like renting flats, and packing up clothes and possessions; it comes of her days as an actress!'

He smiled because she wanted him to, but unsteadily. 'I shouldn't be, because of the cost to you, but I'm glad you're here . . . and so thankful to know you'll stay. Now I can face whatever happens with the delightful Sir James Guthrie!'

'We'll cock a snook at him and fate,' Louise said cheerfully, 'and assume we're going to be here when our lovely weed-free vegetables are ready to eat. But I hope Brett Macdonald finds labouring in the garden so irresistible that he joins us again tomorrow. Jamie will be disappointed if he doesn't come . . . and so, I dare to think, will Aunt Janet!'

But the following morning, when Brett apologized to Ellie for having more work to do, she insisted that she'd go to the manse too. Anything was better than the museum archives, and she'd exhausted the possibilities of Portree.

'But you don't like Louise or the children,' he said doubtfully, 'and I can't swear Janet Maitland will take to *you*; you don't have my winning ways with old ladies.'

'I'm coming, Brett,' Ellie maintained firmly. 'Maybe I'll get to know the children better, and in any case, now I know what's happened to them, I feel sorry for the poor little tykes.' But there was another reason for going that she didn't mention. She couldn't see the attraction of Louise Maitland herself but she strongly suspected that Brett could. Iain Macrae had told her not to worry, but she'd known Brett too long not to be aware of the need to worry. He was quieter now, caught up in the lives of people he hadn't even met a week ago. It wasn't just Skye and the past that had caught his imagination. 'I'm coming with you to the manse,' she insisted.

'You don't know anything about gardening,' he said, sinking but game.

'Nor do you; we'll learn together, shall we? It might come in useful.'

So he gave in, and they presented themselves in tattered jeans and boots for Jamie's inspection on another blue and gold morning that would have lifted even the saddest or most stubbornly pessimistic heart. Ellie's faux pas over Macgregor hadn't been forgiven, but she was taught to thin out tiny leek shoots and transplant them in holes filled with water, while Brett oiled and then used an ancient mower on the lawn.

'You know a lot,' Ellie said to Jamie, impressed in spite of herself.

'I wasn't sure about the leeks,' he admitted, 'so I checked in Grandpa's gardening book.'

She worked diligently after that, but occasionally cast a glance in the direction of the girl who was pruning the overgrown shrubs that would, said their mentor, keep too much sunlight off the vegetable plot. In gardening rig, and flushed with fresh air and exertion, Louise Maitland looked younger than Ellie had guessed; smiling at something Brett had said she was enough to catch any man's eye, and to make any other woman slightly envious. It wasn't easy to pin down why, but it had to do with . . . what? Ellie puzzled it out and came up with words like style and grace that didn't usually come into her vocabulary. She knew precisely what her own assets were, and they were good enough, but they were very different from Louise Maitland's.

When the lunchtime break approached and Louise went into the house to help her aunt, their host suggested that although it wasn't quite warm enough yet to picnic out-of-doors, at least they could inspect the beach. With Macgregor lolloping along as well, ready for another close encounter with the new element he hadn't quite got the hang of, they emerged from the overgrown path to look at a prospect that took Brett's breath away: shingle

beach left glistening in the sunlight by the outgoing tide;
sapphire water; a fringe of green along the opposite shore;
white mountains; azure sky. Ellie looked at his enchanted
face, and tried not to blame Andrew Maitland for taking
them down there; he wasn't to know that one bedazzled,
ghost-haunted Australian would never forget the place,
always assuming that she could drag him away from it
at all.

'Some spot for a barbecue,' she suggested, to bring him
down to earth.

'Just . . . some spot,' he agreed quietly, and then went
to help Fiona in the task of examining shells.

When lunch had been eaten indoors Andrew said that
work in the garden was over for the day. His own afternoon would be spent teaching at the Gaelic College, and
Louise must keep an appointment with the head teacher
of the school Jamie had been enrolled at. While the fine
weather lasted, he suggested, Brett and Ellie must go across
to Elgol, and take a boat trip to Loch Coruisk. From there
on such a fine day as this they'd see the Cuillin in all their
glory.

'We'll be back tomorrow,' Brett promised Jamie.
'Another morning's work should see us through, then Ellie
and I'll make you a real Australian barbecue on the beach.'
He looked across at Janet Maitland. 'Only if you'll come
too, ma'am, and be *our* guest: we'll bring the food and
do the cooking.'

Not sure whether the invitation sounded attractive or
appalling, she missed the moment to say that she would
rather eat indoors like any normal Christian body, and so,
before Brett and Ellie left, the arrangement was understood to have been approved all round.

With lunch cleared away Louise went in search of Jamie
to say that it was time to set off for the school. She found
him in his room, curled up on the window seat pretending
to read; for once he spoke first.

'I don't want to go to the school, thank you.'

'You won't know unless you take a look at it,' Louise

suggested calmly. 'Anyway, we have an appointment with
Miss Mackintosh; it would be rude not to keep it.'

Hunched with misery, he turned to stare out of the
window, and the sight of his thin shoulder blades poking
through his jersey seemed almost more than she could
bear. If she hadn't known it before, she knew it now –
she'd have to stay for as long as he and his sister needed
her.

'Jamie love, you have to attend school . . . the people
who govern us insist on it, I'm afraid. If you don't like
this school we'll try to find you another one, but Grandpa
says it's very good, and he should know. Fee will go there
too, when she's five at the end of the summer, but by then
you'll be able to take her and I won't need to go with
you.'

'You won't be here,' he mumbled, still staring out of
the window.

'Yes, I shall . . . Grandpa says I can stay here too, so
that's what I'm going to do.'

For a frozen moment nothing happened, then he turned
to face her. 'Stay here for ever and ever?' His voice cracked
on the words, and she had to struggle not to weep for its
mixture of hope and disbelief.

'At least for as long as you and Fee want me to,' she
managed to say. 'Will that do?'

His answer was only a nod of the head, but she thought
that would do, too. Then he surprised her by what he said
next. 'I don't like you being an aunt . . . couldn't you be
something else?'

'A sister maybe?' she ventured after a moment's thought.
'Something like Fee, only much, much older of course.'

'Yes – about as . . . as old as Mummy was, I expect,'
he agreed slowly.

Even now she resisted the temptation to assume that a
hug would be welcome, but the first mention of his mother
was so precious a sign of progress being made that tears
began to trickle down her face, and Jamie leaned forward
to smear them away.

'Shouldn't we be going to the school?' he asked.

'Right now,' she agreed unsteadily. 'If Macgregor comes too, he stays in the car – OK?'

'OK,' said Jamie and smiled.

Ten minutes later she could see that what her father had said was true: it looked to be a very good school, and a young and pleasant Miss Mackintosh showed them round it with justifiable pride. The class numbers were growing, she said contentedly – a very encouraging sign when, for so many past years, the island's population had always been dwindling.

'You'll be sending us the wee girl too, I believe, before long,' she added, smiling at Fiona.

'At the end of the summer,' Louise agreed. 'She isn't five yet, and she's having rather a lot to get used to.'

Miss Mackintosh agreed with that and walked with them to the car, where Macgregor greeted them with as much rejoicing as if they'd been gone for days.

'Jamie's dog,' Louise said quickly. 'A rather special Border Collie.'

'Indeed, I can see he is,' Miss Mackintosh agreed, managing to sound properly impressed, and thereby winning Jamie's undying resolve to like her and her school, no matter what. They drove home almost cheerfully after that, and not even her father's news that Sir James Guthrie was coming to Skye could spoil Louise's conviction that, after all, in bringing the children to the manse she'd done the only thing that would put their world together again. What it would do to her own life only time would tell, but she couldn't regret it. Her mother and her London friends would suppose that she'd run mad, and she could see as well as they every damned one of the snags in front of her, as sharp and perilous as Cuillin's peaks. First off, she'd even have to come to terms with the mountains themselves; the day she set foot on them she'd know she'd conquered that particular fear.

There remained a far more important challenge – not

only to help Angus's children grow up as he and Ailsa would have done, but at the same time to make some sort of bearable life for herself on this remote and alien island. Fifteen years from now, when Jamie and Fee no longer needed her it would be much too late to revert to being a Londoner – she had to become an islander well before then.

Eleven

To the children's relief, at least, the fine weather still held the following morning. Even though a change was forecast as being on its way, their barbecue was safe. Towards midday, a steady column of smoke rising from the beach confirmed that Brett's fire was going well, and Macgregor's nose began to twitch at the smells drifting up across the lawn.

Garden chairs were carried down for the elders of the party, and rugs spread on the shingle for the rest of them. Brett's announcement that his alfresco feast was almost ready was the signal for Louise to return to the house for the bread and bowls of salad she had waiting there. She was on her way outside again when a dark-blue car nosed its way along the drive and stopped at the front door. It was a car she remembered well enough but hadn't expected to see again. When Iain Macrae stepped out she stood looking at him for a moment, at a loss to know what to say. A breezy 'still here?' seemed pointless when he so obviously was; and 'no search party or tow needed today, thank you' smacked of sending away a travelling salesman empty-handed.

'Good morning,' she said at last. 'Can we help *you* this time?'

'Tom Hepburn has asked me to call and see your father,' he answered slowly, 'but I seem to have chosen a bad moment. I'll come back another time.'

It was puzzling, to say the least, that he should still be involved in their affairs, but she suspected that a snub would be all she'd get if she enquired the reason. Instead, she gestured at the far end of the garden.

'We're all on the beach, having an Australian barbecue, and it would be helpful if you happened to be hungry – Brett's cooking enough sausages and chops to feed a regiment. Even Aunt Janet is there, unable to quite make up her mind whether to enjoy herself or not.'

Iain Macrae looked uncertain, for the first time in her acquaintance with him. 'An American-sounding gate-crasher! Won't I spoil the party?'

'You might,' Louise admitted, 'but we'd better go and find out. You could carry the basket of bread.'

He'd had no idea how to present himself at the manse – Tom Hepburn's friend, distant relative, or make-believe potential buyer all seemed spurious – but there had to be some reason for his call. Now, plunged into an informal beach picnic his conversation with Andrew Maitland would have to wait, and meanwhile it was Louise herself who would have to decide how to introduce him. As he followed her down the path he thought he could sense the problem she was having.

In fact she decided to say as little as possible; he was Mr Hepburn's Canadian friend, visiting Skye. Her father would make the necessary connection and identify him correctly. She led the way out of the undergrowth on to the beach, and in the moment of stillness that followed an unexpected new arrival there was time to notice Jamie's brief grin and the sudden blush of pleasure in Ellie Moffat's face. There was no doubt of Iain Macrae's welcome from them, but Janet Maitland's expression wasn't encouraging. She disliked visitors on principle who just 'called in', and having to receive one whilst she was sitting in a garden chair on a patch of shingle made him even more unacceptable. Watching the little scene, Louise thought he coped rather well with his baptism of fire.

He bowed over his hostess's hand with a formality that bravely ignored the old tweed hat of Andrew's that she wore to keep her hair from being disarranged by the breeze.

'Tom Hepburn told me to be sure to deliver his best
wishes, Miss Maitland, but I'm afraid I've chosen an incon-
venient moment.' His accent went some way to undoing
the good effect, but she remembered that Louise had
stressed the word 'Canadian'. She would reserve judgement for the moment.

'We don't make a habit of entertaining guests down
here,' she explained, to set the social record straight. 'Our
Australian friends are responsible for this rather unusual
party. The *children* are enjoying it very much.'

His mouth twitched at her own faint stress on the word,
but he answered solemnly. 'I think I might live down here
if this belonged to me. I see now why Tom Hepburn urged
me to pay you a visit.'

Ellie arrived with plates of food at that moment and he
was free to move on and greet his host.

'You've been very kind to Louise,' Andrew Maitland
said immediately. 'I can't tell you how grateful I am.'

'Well I know why she had to bring the children . . . it
seemed little enough to do what I could to help.' He
watched the chef spearing a sausage to put on Jamie's
plate, and turned to smile at his host. 'I expect your
daughter mentioned that we met Brett and Ellie on the
road. He's very beguiled by the idea of his Skye ancestors!'

'And you are not?' Andrew asked curiously. 'This is
equally where your own forebears left from, I believe.'

'It was all too long ago for me, I'm afraid. Canada is
full of people with Scottish names, and although they enjoy
the game of Burns nights, and all the nonsense that goes
with them, that's what it is, I think – a game!' But Iain
felt uncomfortable as he said it; he'd probably protested
too much, and even managed to sound like his stepmother
into the bargain. He was silent for a moment, then risked
a question he wasn't sure he was entitled to ask. 'How is
Jamie settling down?'

Andrew didn't resent the enquiry. 'He longs for his
parents, of course, and will probably never quite stop

missing them; but now Louise has decided to stay, we know this is the best place for him and Fiona. It wouldn't have been, I'm afraid, without her.'

Iain looked across to where Louise Maitland knelt on the rug, cutting up the food on her niece's plate. She was laughing and pushing Macgregor's inquisitive nose away at the same time; with her hair lifted away from her face by the breeze he could see the delicate planes of her face; intelligence and kindness were there, and – he could acknowledge it now – a certain sort of beauty. But even on a beach she managed to look sophisticated. How in God's name could she settle here?

'Quite a change of lifestyle,' he remarked casually. 'This place is glorious now, but I suspect it looks very different in the winter, and it won't ever have the things your daughter's used to.' Then Andrew Maitland's bleak expression made him quickly apologize. 'I'm sorry – forgive me for pointing out the obvious.'

'She's giving up her own life, Mr Macrae – I know that; Jamie doesn't yet, of course, but one day I hope he will.' Then after a little pause, he went on in a different tone of voice. 'Tom didn't mention that you were coming to Skye, but perhaps he didn't know.'

'Nor did I when I left Edinburgh,' Iain admitted. 'At the moment I'm a free man, so I go where events seem to lead me. It feels odd but very enjoyable after years on the treadmill of a United Nations relief organization.' Then he smiled suddenly. 'I'm not quite a free man: Tom Hepburn asked me to call on you! Could we talk after the picnic?'

'Of course,' his host agreed, trying not to look surprised. The Canadian's fine-drawn, tired appearance was at least explained now, and so was his readiness to find a lost, small boy; the rest was a mystery of Tom Hepburn's making. But he didn't say so, and left Iain Macrae free to move over to the rock where Jamie sat sharing the contents of his plate with Macgregor.

He was greeted with a shy smile and a recommendation

to try the sausages. 'Macgregor's had two already; I should think that's enough, wouldn't you?'

'Quite enough, and in any case Brett's been cooking them for you, not him.'

Jamie looked across at the Australian, now sitting with Louise and Fiona while he cooled down from the heat of the fire. 'He's nice, and he can even make Aunt Janet laugh. P'raps he'll stay – he likes it here.'

That much was true, Iain thought, but it seemed very obvious that Brett also liked Louise Maitland much more than was good for a man whose destiny lay back in Australia with Ellie Moffat. He was at that early stage when he didn't even question why the world had never looked so beautiful or life so richly promising, but the explanation would dawn on him soon.

'Don't count on him staying, Jamie,' Iain said gently. 'He's like me, you know – just visiting.' The child nodded, looking suddenly so sad that Iain hurried on. 'But your Aunt Louise *is* staying, I understand.'

Contentment reappeared in Jamie's face. 'Yes, but we don't call her that – Aunt Janet is an aunt.' Iain could see the distinction clearly enough but before he had to say so Jamie spoke again. 'Now she won't have to go back to London. It's horrid there. People only look down at the pavements, not at the sky, and when they bump into each other they don't say they're sorry.'

It was a child's graphically simple description of city life, forgotten a moment later when Macgregor barked at an incoming ripple of water and Jamie went with the dog down to the water's edge. At once Ellie came to take his place on the rock.

'Did you ever see a happier man?' she asked, looking across at Brett. 'Make him any offer you could think of and he'd choose to stay right here. The funny thing is that before we came to Skye Brett was all for going home and I was the one who kept saying "not yet, I'm not ready to go home yet".'

'And now you are?' he queried gently.

'Not just ready – desperate!' Her mouth sketched a tremulous smile. 'I've had enough of "abroad" – I want to be back in Oz again. Brett keeps telling me that people are different here; well, I know now that's true . . . and you're different again, just to get me in even more of a muddle!' She tried hard to say it lightly, even though her eyes had filled with tears. He wanted to salute the effort she was making, but was also sharply aware of a discovery about himself. Years of loneliness kept intensely private, and detachment learnt as the only means of surviving other people's distress, were suddenly at an end. Attachments were coming at him thick and fast on this Scottish odyssey . . . the gods had finally caught up with him and ordained that, late in the day though it was, his heart should be wrung and wrung again with pity.

'Take Brett home, Ellie,' he said at last. 'That's where you both belong. It's true he's fallen in love, but it's a temporary sickness, not life-threatening.'

She didn't argue or say that he was wrong, although she thought he was; instead, she needed to explain herself. 'Have you ever not wanted something that was yours for the taking? I left Australia to see the great big world but also to escape, maybe, ending up with Brett, as everybody had it planned. Now, even if I asked him to come home I don't think he would . . . he's under some kind of spell.' She didn't mention the name of Louise Maitland, couldn't bring herself to, he thought; letting the blame rest on Skye made what was happening less unbearable.

The silence was broken by Brett himself announcing that because the tide was on the turn it was time to start clearing up. He began to dismantle his fire, while Louise set the children to collecting plates and cutlery and piling them in the wheelbarrow that waited at the bottom of the path.

Iain and Ellie stood up as well, but he had one last thing to say to her. 'I've checked in at the Ardvasar – bring Brett down for dinner this evening.' She nodded and then walked away to join in the work of restoring the little beach to order again, while he went to offer Janet Maitland an escort up the cliff path. She allowed her arm to be held, but disengaged herself as soon as they were back in the garden again. 'Thank you, Mr Macrae; from here I can manage,' she said very firmly. 'You'll be wanting to get on your way now, I expect.'

He felt rather pleased to be able to disappoint her. 'Well, first I have to talk to your brother, Miss Maitland. I'll wait for him here while you go indoors.'

Dismissed in her turn, she stared at him for a moment but, aware that he wouldn't volunteer anything else, finally walked towards the house. He was still smiling to himself when Andrew Maitland came towards him and suggested the garden bench as the place where they ought to talk.

'I think Tom has told you of our situation here,' Andrew said when they were sitting down. 'He's still hopeful that something can be done about it, but I am not. We must soon find somewhere else to live.' He smiled faintly at his guest. 'My daughter and Tom Hepburn would like us to fight Sir James Guthrie, but I'm afraid I see little point in a battle we can't win.'

Unable to admit that he agreed, Iain began to lay out Tom Hepburn's plan. 'The first objective is to buy some time – stop the Church authorities closing a deal with Guthrie while the possibility of another buyer they might like better is floated in front of them. Rich entrepreneurs are usually impatient men; who knows, Guthrie might decide to look elsewhere on Skye.'

'I'm sure he equally knows that this would be his ideal site – between the bridge and the Armadale ferry, near the airstrip, and on good level ground. I think he'll wait for it to fall into his lap.'

Irritated by a reasonable viewpoint that exactly matched his own, Iain was considering what to say next when Andrew Maitland spoke again. 'In any case we don't *have* another possibility to offer the Church.'

'We can have; at least, a hint of one,' was the unexpected reply, and it made Andrew stare more closely at his visitor.

'Not . . . not you, surely?' But when he saw confirmation in Iain's face, he shook his head very firmly. 'No, Mr Macrae . . . I really can't allow it. You mustn't get embroiled in our affairs in this way. Tom intends it for the best, of course, but ends never justify the means, and this would be a shabby pretence that neither you nor he should have to get involved in.'

Iain's answering smile was rueful. 'Exactly what I thought, too! But an overbearing solicitor in Portree made me begin to change my mind, and what I subsequently found out about the Guthrie enterprises suggested that *someone* ought to put a spoke in his wheel.'

'Louise would agree with that,' Andrew Maitland admitted. 'She had dealings with him once, by an extraordinary coincidence; her adjective for the man is "poisonous"!' He reflected for a moment on what Iain had said before he spoke again. 'If Tom's idea is that you're to be the alternative bidder, your offer would soon be exposed as worthless. What could that possibly achieve?'

'Time for your good friend to find an authentic buyer who might offer less money but a proposal that the Church authorities would prefer.'

Andrew Maitland still looked doubtful but Iain went firmly on. 'It's not as hopeless as it seems. There's growing opposition to wholesale tourism; apart from anything else it's chancy and very volatile. On the other hand there's growing support for alternative, traditional ways of supporting Skye's own indigenous population – crofting being the most fundamental one of course.'

'It was tried and failed,' Andrew sadly pointed out, unknowingly repeating Edward Carmichael's words.

'It failed two centuries ago; it doesn't have to fail now.'

'Nevertheless, Donald Mackinnon is giving up,' Andrew had to insist.

'I know – I went to see him this morning.' Iain's smile reappeared. 'I went, of course, so that he should mention my visit to the lawyer in Portree, and you must do the same. He has to be convinced that I'm what I've said I am – an interested party!'

But Andrew didn't return his smile, and Iain knew why – Janet Maitland's Presbyterian principles were as deeply embedded in this gentle, honest man as they were in her.

'You don't like the pretence,' Iain said bluntly, 'and nor do I. But remember, please, the sort of man we're trying to beat. He fights any way he can, for profit. We are trying to preserve not only your home, but buildings that are part of Skye's history and land that should be worked and cherished and made properly productive again. If that requires a bit of subterfuge, Tom Hepburn can count me in.'

'You'd make a very good advocate yourself,' Andrew commented, looking a little happier. 'Forgive me when I say that it's a ruse that won't work in the end; but if it only buys us the time for my grandchildren to settle down here, that will be something achieved. I'm very grateful to you for bothering with us at all.' He thought for a moment, then went on. 'Janet will wonder about this conversation, and so will Louise. What am I to say to them? Even if I *could* take refuge in a lordly silence, it wouldn't be very fair; this is their home as well as mine.'

Iain acknowledged to himself that fighting with Andrew Maitland on his side meant tying one hand behind his back, but he did his best to sound calm. 'I think you say, as briefly as possible, that Tom Hepburn is working hard to produce a buyer that the Church might like better than Sir James Guthrie. Miss Maitland must pray hard that he finds one; your daughter can speak of her acquaintance with Guthrie to anyone who asks! How about that?'

'Masterly,' Andrew agreed quietly. 'I shall go and report to Mr Carmichael that a charming but unidentified Canadian called on me this morning. He asked if he might look around a house and garden that his ancestors had known! Will that do?'

'Masterly,' Iain repeated with a grin. 'I've got some more investigations to make, but between whiles I'm staying at the Ardvasar Hotel. Say goodbye to the others for me, please, and tell Jamie I agreed with him about the sausages!'

With that he walked back to the drive where he had left his car. Louise climbed up from the beach just in time to see that blue car back its way down the drive – Iain Macrae made a habit, she thought, of abrupt departures. It was tempting to ask why he'd come at all, but the question might have seemed impertinent, and she could – with a heroic exercise in self-control – manage to wait until her father felt inclined to tell her what they'd been talking about so earnestly.

Twelve

The following morning, on his way to an interview with the editor of the forthright *West Highland Free Press*, Iain noticed that for once the doors of Kilchrist's kirk stood open. He stopped the car and walked towards them, now even more surprised to hear music being played inside the church. But first something else halted him on the threshold – hanging on the wall in the porch was a framed list of the pastors who had served there. One name leapt out, making his heart miss a beat: 'Thomas Macrae, 1848-1852'. Not a long span of years, but he knew why; in 1852 Thomas had chosen to go with his flock to Canada when they were evicted and their homes burnt down behind them so that they couldn't return.

He stood still, seeing in his mind's eye the straggling, pitiful procession that had made its way to the waiting ship in Broadford Bay. Thomas and his wife had survived the voyage because they were young and strong, but many hadn't. He, their great-great-grandson, was standing here simply because of them. Useless now, with this lump in his throat, to pretend that he didn't care, that a best-forgotten past was nothing to do with him.

At last he moved away and walked into the church – cold as a tomb, bare of ornament or stained glass, but flooded with light from the plain lancet windows, and for the moment filled with music as well. Almost conditioned now to expecting surprises, he barely questioned why the musician in front of him should be Andrew Maitland's daughter. She stopped playing and looked round to see him standing there.

'Musician as well as cook?' he asked, brief and to the point as usual.

'Nothing if not versatile,' Louise agreed politely. 'But I wouldn't dignify this instrument by saying that it produces music; sounds will do.'

'Whatever it is, why are *you* playing it?'

She smiled at his insistence; he was a man who liked to get to the bottom of things. 'Aunt Janet volunteered my services for Easter Sunday, which is fast approaching, because the usual performer is sick. I shall manage well enough to satisfy the congregation, I hope.'

She sounded cheerful, but he could see the thinness of her face too clearly when she looked down at the keyboard, and something that felt strangely like anger stirred in him – it was all wrong that she should be here alone in this ice-cold place, practising Presbyterian hymns; even more wrong that fate had sentenced her to a kind of island servitude.

'Can you really stay on at the manse?' he heard himself ask. 'What sort of a life will you have?'

He expected to be told with Janet Maitland's sort of firmness that, however it turned out, it need be no concern of his, but she answered instead with the candour that he was beginning to recognize. 'I have no idea as yet. I shall look after the children, find a job when I can, maybe even come to terms with Aunt Janet if we both live long enough.' Unaware of the desolation in her face, she tried to sound as if she didn't mind what she'd just described. 'You're not impressed, but then you weren't impressed by what I did in London, either. You're a hard man to please, I'm afraid.'

'Be serious for a moment,' he insisted quietly.

Her fingers hit the keys in a moment of sudden ugly sound before she resolved the discord into harmony again and answered him. 'I'm not anything of a saint, nor – I hope – am I stupidly biting off more than I can chew. Staying here is what I have to do; that's all there is to it.' Then her hand swept the subject aside. 'Am I allowed to know why you called on my father yesterday? All I've gleaned so far is that the manse is in danger of being sold to a man who could have doubled nicely for the loathsome MacDonald factor of a hundred and fifty years ago!'

'Your father said you were acquainted with James Guthrie,' Iain commented. 'The prospective sale was what caused Tom Hepburn to write to my father, inviting him to take an interest in what was going on. My father died a month ago, so I came over instead to present my apologies in person for declining to do any such thing. Since then, of course, your father's wily lawyer friend has led me ever deeper into the Maitland family maze. Now here I am pretending to be seriously toying with the idea of outbidding the man you dislike so much.'

As she stared at him the disbelief in her face gave way to anger. 'It's a ridiculous idea; nothing will come of it except further disappointment for my father. What on earth made you agree to it?'

'I've no idea,' he said with an honesty to equal hers. 'My only excuse is that I haven't behaved as I normally do from the moment I arrived in Scotland. I even remember offering to help a cross-grained young woman off the train at Edinburgh – absolutely untypical!'

'I was slightly distraught, not cross,' Louise insisted, 'and so would you have been if you'd shared a guard's van with Macgregor for several hours.'

Iain smiled at that, acknowledging the truth of it, and the sudden warmth and humour in his face prompted her to ask a question.

'When you're in Canada, behaving normally, what do you do?'

'I'm hardly ever there,' he answered. 'Canadians by and large know how to treat their land; Africans by and large don't. My job has been to try and teach them. From what I've seen so far there's scope for improvement here as well.' He saw the other question in her face that she baulked at asking, and answered it anyway. 'I fell foul of malaria – extended sick leave is the result.'

She was silent for a moment, then spoke seriously, as
he'd asked her to. 'I'm sorry about your illness, and about
your father's death. Can't you find something more
relaxing to do while you mend than get involved in our
affairs?'

Iain shook his head. 'Don't stop me. I've been told more
than once that it's time I took an interest in other people's
lives – that's what I suppose I'm trying to do! Now, you'd
better start playing again before you freeze to death, and
I must go or be late for an interview in Broadford.' But,
on the point of leaving he thought of something else. 'I
had dinner with Ellie and Brett last night. *She's* very
unhappy and he's in a trance. I can't blame you – he's
falling in love without any help from you, that I can see;
but you might urge him to remember *her*, and make up
his mind to take her home.'

She was too slow to follow what he meant. By the time
she'd got a reply phrased sharply enough to demolish him
he'd walked away out of the church. There was a little
truth, unfortunately, in what he'd suggested; she could
sense Brett's concern for her at least, and it had been
comforting. But it was only a temporary thing whilst he
was there. She hoped Ellie would understand that as clearly
as she did herself. With that settled in her mind, she considered the rest of her conversation with Iain Macrae. He'd
seemed angry a good part of the time, though oddly not
with the man who'd been responsible for bringing him to
Scotland. She knew a little more about him now, but understood him no better. Who had told him to involve himself
with other people? A woman, almost certainly; someone
who'd been unhappy about his role of uncommitted
onlooker. He was a mystery she couldn't solve, and only
occasionally like; but meanwhile her fingers were stiffen-
ing with cold. It was time to put away her music and go
home.

A quarter of an hour later, apologizing to the editor he'd
kept waiting, Iain was unaware that Edward Carmichael

was himself nervously welcoming into his office in Portree a man who both fascinated and frightened him. Here influence and wealth were personified; here was the ruthless use of both to gain still more; and here the occasional display of charm needed to soften brutality. Saville Row and Jermyn Street had done their best for James Guthrie, but no tailoring genius could disguise the stocky, powerful body of the Lowlander, and no rich living had coddled his brain or blunted his ambition.

Entreated by the lawyer to take his most comfortable chair, the visitor preferred to walk about the room. He didn't want coffee or a dram; he simply needed the name of the man who was threatening to meddle in a negotiation that had been all but settled.

Looking acutely miserable, Mr Carmichael confessed, 'I didn't get his name, Sir James. He was careful not to give it to me. All I can tell you is that his ancestors left – were evicted, I have to say – from the Sleat peninsular land that you're interested in.'

'I'm not "interested" in it – I'm buying it,' his client pointed out. Pale-blue eyes examined Mr Carmichael's gently perspiring face. 'You shouldn't have mentioned this troublesome Canadian to the Church men; an expensive mistake – for *you* I mean.'

'I did not, Sir James,' the lawyer said, struggling to sound firm. 'The mistake occurred in Edinburgh, not here. Tom Hepburn was the informant – he's distantly connected to this man.'

Sir James wasted a moment in considering how to get the Edinburgh lawyer thrown out of the club they both belonged to, then turned his fire on Mr Carmichael again. 'Someone in his office must know the Canadian's name; a bribe unlocks most tongues, I find, but perhaps you hadn't thought of that.'

There was the hint of a pointed sneer which the lawyer decided to ignore. Then a little light shone on his darkness. 'I recommended the Ardvasar Hotel as a place to stay – he could have gone there.'

'Good of you to remember . . . no, don't bother,' Sir James snapped as Mr Carmichael's hand reached for the telephone, 'I'll check myself; like as not they'd fob you off with some cock and bull story. I want to go down there anyway to see the crofter.'

Mr Carmichael took comfort in what he was about to say next; he was tired of being put through Sir James Guthrie's wringer. 'The Canadian has already been to see him – Donald Mackinnon telephoned to tell me so.'

Unexpectedly his visitor smiled. 'Then the man's a fool, leaving a trail a mile wide – hardly worth the trouble of beating. Still, I want the deal closed soon, and the buildings on that land demolished before winter sets in. I'll do the donkey work here while you try to concentrate your clerical employers' minds on what *they* have to do.'

Mr Carmichael spared a thought for the most reasonable excuse he could offer them for not reporting that someone else was interested in the Kilchrist land. But his visitor was getting ready to leave; a moment later he'd gone without bothering to shake hands, and Edward Carmichael could restore himself with a wee dram from the whisky decanter on the table behind his desk. It helped to soften the reflection that serving God and Mammon *was* quite as difficult as the Bible maintained, even for the most astute of lawyers.

Outside, the chauffeur was instructed to head for Sleat, stopping first at the Mackinnon croft along the way. Leaving the servant the task of finding it, Sir James settled back to observe the landscape and consider what he could do with it. A Lowlander through and through, he didn't like mountains; a hill or two added something to the scenery, but bloody great lumps of rock like the Cuillin were no use to anyone but the madmen who wanted to climb them. Still, there were plenty of rich madmen and he'd make sure they came to his hotel when it was built. Pity the island climate was so iffy, but even that could be turned to good account – rich madmen liked to think themselves rugged adventurers when they weren't busy making money; well, let Skye be a challenge for them.

Obedient to the name painted on a board at the side of the road, the driver turned the car into a rutted lane and stopped it a hundred yards further on outside a white-washed, dormer windowed croft that sat squarely among small fields dotted with sheep and black-faced lambs. A tall, thin man had emerged from an outbuilding at the sound of the car, and now stood waiting.

'James Guthrie,' the visitor announced himself, 'and you'll be Donald Mackinnon; I reckoned it was time I talked to you myself.'

A soft Highland voice admitted to the name of Mackinnon and invited Sir James to step indoors. He was led into the kitchen and politely asked to be seated. The crofter washed his hands at the sink, and then sat down himself, with Highland dignity and grace as unimpaired as if he'd been entertaining his guest in some palatial drawing room.

'I've come about the sale, of course,' said Sir James, having refused the offer of tea. He smiled at the man facing him across the table. 'Leave these things to lawyers and they drag on for months; we can settle this between ourselves in no time at all. I agree to your price, so all we need to settle is the timing. I'm not going to be unreasonable – I know you've got to sell your animals before you can leave; but I'm not inclined to waste all the summer months . . . so what do you say – I have possession on Quarter Day, August the first?' He saw no encouraging agreement in the grave face opposite him; in fact he saw nothing readable at all. 'Well, speak out man,' he said sharply. 'You haven't changed your mind about selling, I take it?'

The tall Gael shook his head. 'Selling iss certainly what I must do,' he agreed sadly, still leaving a faint doubt in the air that his visitor thought he could interpret easily enough.

'You've been approached by someone else, and now wait for us to bid against each other. I'm not playing that game, Mackinnon. You set a price and I agreed to it; I won't be bulldozed into offering more.' He saw something that looked like distaste on Donald Mackinnon's face and had the good sense to apologize. 'Sorry – it's what often happens in the cold, hard world outside this island, but I'm sure it's not how business is conducted here. Shall we shake hands on a deal?'

Still the man hesitated, and finally put together the unfamiliar English words he needed. 'It iss like this, Sir James. A Canadian gentleman would like to buy my land – that iss true; but I'm thinking that I like more what he wants to do with it than what you want to do.' If Highland courtesy hadn't prevented it Donald Mackinnon could have added the further truth that he liked more the man who'd called to see him earlier than he liked the one he was talking to now.

James Guthrie took a deep breath, contained his rising anger, and spoke in the calm tones of a reasonable man arguing with a lunatic. 'While you're thinking, Mr Mackinnon' – the 'Mr' this time was a deliberate concession – 'remember this: we all know that crofting's a hard and painful way to make even a bare living; the Canadian *may* be serious in what he's offering, but what if it's just a ploy to hold things up? And even if *you* don't like my development very much, other people will who'll bring much-needed money into Skye.' He stood up, and tried to match the dignity of his grave host. 'I can give you three days to make up your mind – you can reach me at Lord MacDonald's Kinloch Lodge. After that I must go back to Edinburgh.' Then the hand he hadn't offered to Edward Carmichael he held out to a man he realized couldn't be bought, and smiled at him. 'I'll say good day to you now.'

Donald Mackinnon had one more thing to say. 'You must give me four days, I'm afraid – we don't do business here on the Sabbath, and this one in particular will be Easter Day.'

Sir James managed to stay calm. 'Four days then; I'd forgotten that the Sabbath is still properly kept up here.'

Then he walked out of the croft and was driven away. It was time to track down the unnamed Canadian and bribe or browbeat him into confessing to Mackinnon and the Churchmen in Edinburgh that he'd had his joke at their expense and was now ready to leave the field clear for the only serious buyer they'd got.

Thirteen

Dinner was over at the Ardvasar that evening when Brett Macdonald walked in. The man he was looking for sat drinking coffee in the bar.

'Glad to find you here,' he said, 'otherwise I'd have added a pointless walk to the miles we've done today.'

'Ellie not with you?' Iain asked.

The Australian's slow smile appeared. 'I got her tired out today – first time I've managed it. A guide from the hostel took us up what he called a "wee small hill", but it felt like mountaineering on Everest to us! Ellie loved it as much as I did. According to our friend she has the makings of a natural climber – less brute strength than me but more finesse and plenty of nerve! She's very pleased with herself.'

'And so she should be,' Iain agreed. 'Your first walk on a hill calls for a dram to celebrate. Stay there while I get it, and then you can tell me why you came looking for me.'

When the whisky had been brought Brett took a sip, gave a little sigh of pleasure, and then plunged into his tale. 'Ellie wanted you to know something that happened this morning when she came to collect our picnic lunch. She had to wait because someone else was being attended to – not a local, but not a foreigner either, like us. Being a girl who makes up her mind about people pretty quick, she took a scunner to this man straight off – too much money, too used to throwing his weight about, she reckoned; not her cup of tea at all.'

Iain suspected that he could now guess why the story concerned himself, but he was content to let Brett finish it.

'She was standing right behind him, so she couldn't help hearing what he said to Chrissy Macdonald at the desk; he was looking for a Canadian visitor who was anxious to contact him. But his fool of a secretary hadn't got down more than the name of the Ardvasar Hotel before the Canadian had rung off. Chrissy was impressed by the man and glad to be helpful. "Och, it's Mr Macrae you'll be wanting – Iain Macrae. He's a Canadian right enough. He's away out just now but you're welcome to leave a message".'

Having reported this snippet of conversation passed on by Ellie, Brett then went on to say that no message had been left. The man had gone straight back to the expensive car waiting for him outside, barely remembering to thank the girl for her help. 'Ellie thinks it's fishy,' he finished up. 'He wasn't the sort of man to employ a dud secretary, and why didn't he say where you could reach him – supposing, of course, that you *had* been wanting to.'

Clearly doubtful about that, Brett sat with his head cocked on one side, looking like an expectant robin about to be thrown a titbit; something was going on that he and Ellie didn't yet know about. Iain Macrae hesitated for a moment, then briefly explained James Guthrie's development plan and how it affected the Maitland family.

'He can't do that – can he?' Brett asked, with a mixture of anger and anxiety in his voice. 'I mean, couldn't someone stop him wrecking what's left of their lives?'

Iain shook his head. 'It's all too likely that he'll be encouraged, not stopped. His hotel and golf course would bring in wealthy visitors – good for the island, it's thought, as well as for himself.'

Brett thought about this for a moment. 'Why is he looking for you?' he then asked as his obvious next question.

'This is where it does indeed get fishy,' Iain had to confess. 'With the help of Andrew Maitland's lawyer friend in Edinburgh, I'm pretending to be a mad Canadian with more money than sense, hell-bent on recovering the land my ancestors were kicked off a hundred and fifty years ago.' He took a sip of whisky from his glass and smiled ruefully at the expression on Brett's face. 'It was meant to buy some time before Guthrie could close his deal with the Church, and it seemed justified given what's at stake for the Maitlands and the sort of unscrupulous buccaneer that Guthrie is. But that was before I'd met the other person involved – the crofter, Donald Mackinnon, whose land is also an important part of the deal. He hates the thought of leaving, but he's desperate to go because his wife needs a drier climate than this one.'

'And if Guthrie pulls out, or the Church prefers your pretend-bid, the crofter's left high and dry without a proper buyer.'

'The situation in a nutshell,' Iain agreed.

Brett sipped his whisky reflectively. 'It's hopeless, isn't it? From what I've seen of the island, most of it would break a farmer's heart – bare rock or peaty, swampy land good for grazing sheep and precious little else. Who's going to make a serious bid for that?'

'It's difficult, not hopeless,' Iain insisted, 'but the wrong things have been done here for too long: trees cut down that would have held the soil; sheep allowed to take over instead of mixed livestock that would manure the ground instead of eating it to death; too few cereals and vegetables grown on what good land there is. But the crofters were squeezed on to smaller and smaller plots and their communal grazing up on the braes was taken away from them to make more income for the lairds. Of course starvation was the result, followed by forced clearances.'

'You know a lot about it,' Brett said with some surprise.

'It's my job,' Iain pointed out briefly. 'I'm an agronomist, but I can only tell people what they ought to do, not make them do it.'

The Australian's face looked suddenly full of sadness. 'I'd give it a go. Sounds crazy, I expect, when I've only been here a few days, but I know just how Donald

Mackinnon feels, and I don't want to leave any more than
he does. But we have this big spread at home and although
my father isn't ready to kick his boots off yet, he reckons
it's safe to assume I'll be there to take it over when he
does.'

'And in any case,' Iain reminded him gently, 'there's
Ellie to think of, too. My impression is that she wants to
go home.'

Brett picked up his glass and nursed it between large,
square hands. 'Yes, there's Ellie,' he agreed. 'I think we've
waited long enough; it's time to marry and settle down. I
shan't forget this place, though, and one day I'll come
back, but it won't be in time to help the Maitlands, and
that hurts a lot more than I know how to say.'

Not in time to help Louise Maitland, Iain guessed that
he meant. He'd go on with the families' plan, love and
honour Ellie as his wife, and help her raise their children,
but his heart would remember a grey-eyed, gentle-voiced
girl who was nothing like the women he knew at home.
As if to confirm that thought, Brett said one more thing
in a voice that he couldn't quite hold steady. 'Life's a bitch
sometimes; but I think you know that already.'

Iain's nod answered him, and they sat in silence for
a moment or two until the Australian spoke again.
'What's going to happen – about the manse and this man
Guthrie?'

'I don't know, Brett,' came the slow reply. 'I suppose
that what I hope will happen is that the Church authorities simply accept his offer; then, mission failed, I can
go back to Canada, forget this Scottish interlude and get
on with filling in the time until I'm passed fit for work
again. Sir James Guthrie is getting impatient – that's
why he's come here himself, to lean on Donald
Mackinnon and to elbow me out of the way. Having
done that, he'll go on to the manse to mop up Andrew
Maitland.'

Brett's all-too expressive face showed how disappointed
he was. 'You make it sound as if it's all over.'

'Of course it's over,' Iain said sharply. 'Charades don't last, and Guthrie knows that quite as well as I do. I'd drag it out if I could, but not at the expense of Donald Mackinnon.' Then his thin hand waved the vexed subject away. 'Come to the kirk on Sunday – it's Easter Day and Louise will be playing the hymns; I heard her practising this morning.'

Brett agreed, refused a lift back to the hostel and said a quiet goodnight. Walking back through the dark, he stopped to watch the lights of Mallaig across the Sound; for once the air was still, and moonlight laid a silver track across the water. What he'd said to Iain Macrae was true – he'd come back one day; simply had to. But the thought of the Canadian made him frown; unreasonable it might be, but somehow he'd wanted more from him. All right, there was no place in this fight for a brave Highland charge, with claymores swinging and the skirl of pipes to put the fear of God into the invader; but a stubborn refusal to quit the field of battle *might* have defeated Guthrie's weapons of money and influence in the halls of power. His heart bled for the Maitlands, Andrew and his orphaned grand-children; Louise he wouldn't allow himself to think about at all. He was going to take Ellie home and marry her, and it was only the damnably haunting atmosphere of this place that made it feel as if he was going into exile. Turning away from the shimmering water at last, he trudged back to the hostel, not knowing that he'd left a troubled man back at the hotel. Iain was fully aware of his Australian friend's disappointment in him, and it hurt even though it was unfair. The temptation was to blame Tom Hepburn for getting him into the mess at all, but he knew it wasn't true; he'd been hooked and reeled into the Maitlands' affairs from the moment he'd walked into the lobby of the Alexandra Hotel and found a tired young woman quietly agonizing over a missing child. All that had happened since had merely confirmed that fate had decided to teach him a lesson; it was time for one self-sufficient onlooker on life to learn about the heartaches that beset everybody else.

Guthrie would come looking for him in the morning – he felt sure of that. He had until then to make up his mind whether to fight or to run.

The morning ritual at the manse, Louise had now discovered, was for her father to drive to the Armadale stores to collect whatever shopping Janet Maitland needed and to wait for the newspapers brought over on the first ferry from Mallaig. His suggestion that the children should go with him and watch the boat come in was accepted by Jamie for both of them, and the three of them, plus Macgregor, set off leaving Louise alone for the first time with her aunt. It was the moment, she knew, to clear the air between them, but Janet's unyielding expression held out no hope that the confrontation would be painless – like Hamlet and Laertes fighting their final duel, they'd 'bleed on both sides' before they were done.

She began by starting to clear the breakfast table, knowing that she'd be told to leave it alone because guests didn't busy themselves with the dishes. Still gripping a porridge bowl, Louise turned to answer her opponent.

'You may be right about guests, Aunt Janet, but that's not what I am. We make a lot of extra work, the children and I – you have to let me help.'

'Caring for the bairns isn't something we'll be sharing for long,' Janet insisted implacably. 'Andrew thinks you'll stay, but I know better. You'll be off and away back to London, just like your mother. The truth is I'd rather you went now; the longer you stay, the more upset the bairns will be when you decide you can't bide here any more.'

Louise took a deep breath, telling herself that, however much provoked, she would *not* shout at her aunt. 'I shall stay until Jamie and Fee no longer need me,' she said with absolute certainty. 'That's why I've written to the people I used to cook for to say I'm not coming back; that's why my mother is packing up clothes and books to send me. When that's been done she'll find a tenant for my flat – I'll have nowhere to go back to.'

She could hear the note of hostility in her voice but, watching the contained misery in Janet Maitland's face, she couldn't hold on to anger. 'Can't we share the children and the work?' she suggested more gently. 'Won't that be happier for them?' When her aunt didn't reply she made one last appeal. 'Isn't that what Angus and Ailsa would have wanted?'

The mention of their names finally broke her aunt's stubborn composure. The tears she'd so far refused to shed suddenly began to trickle down her cheeks and, beyond saying anything at all now, she turned away and fled out of the kitchen. Louise was left alone, wondering how her trembling fingers still managed to hold one of the pottery bowls her aunt treasured so much. She walked over to the sink to place it carefully on the draining board, then went back for another one, and then another, not trusting herself to carry more than one at a time. The table was cleared and the breakfast cloth folded up by the time a ring on the bell summoned her to the front door.

On the step stood a man not seen for several years but still instantly recognizable. There was no mistaking him even though he didn't return the compliment of identifying her. The cook who hadn't been sufficiently obliging had been dismissed from memory, she supposed. In the circumstances it was just as well, but she was irked all the same to have been found so negligible by Sir James Guthrie. Coming on top of her scene with Janet Maitland it was hard to hold her voice steady as she said 'good morning' with a faintly questioning air.

'My name's Guthrie,' he announced briskly, 'Sir James Guthrie. I hope I've come to the right house. It's Mr Andrew Maitland I want to see – your father . . . grandfather perhaps?' He tacked that on as an afterthought because she hadn't the voice or manner of a servant; but in fact she was vaguely familiar as well and he struggled to pin down an elusive memory of having seen her somewhere before.

'Mr Maitland is out,' Louise said coolly, not answering his last question. 'I can't be sure when he'll be back – he

mentioned something about the Mallaig ferry.' She
managed to smile at the visitor. 'A wasted journey, I'm
afraid – you should have telephoned.'

With a slight suggestion of gritted teeth, Sir James smiled
back. 'Didn't occur to me to make an appointment with
a gentleman living in retirement in a secluded corner of
Skye!' He made a little show of consulting his watch. 'I've
some time in hand – I could wait to save calling again.'

Louise tried her hardest to sound regretful. 'I'm sorry
but I'm not permitted to admit strangers. You could leave
a message, then perhaps you wouldn't need to come
back.'

The helpful suggestion had almost a faint ring of impu-
dence about it, and then there came again that nagging
sense of familiarity; but it was this tiresome, bloody island,
he told himself. Everyone he'd met from Edward
Carmichael onwards had been getting on his nerves.

'I've someone else to see in the neighbourhood,' he said
curtly. 'I'll call again on my way back to Kinloch Lodge.'
He gave her a brief farewell nod and strode off up the
drive. A moment later she heard his car engine start up
and gradually fade away.

Ten minutes later her father's ancient Ford chugged to
a halt outside the front door.

'Perfect timing,' she said unsteadily when the children
had tumbled out and gone searching for eggs that the hens
liked to lay in unexpected places. 'You've just missed a
visit from Sir James Guthrie, but I'm afraid he'll be back.'

Andrew Maitland looked unsurprised. 'I thought he
might have been here – we met Iain Macrae down at
Armadale and he warned me to expect a visit.'

'Then let's hope he's worked out what to say when the
great man corners *him*,' Louise suggested wearily. She saw
the question in her father's face and answered it. 'When
I bumped into him in the church yesterday he mentioned
the ridiculous scheme that he and Tom Hepburn had
hatched up together. Maybe he wanted to try to help, but
his bluff is about to be called, I reckon.'

Andrew Maitland heard the dejection in her voice, and his answering smile was full of affection. 'I'm afraid I agree; but what else is wrong – apart from almost everything judging by the woeful expression on your face?'

She held up her hands in a little gesture of despair. 'I tried to tackle Aunt Janet about staying here – because she's refused to mention it herself. But all I did was make bad worse and thoroughly upset her. She's probably still weeping in her bedroom now.'

'Good!' Andrew Maitland said astonishingly. The surprise in his daughter's face made him go on. 'Ever since Angus died she's been locked within herself, mourning him all alone. I'd begun to fear that she would never change . . . that when her time came to die she'd still be embittered and lonely. If you've broken down that barricade all I can say is that I'm deeply thankful.'

Louise heaved a sigh of relief. 'So much for that worry. What about Sir James Guthrie? He'll come back, I'm sure, if only for the pleasure of giving us our marching orders in person. Like Shakespeare's Iago, he can "smile and smile and still be a villain".'

'Then we shall smile back, my dear,' Andrew said calmly, 'and he'll never know whether we mind being told to go or not.'

'Now why didn't I think of that!' More or less serene again, she linked her arm in her father's and walked with him into the house.

Fourteen

When Andrew Maitland had driven away with the children, Iain walked down towards the bay and found a convenient piece of sea wall to perch on. He was visible to anyone travelling along the road, and he had no doubt that the visitor he expected would spot him easily enough. The meeting place, he'd decided, should be of his choosing, and one in which James Guthrie wouldn't feel at home – the sea wall would do very nicely. Dressed himself in jeans, open-necked shirt and sweater, he hoped that his opponent would be nattily turned out in well-cut suit and tie, and so it proved to be when a quarter of an hour later he walked down from the car that had stopped along the road.

'Iain Macrae?' Guthrie asked, coming to a halt in front of him. 'They told me at the hotel where to find you. I'm sure you know who I am.'

'Sir James Guthrie at a guess,' Iain said with a faint smile. 'I heard that you'd been looking for me. Well, here I am.'

Aware of being at a disadvantage, even of being made to look slightly ridiculous and overdressed by a man who seemed altogether too much at ease, Sir James sounded testy when he spoke again.

'We need to talk, but preferably not here.'

'Preferably not where we can be overheard,' his tormentor pointed out. 'Try the wall yourself; it's clean and dry.'

The visitor considered the wall for a moment. 'I'd rather stand.'

'Well then,' said his host, 'shall we not waste time circling round each other like a couple of prizefighters looking for a weak point? You want some land on which to build a golf course and an hotel, and I'd like to see the land put to better use.'

'Such as?'

'Growing good food for the people who belong here . . . keeping a traditional way of life going . . . preserving the look of this lovely place . . . shall I go on?'

'Spare me the romantic stuff and let's get down to brass tacks,' Sir James said, not unreasonably his listener thought. 'My bid for the land is in, with Mackinnon and the Churchmen; they know exactly what I'm prepared to pay and exactly what I'll do with what I buy. I doubt they can say the same for you. All they've got so far is a vague suggestion that you've got a mind to try your hand at crofting – God knows why; it's not been much of a success story up till now. My own idea is that you're playing a game hatched up by that bloody lawyer in Edinburgh – I think Hepburn's his name. He knows I'm not a patient man; he reckons I'll give up on Kilchrist and find something else to buy.'

As a résumé of events it was precise and fair, Iain admitted to himself, and he couldn't disagree with anything the other man had said. Almost, the private battle he'd been fighting for hours was ending in the certainty that he must concede the game was up. But while he framed a probably hopeless appeal for Andrew Maitland's family to be left in the manse, James Guthrie spoke again – arrogantly now, because he sensed that he was going to win.

'Let Mackinnon and Carmichael know you've changed your mind and I'll not make trouble for Hepburn, which I very easily could. You fade away, the crofter and the clerics get their money, and I can stop wasting time; everybody's happy!'

'Except the Maitlands,' Iain pointed out gently. 'I assume you'll start by knocking down their home.'

'It's a house they merely rent,' Guthrie contemptuously

corrected him. 'If it was theirs I'd have to buy it first from them. But yes, of course I shall knock it down – that and the garden will be the site of the hotel. I'll have to knock the church down as well.'

Iain thought of Jamie's cherished vegetable plot, and saw in his mind's eye the child's face when once again his fragile world fell to pieces. In that moment the see-saw of indecision that he'd been riding suddenly came to rest. He smiled at Guthrie's expectant face and knew as clearly as if the words had been written out in front of him exactly what he was going to say.

'There's nothing vague about my own suggestion, Sir James. I shall offer Donald Mackinnon what he asks for his house and land. I shall offer the church authorities the market price for their land. The manse, and its garden, I assume they could continue to rent to Mr Maitland. The church, which I'd also have no use for, they could and should preserve as part of Sleat's history. The Maitlands would be left where they are, the rest of the land would be worked as God intended it to be, not turned into a useless playground for rich tourists. Is that precise enough for you?'

Sir James took a little while to decide what to say; when he did finally speak, it was more slowly than usual. 'I still think this is some sort of time-wasting game and you'll never put your money where your mouth is. But it doesn't matter; I'll win in the end. And even if you're serious, I'll outbid you if I have to, and get my Edinburgh friends to exert a little pressure where it's needed.'

'I'm sure you can,' Iain agreed politely, 'in which case of course you'll win . . . unless Donald Mackinnon decides that he'd rather sell to me. I assume a hotel without a golf course wouldn't be much of a draw.'

Sir James was rattled, but still in heroic control of himself. 'We shall know soon enough – I've given him until Monday to make up his mind.' His final throw was typical – he wanted to know why this man was so inex-plicably getting in his way. 'I can understand Mackinnon not wanting to leave, but you're a long way from home;

where's the sense in wasting your money to try to preserve
something you can't have any affection for, and certainly
don't belong to?'

Iain smiled at him. 'You shouldn't have mentioned
that you were going to destroy the kirk. My great-great-
grandfather was the pastor there a hundred and fifty
years ago – you'll see his name in the porch. I think I
sort of belong, don't you?'

Guthrie stared at him for a moment, and then turned on
his heel and walked away. The duel, for the time being,
was over, with honours roughly even. But he wished he
knew more about the Canadian. He was still inclined to
believe that when push came to shove Macrae would fade
away, but he couldn't be sure and uncertainties were
worrying. Talk of ancestors and reviving crofting as a way
of living was just romantic twaddle of course, but it was
in fashion at the moment, and Hepburn would know who
could be swayed by it in Edinburgh. Still, the economic
arguments were entirely in his own favour and the truth
was that he didn't mind having a fight on his hands – it
made success all the sweeter in the end. Such was his
conclusion: not quite the easy ride he'd been expecting,
but no real cause for concern.

Sitting where he'd been left on the sea wall, Iain would
have agreed with him. But for the moment he was thinking
only about himself and the complete lunacy that had overtaken him. He couldn't account for it, and would never
be able to explain it to a level-headed friend like James
Hollister. All told, it was no more than a couple of weeks
ago that he'd left Ottawa to make a brief visit to Edinburgh,
partly out of curiosity and partly because it seemed to be
a duty he owed his dead father. In that brief space of time
his involvement with the Maitland family had gone from
inconsequential help to stark madness. A large part of what
wealth he possessed was now going to be seriously at risk,
and he could find himself with an unwanted stake in a
remote island that, whatever he'd claimed to Guthrie, he
most obviously didn't belong to.

He remembered his dream of recuperating in the solitude and peace of Canada's far north – nothing of that lovely plan would remain if the Church commissioners became similarly inclined to madness and decided to accept his bid, but he was committed to going on with it now; the charade was over.

Easter Day dawned with sunlight and showers chasing each other across the island; it was Skye's rainbow weather, and Louise counted three of them as she walked to church ahead of the others. They were something to lift anyone's heart, a proper celebration of the fact that Christ was risen; but she was cheered as well by what had happened that morning over their breakfast eggs – painted by her aunt as tradition decreed, as a surprise for the children.

There'd been no change in Janet Maitland's attitude towards herself – yesterday's scene might never have happened – but there was a detectable change in the way she spoke to the children. Jamie, quick to sense it, had been encouraged to suggest that Macgregor should escort them to church, at least as far as the porch. Aunt Janet had declined to sit through the service with a dog howling outside the door, but there'd been enough of a glint of humour in her face for Jamie not to mind the ruling. It might only have been the spirit of Easter that had descended on her, in which case the alteration wouldn't last; but Louise walked into church still hopeful – she might yet hear her aunt laugh one day.

Inside the kirk she was introduced to the minister, who had been borrowed for the occasion from Portree. He was a large, bearded man she liked on sight, but couldn't help thinking would have looked more impressive robed than dressed in a lounge suit. That was something she'd have to get used to, together with a service that was clearly to be very different from the ordered, Anglican liturgy she was used to.

The pews – penitentially uncomfortable, she'd tried one

the morning she'd come in to practise – were already
filling up; it was time to offer some music. Her father had
said the organist usually contented himself with running
through the hymns they were going to sing, but Louise
hoped that if she played softly enough no one would notice
that this morning they were getting some of Elgar's lovely
songs without words instead; time enough for the hymns,
she reckoned, when the congregation stood up to sing.

Immersed in the music, she took no note of the people
filing in, cramming the pews, and overflowing into the
upstairs gallery at the rear of the church. Once the minister
had begun to speak there was time to smile at her family
sitting three rows back, and she also identified Elspeth
Mackintosh, the charming headmistress of the school,
and Donald Mackinnon beside a frail-looking woman
who was presumably his wife; but it was only when the
last rousing hymn had been sung and her own share in
the service was over that she could identify some unexpected faces: Iain Macrae sitting with Brett and Ellie
right at the back and, even more astonishingly, Sir James
Guthrie, who'd perhaps been railroaded into coming by
some other guests at Kinloch Lodge, much more in
evidence near the front.

There was an embarrassing moment when the minister,
before dismissing the congregation asked them to applaud
the morning's replacement organist; but after that she was
free to go and warn her father that James Guthrie was
there.

'Come to make peace with his Creator?' Andrew
suggested with a smile.

'Come out of sheer hypercritical impertinence,' Janet
Maitland amended fiercely. Louise thought that she was
more likely to be right but instead of saying so pointed
out that Brett and Ellie were at the back of the church
with Iain Macrae.

Andrew Maitland looked at his daughter. 'We should
invite them to dinner don't you think – if the paschal lamb
will stretch that far?'

She hesitated, considering how to suggest that the Canadian could be excluded from the invitation; but she recalled just in time that he *had* been helpful at Fort William. 'The lamb will stretch as far as it has to,' she answered. 'All I ask is that Christian charity doesn't oblige you to invite that man who wants to make us homeless.'

Andrew agreed to this, and made his way to the back of the church. He was smiling when he returned. 'They're going climbing together this afternoon; I told them to come off the hill in time for supper at eight o'clock!'

Walking home afterwards, when the children had gone running on ahead, Louise commented on the fact that Sir James hadn't made his promised return call at the manse.

'Why should he bother?' Janet Maitland asked, over-hearing what she'd said. 'Your Canadian friend has obviously given up whatever mischief Tom Hepburn talked him into, and this wretched Lowlander knows that he has nothing to fear.'

Louise looked at her father. 'Is that what you think, too?'

Andrew Maitland made sure the children were out of earshot. 'Yes, I'm afraid so; but unlike Janet, I think Sir James might have been reluctant to come and give us the bad news himself; he knows that we shall hear it from the Church authorities in due time.'

Louise smiled, comforted to some extent by her new-found but deeply satisfying affection for this father she was only now learning to know. 'You'd find something merciful to say about Judas Iscariot himself!'

He considered this seriously for a moment before answering. 'Well, without him there would have been no crucifixion, and no Easter story for us to be retelling two thousand years later.'

'I knew you'd have the answer,' she said contentedly. Now it only remained to be seen whether she would be allowed to cook the lamb or not. Almost certainly there'd be no garlic in her aunt's vegetable store, but she had seen rosemary growing in the garden, and young shoots of mint that buttered new potatoes cried out for. But they walked the rest of the way home in silence, and it wasn't until their lunch of soup and fruit was over that the question of the evening's entertaining was mentioned again. Janet waited until the children had gone out to the garden with their grandfather to be taught the Gaelic names of trees and flowers before broaching the subject on both their minds.

'I must get on with my work,' she announced, referring to her usual afternoon ritual. She was slowly re-covering the seats of the dining-room chairs with exquisitely-worked tapestries of wild flowers, each design different and each one beautiful. 'Then when I've given the children their tea I shall need to take a little rest if I must sit up half the night entertaining your father's guests.'

It sounded unamiable, but Louise was aware of a small important alteration. It had been Janet Maitland's habit up till now to refer to Andrew as 'her brother'; the admission that they also had his daughter living with them seemed to be a precious step forward.

Praying that she didn't say the wrong thing that would set them back again, Louise made a gentle suggestion. 'I could do something useful while you rest – prepare vegetables, lay the table . . . ?'

'Two women in one kitchen are too many,' Janet said decidedly. 'You'd better do it all yourself, I think . . . but it's not to be too fancy, mind; we're accustomed to good, plain food that we can recognize.'

Louise promised to remember this with a smile so warm that the woman facing her was silent for a moment; had she been smiled at like that before and not noticed that when it happened she was reminded of Andrew, not Drusilla?

'The hymns went very well this morning,' she said gruffly, 'and I liked whatever it was you were playing when we walked in.'

'Elgar,' Louise answered. 'It's hard *not* to make his music sound lovely!'

'You should have been a musician, not a cook,' Janet said, if only to have the last word, and then walked out of the kitchen, leaving Louise to ponder whether creamed leeks, wine-based gravy, and chocolate-rich profiteroles could loosely be considered 'good, plain food'. Perhaps not, but they were what her aunt was going to eat this evening.

Fifteen

With the Gaelic lesson over, Andrew and the children were now looking for shells down on the beach. Aunt Janet was sewing in the drawing room, and the old house felt peaceful. It was time to think about cooking again, a pleasure Louise had missed recently. She was out in the garden, raiding the overgrown herbs surely planted by some long ago minister's wife when footsteps sounded on the gravel drive behind her. Suspecting the return of Janet Maitland's 'that man', she turned round to find herself looking at Elspeth Mackintosh.

'A pleasant surprise,' Louise said, smiling at her. 'I thought you were someone else!' She held out her hands, full of the rosemary and mint she'd picked. 'Preparations for supper, which I'm allowed to cook as an Easter treat. We saw you in Church this morning, but you were too far away to speak to.'

Elspeth smiled shyly back. 'The music was lovely. Bearing in mind what we usually listen to, I'm surprised the congregation didn't get up and cheer!'

Louise accepted the compliment with a little bow, then asked who the head teacher had come to see. 'Aunt Janet's indoors, but my father's down on the beach with the children.'

Elspeth Mackintosh shook her head. 'No need to see either of them – I only came to bring you these books. I should have remembered to give them to you when you brought Jamie to the school. I know that Mr Maitland teaches at Sabhal Mòr, but I doubt he has need of the simple primers that Jamie could start learning from.'

Louise glanced at the little books she was being given, then led her visitor to the garden bench. 'Sit down for a moment, please, and explain something to me. Is it important for Jamie to learn Gaelic quickly – is that what the other children speak among themselves?'

'It depends who their parents are,' Elspeth Mackintosh admitted. 'There are some who even press for their children to be *taught* in Gaelic. Jamie needn't worry about that yet, though it may come. But he and wee Fiona will be happier here when they can move easily from one language to another.'

'It was stupid of me not to realize that, and I doubt if it's properly occurred to my father either, although he *has* begun to teach them Gaelic words. He's an expert on Gaelic literature, but I'm afraid I associate the language with serious adult students, not with children yelling at each other in the playground. Now *I* shall have to start learning as well!'

Surprise showed in the face of the girl sitting beside her. 'You'll not be needing the Gaelic back in London, surely, and Mr Maitland said you were only coming here to bring the children.'

'I was, but now I'm staying,' Louise admitted briefly. 'Just until the children don't need me any more.'

Elspeth considered this for a moment. 'Just until' might sound almost nothing at all, but Fiona wasn't yet five years old. 'You'll be here for quite a wee while then,' she pointed out. After a little hesitation she went on. 'I only came here from Inverness, not London, but to begin with I doubted that I could stay. There's nowhere more beautiful when the sun shines, but mist and rain and wind are what we more often get!'

'You've settled down though?' Louise asked.

'Yes; I'd not leave now. I love my work at the school, and I've got used to living here on my own. But you'll have had more to give up than I did, I'm thinking.' She received no answer to this and, after a little thought, decided that it would have been better left unsaid. 'It's time I went and let you get on with your preparations,' she suggested more cheerfully. 'I hope the dinner is a great success.'

'I hope so too, otherwise I shan't be allowed in my aunt's kitchen again!' Louise smiled at her visitor, then remembered what she'd said a moment ago. 'If you're alone, why not come and sample it this evening? You'll meet two very nice Australians, and a Canadian who's less easy to get to know – more of a challenge to like, let's say!'

Elspeth looked pleased but hesitant. 'It would be very nice, but are you sure Miss Maitland won't mind?'

Not sure at all, Louise managed to sound very firm. 'She'll be delighted. The others have been asked for eight o'clock because they're out trying to climb a hill this afternoon – and that's something else I expect I ought to learn, but the truth is that mountains frighten me!'

It was Elspeth's turn to sound firm. 'Fear of the unknown,' she said in her best head teacher's voice. 'I can start you off when you have a Saturday afternoon to spare.' She smiled with pleasure at the idea, and then said good bye until the evening.

Louise watched her go, took a deep breath, and went indoors to break the news that there would now be four guests for dinner instead of three. Janet put down her work and slowly removed the rimless spectacles that had slipped down her nose.

'Why Elspeth Mackintosh, may I ask?' she enquired coldly.

'Because she lives alone and, although she pretends not to be, is probably lonely,' Louise answered. Then she felt obliged to apologize. 'I'm sorry, Aunt – I forgot for a moment that I wasn't in my own flat, free to do as I like. But Elspeth's a nice person and I think she'll be kind to the children. She brought some Gaelic books for Jamie to learn from.'

'Then we shall make *her* welcome, of course, and hope that your father hasn't now found some vagabond on the beach who looks as if he might be hungry.' With that she put her spectacles on again and carefully selected the next strand of wool that she needed. Dismissed, Louise returned to the kitchen to relieve her feelings by banging saucepan lids very vigorously and reciting the witches' cauldron incantation from *Macbeth* to nobody but herself.

By the time the shell-hunters returned, flushed with sun and sea wind, the lamb was ready for the oven, pricked with slivers of rosemary and onion, the profiteroles were cooling on a wire tray, waiting to be split and filled with cream, and the dining room was laid and decorated with the last jonquils from the garden.

Janet emerged to give the children their tea as usual – a daily event that Louise suspected she now looked forward to – while Andrew was told about the books that Elspeth had brought for Jamie.

'There was mention of parents wanting their children taught in Gaelic,' Louise also reported. 'Can that really be sensible when their further education will almost certainly not be done here?'

'Not sensible perhaps,' Andrew admitted, 'but understandable because the Gaels have come so close to seeing their language disappear. There's been talk before of enforcing it in the school. It's never come to anything, but this time it might. Even if it doesn't, Elspeth Mackintosh is still right – the children should become bilingual.'

'And so should I if I want to find some work here,' Louise pointed out, 'but first things first; my immediate challenge is in the kitchen. I think the children should be allowed to stay up long enough to greet our guests, don't you?'

They were bathed and ready for bed a couple of hours later when first Elspeth arrived, closely followed by the others. She had taken pains with her appearance, Louise noticed; released for the moment from the need to seem a serious, sensible head teacher, she looked unexpectedly pretty and youthful. Brett greeted her with unfeigned pleasure, and even Iain Macrae managed a friendly smile before he was claimed by Jamie to decide whether he'd drawn correctly a yacht that was moored out in the Sound.

With the children put to bed and the food served, Louise began to relax and enjoy the evening. Her cook's hand hadn't lost its cunning: the meat was succulent, just on the correctly yonder side of pinkness; the vegetables cooked *au point*; and even Janet allowed herself to be helped to a second profiterole, admitting that it made rice pudding seem a trifle homely.

It was Brett who brought the conversation round to the subject of the church – his friend, he said, looking at Iain Macrae, had mentioned that its future was threatened.

'Seems bad enough to me,' he pointed out, 'but it must be worse for people who live here. The church was full as it could hold this morning.'

'Of course it's all wrong,' Janet agreed bitterly, 'and in times past it wouldn't have been allowed to happen. Congregations without a church even set about building one themselves, *and* raising the money to pay for the minister. They lack that sort of spirit today, more's the pity.'

'Soon they'll also lack a minister,' her brother suggested gently. 'I'm afraid that's the greatest problem. With someone available to take over from our present ailing man I think the Church authorities would keep Kilchrist open and tell hungry developers to look elsewhere.'

Then Elspeth Mackintosh glanced shyly at the man sitting next to her. 'A Reverend Macrae is listed among the pastors' names in the porch. Would he have been an ancestor of yours?'

Iain nodded, liking her soft accent and the character clearly written in her face. 'He and my great-great-grand-mother sailed for Prince Edward Island with their flock. My branch of the family found its way to Ontario, but there are still Macraes living on the island.'

'And there are still Macdonalds in Australia,' Andrew commented with a smile at Brett. 'Their hardships have made great wanderers over the face of the earth of the Scots, the Irish and the Jews – to the great benefit of the rest of us, I have to say.'

Louise guessed from her aunt's expression that the inclusion of the Irish among the benefactors wasn't fully approved, but for once Janet Maitland withheld her fire and merely suggested that it was time to return to the drawing room. With logs now burning in the hearth because the evening had turned cold, and lamps lit, the room's air of prim formality had disappeared; perhaps it had only waited to be used, Louise thought, by people who were enjoying each other's company. Even Aunt Janet looked intrigued when Andrew enquired about the guitar case left sitting in the hall.

'It's Ellie's,' Brett explained with a grin. 'She brought it along because we have the habit at home of singing for our supper; it's a bit like the ceilidhs you have here. But you have not to mind listening to a couple of amateurs.' He looked across at Louise. 'We're not in the same league as you.'

He meant by it more than music, Iain realized, watching the little scene. Nothing about Brett's visit to Skye would be forgotten, but his expression whenever he glanced at Louise gave away her part in what his memories would be. Her outfit – a skirt and tunic of fine, silver-grey wool – was simple but exquisite, and everything else about her was equally a reminder that she came from a more complicated, more sophisticated world than the one she found herself in now. But she merely shook her head at what Brett had said, and went to fetch the guitar.

'Play it for us, please,' she asked, handing it to Ellie.

'I only strum the chords,' Ellie admitted, 'Brett plays the melodies!'

She waited for him to pull a mouth organ out of his pocket, tested the tuning of the guitar's strings, and then the rollicking strains of 'Waltzing Matilda' filled the room.

'You were bound to get that,' Brett said with a grin, when the applause had died down. 'But now here's what we've been learning at the hostel.'

He nodded to Ellie and a moment later the 'Skye Boat Song' and then the 'Eriskay Love Lilt' filled the room with haunting music. Ellie did much more than strum chords, but Brett was the magician, drawing out of the little instrument against his mouth sounds of plaintive longing and beauty. There was silence this time when they stopped playing, then Brett looked at Louise.

'Your turn now, please.' He opened the lid of the rose-wood grand piano that occupied one corner of the room, thereby gently insisting that he didn't expect her to refuse.

She hesitated long enough to decide how to follow what they'd just been listening to, and then went to the piano . . . perhaps Debussy would do; the man of delicate, impressionistic tone-colours and shifting harmonies; and, since blonde Ellie was sitting there, why not 'La Fille aux Cheveux de Lin' – the girl with the flaxen hair? After it, with a glance at the nearly full moon outside that washed the garden in green and silver light, she played the same composer's 'Claire de Lune', a poem written in keyboard notes instead of words.

When the last note died into silence, enchantment held them still until she stood up herself and closed the piano. Rightly so, Iain thought; it was time to bring the evening to an end. He couldn't be sure about Elspeth Mackintosh – didn't know enough about her – but the rest of them for a variety of different reasons, all had emotions that were too near the surface at the moment.

With thanks and goodnights said, he shepherded all three guests into his car, overriding Elspeth's suggestion that she could go home as she arrived, on foot. Their host went outside with them to wave them on their way, and Iain was tempted to suggest that they should meet in the morning when Andrew went down to Armadale as usual to collect his newspaper. But what would be the point of it apart from letting the Maitlands know that his bid had become real? Was he so anxious to remove the questioning look in Louise Maitland's eyes that clearly indicated her doubts about him? Certainly not; he'd wait and see what the next day brought, in the shape of Donald Mackinnon's promised decision for Guthrie.

Outside Elspeth's cottage Brett got out as well to escort her to her front door, and Ellie seized the moment to ask Iain to invite her out to dinner the next evening. 'Just me,' she added to make herself clear, 'not Brett as well; he'll have an engagement of his own.'

'Any particular reason?' he enquired curiously.

'Yes – we'll be going home in a day or two, and I want him to be able to say goodbye to Louise alone,' was her surprising answer. 'He deserves that, I reckon.'

'And then?'

'We'll get married,' she said briefly, and because Iain didn't question it she went on. 'It will be all right; I knew that this evening when we were playing together.'

She was, he reflected, an odd mixture of immaturity and wisdom, but all he said was, 'Brett's lucky – I hope he knows that.'

'He will,' she promised with a smile as the man himself walked back to the car. 'I'll tell him about our dinner arrangements tomorrow.'

Ten minutes later, after dropping them at the hostel, Iain parked the car and then went to his favoured spot on the sea wall. It wasn't a night for going indoors when the quiet water of the Sound was still painted silver by the moonlight, and he could hear the gentle murmur of the incoming tide. He was reminded by it of the music they'd listened to that evening, and the undercurrents of emotion that it had stirred – even Janet Maitland's stoical composure had looked threatened. He also remembered too vividly for comfort the expression on Brett's face as he watched Louise play, and he couldn't help wondering whether Ellie quite realized what she would be up against in persuading an island-haunted Australian to return to normal life.

Then his thoughts ranged back earlier in the day . . . to the Easter service in Kilchrist church. He'd only half-listened to what had been said and read because he'd found himself imagining a Sunday more than a hundred and fifty years ago when the Reverend Thomas Macrae had spoken those same words there for the last time – 'imagining' wasn't right; he'd *been* there, and shared the pain of the people who were being driven from their homes; he'd trudged with them to the ship in Broadford Bay.

He shook the memory away now and forced himself to think about the future, not the past. Guthrie would probably get the crofter's land and, inevitably, with it the rest of what he wanted; in which case one deeply relieved Canadian could inform Tom Hepburn without dishonour that he was going home. But that word pulled him up again. He had no home, and wherever he went next he would take with him the image of Jamie's precious vegetable patch churned to dust and Thomas Macrae's kirk reduced to a heap of rubble. This remote Scottish island was part of his inheritance now, and even if he went away the memory of it would travel with him. He felt close to panic for a moment or two, wanted to shout at the inscrutable face of the moon that the fact wasn't true; but he knew that it was, and with that certainty clear in his mind and heart at last, he finally went back into the hotel.

Sixteen

Donald Mackinnon's letter was delivered to Kinloch Lodge early the next morning. He'd taken great pains with it, not being accustomed to writing in English, but it was needed to be very polite as well as firm.

Reading it at the breakfast-table in the dining room, James Guthrie took no note of the careful, courteous phrasing. He saw only that a stubborn, prejudiced Highlander – mishandled by Carmichael in Portree, and misled by a Canadian who was an even bigger fool – was standing in his way. Chicanery he was accustomed to, expected even in the business world he inhabited, but sheer, blind stupidity was much harder to overcome. Without Mackinnon's land the church site was useless; he'd have to look elsewhere. But not on this benighted island – he'd had enough of Skye. Serve them bloody well right for a golden Guthrie opportunity missed.

Then, as he thought what would happen next, his ill-temper faded. Either Macrae would quietly disappear, leaving the crofter and the Churchmen without a buyer after all, or he'd have to go on – squander whatever wealth he had, and eventually retire a broke and broken man; delightful! Carmichael's reputation would suffer with the people who employed him, but it was irritating to think that Thomas Hepburn – the puppeteer in Edinburgh, pulling the strings – might escape without punishment. While Sir James considered what he could do about that, a telephone conversation was taking place between the lawyer and Iain Macrae.

'You've done . . . what?' Mr Hepburn was enquiring

anxiously. 'The line is bad this morning, but I thought you said something about . . . about actually buying Donald Mackinnon's land.'

'I did,' Iain agreed. 'He's just called to tell me that he's turned Sir James Guthrie's offer down. He prefers the look of mine, apparently.'

'Dear Heaven,' the lawyer's voice came faintly along the wire, 'it was never meant to be in earnest . . . I thought that was clearly understood.'

'By us, but not by Mackinnon: he still assumes that a man means what he says. I'd hate to be the one to teach him otherwise.'

There was silence for a moment before Tom Hepburn, greatly agitated, spoke again. 'I feel deeply responsible – what I hoped might be a harmless delaying tactic while I found another solution to Andrew's problem has landed you in this impossible position. You must withdraw at once, my dear man; then Guthrie can be approached again. I shall apologize to him, of course, and to the Church commissioners.'

'Please do nothing of the sort,' Iain insisted firmly. 'None of them is to know the truth, particularly Donald Mackinnon. Assuming that my offer for the glebe is also accepted, I shall own enough to make a sizeable croft.'

'And . . . and you'll try to find someone to work it for you . . . before returning to Canada?' Tom Hepburn suggested, clinging desperately to what seemed rational in a situation that threatened to get completely out of hand.

'For the next ten months I shall work it myself,' came the calm reply. 'Time enough, I hope, to discover whether my crofting theories are feasible or not. If they are, I'll find someone to carry them on for me; if not, I'll return to my real job a rather poorer but wiser man!' He imagined that he could hear Tom Hepburn wringing his hands, and spoke again with amusement as well as firmness in his voice. 'I haven't run mad, and I shan't blame anyone but myself if it doesn't work out in the end. When I left Canada I needed an objective; I've found it, largely thanks

to you. Now, since I'm sure Guthrie will drop out altogether, I want you to offer the Church commissioners
the market price for *their* land. In return, I hope they'll
agree to leave the Maitlands where they are, and preserve
Kilchrist kirk from going to ruin.'

'I shall do my best,' the lawyer was heard to promise
faintly. 'It's pointless, I expect, to try to thank you – you'll
tell me that you couldn't think of anything better to do.'

'Which would be exactly true. Spur the reverend
gentlemen on if you can – I'm tired of living in an hotel
and I'd like to move into Mackinnon's croft as soon as
he's ready to leave. But what I plan to do with the land
will depend on how much I can finish up with. I'll wait
to hear from you.'

With that the line went dead, and Mr Hepburn was
discovered by Miss Morrison a moment later sitting with
his head in his hands. 'Is something wrong, Mr Thomas?'
she asked, rather put out to think that it could be something she didn't know about.

'I have no idea whether it is or not,' he answered in the
bemused tone of a man who'd lost his grip on the certain-
ties he was used to. 'But I'm instructed to speak to the
Church commissioners urgently; that at least I can do.'
She turned to leave the room but his voice halted her at
the door.

'Have you ever been to Skye, Margaret?'

'No, I have not,' she said sounding surprised at the
question.

'Then I don't think you should go; it seems to have an
extraordinary effect on its visitors.'

'The island of lost causes, don't they call it?' she asked
with a faint smile, but Mr Hepburn looked suddenly
distressed.

'I hope not . . . oh, I do pray not, Margaret.' Then he waved
her away before she could ask why it mattered so much.

Iain spent the rest of the day learning the hard realities of
a crofter's life from Donald Mackinnon, and walking the

boundaries of what would soon be his land. It was a reminder of the previous day's strange déjà-vu experience, but he insisted to himself that no atavistic memory of his forbears troubled him now. The historical wheel might be coming full circle, but the fact that he'd be back precisely where the Macraes had started out from wasn't going to change his life for ever. Aware of the Highlander's unspoken distress at leaving the croft, he didn't repeat what he'd said to Tom Hepburn; his own crofting experiment would result in a success he could find someone else to take over or it would be a failure he must accept. Either way, his real work lay in Africa as soon as he was declared fit to go back.

He regretted having to refuse Mrs Mackinnon's invitation to share their evening meal, but it was time to remember that he was taking Ellie out to dine. The island wasn't rich in high-class restaurants, and he could foresee an evening of extreme embarrassment if he and Brett had selected the same place for their rendezvous. But when he put this tactfully to Ellie outside the hostel, she shook her head.

'Brett's taking Louise to Isle Ornsay,' she said. 'He wouldn't go to Kinloch Lodge – he's shy about what he calls presuming on his Macdonald name. When he gets to the pearly gates I expect he'll apologize to St Peter for being there at all!'

'He's a nice man,' Iain commented with a smile as he put the car in gear. 'I reckon you deserve each other.'

The restaurant was attractive and Lady MacDonald's food delicious, but his chief interest was in enquiring about his 'friend' Sir James Guthrie. He'd come too late, they said – Sir James' private plane had arrived that afternoon to take him back to the mainland. It was safe to assume, Iain thought, that he wouldn't be coming back.

The evening from then should have been enjoyable; host and guest tried hard enough, but their minds were on another couple dining somewhere else. Ellie's abstraction Iain could understand, but his own failure to stop thinking

about Brett and Louise irritated him – all the more so
when it was fairly certain that they weren't spending *their*
time being bothered about himself and Ellie.

Louise, at least, could have told him that he was wrong;
the thought of Ellie hovered at the back of her mind, even
while she recalled for Brett's benefit some of the more
trying episodes in her career as a professional cook. But
try as she might to keep the conversation light, he refused
to be entertained for long.

'What made you change to cooking? Something did,
I'm sure; otherwise you'd be the famous pianist by now
that you ought to be.'

Louise shook her head. 'There were students better than
me, but apart from that I made the fatal mistake of falling
in love with my teacher. It was all or nothing for me, but
a brief, amusing affair to him. I retired hurt from trying
to become a virtuoso pianist and took up cooking instead.'

'Is he what kept you from marrying someone else?'

'Probably. I ricocheted from shy dreamer to wild girl-
about-town; learned to hate myself and the gaudy, third-
rate people I went about with; and finally got back on the
rails again with help from the very nice stepfather my
mother thoughtfully provided me with. The story of my
life in a nutshell; I don't know why I bored you with it!'
She did know, hoping that it would correct his romantic
image of her, but his face now said that she had failed.

'Brett dear, don't make a heroine of me, please,' she
went on gently. 'I'm nothing of the sort; I'm only doing
what women the world over accept as their job in life –
taking care of children until they are old enough to fend
for themselves.'

He couldn't bring himself to point out the difference
that Jamie and Fiona were another woman's children, and
she knew as well as he did that she was probably giving
up the chance of having children of her own.

'What will you do,' he asked instead, 'when you're free
to choose again – go back to London?'

'I don't think so,' she answered regretfully after a

moment's thought. 'To stay afloat there you need to keep in practice; I shall have been away too long. Anyway, by then I hope Skye will have come to seem like home.'

Brett's sad expression told her what was coming next. 'That's how it feels to me already. We're flying back to Oz in two days' time, and I shall want to howl like a kid being thrown out of a sweetshop.' He tried to smile, but his heartache was painfully real; she knew it, as surely as she knew that she was part of it, but it seemed safer to talk of Skye.

'You have been lucky, you know; seen it coming to life again after the winter, been blessed with the sort of weather that shows it at its best – that doesn't happen very often. Weeks of wind and rain would make it look much less desirable!'

'I know . . . but you'd still be here,' he said simply, taking the plunge at last into what he had to say. 'You'll think I'm being disloyal to Ellie – I suppose I am; but I think she understands that my affection for her isn't altered at all by what I feel about you. It doesn't change anything, can't do; I shall say goodbye and take Ellie back to what *she* still thinks of as home. I'll get on with life there and learn to count myself fortunate because it's a good life, but inside I'll be wanting you and this place for as long as I live.' His smile was a failure but he kept his voice steady. 'I didn't intend to make quite such a speech, but I'm glad I have. You had to know how happily I'd have stayed, to love you and to help you take care of those children.'

Alone with him she couldn't have kept from weeping, but here, with the waitress hovering to clear the table and bring their coffee, tears had to be blinked away. At last she could trust her voice enough to answer him. 'I shall miss you and so will they, but at least we've all had the pleasure of knowing you.' She took a pen and notebook out of her bag. 'Write down your address, please. Jamie will want to find you on the map of Australia, and I'll want to let you know what happens about the manse.

Perhaps the gods will be kind for once and drop into Sir James Guthrie's lap the perfect site somewhere else that he can't possibly refuse!'

She doubted it very much, but it was time to talk of something other than themselves. Then she pointed at the whitewashed lighthouse they could see from the window – islanded now because the tide was high enough to cover its little spit of land. 'It would be fun to live in that, as a well-known author actually did some years ago; but there'd be nowhere for Jamie to grow vegetables, and Aunt Janet might have a little difficulty with the stairs!'

She was talking too much, but at least she'd made Brett smile at the thought of Janet Maitland's reaction to being asked to live in a lighthouse. In control of his voice again, he could ask calmly for the bill and thank the waitress for an enjoyable meal. But he didn't speak on the short drive back until they'd climbed down from the Land Rover and stood on the steps of the manse.

'We'll drop in before we leave, just to say goodbye to the rest of the Maitlands,' he managed to say naturally, then his voice changed. 'Promise you'd let me know if something bad ever happened and you needed help . . . I can't go unless you do.'

'I'd let you know; I promise, dear Brett.' She reached up to kiss his cheek, and felt his arms close about her in a brief, desperate hug. Then she was released, and he jumped back into the Land Rover, reversed, and drove back along the drive. When she could no longer hear the sound of its engine she let herself into the sleeping house, and slowly climbed the stairs; but she sat for a long time at her bedroom window, watching a track of moonlight move across the waters of the Sound. She'd learned through hard experience the lesson that unhappiness, like everything else in life, didn't last for ever; human beings and all their doings were a very impermanent part of God's creation, no matter how hard they tried to ignore the painful fact. But for the moment the memory of Brett's distress was too vivid in her mind, and she was sharply aware of her own sense of loss as well. Even if he became nothing more, he'd have been a true friend, and how much easier to bear the years ahead would have seemed if he'd been free to stay and share them with her.

Seventeen

She didn't see Brett again, or get to say goodbye to Ellie at all. When she returned from a trip to Portree the following day they'd said their farewells at the manse and gone back to the hostel to pack for an early start the next morning. The Land Rover had to be handed over in Edinburgh, then they would fly home.

Their leaving had plunged Jamie back into surliness, and he refused to be interested in finding the state of Victoria on the map or tracing the route of Brett's journey home.

'It's a long way away,' he said crossly at last. 'I wanted him to stay here. Why do grown-ups have to keep moving about all the time?'

He sounded merely out of sorts, but Louise knew that, with all confidence lost in the security of things, any alteration now distressed him; if this or that could suddenly change what would alter next? She couldn't promise him that nothing would, only try to offer reasons that he might accept for the way things were.

'People live in one place but want to see other places,' she pointed out. 'So will you when you grow up.'

'I shall stay here, I expect,' he corrected her firmly, 'now that I'm getting used to it.' He was silent for a moment, then the other cause of his anxiety surfaced. 'I don't think I'll go to school tomorrow. The potatoes need earthing-up and Grandpa doesn't know how to do that.'

'You can teach him before we leave,' she suggested with equal firmness. 'Going tomorrow is important, Jamie . . . it's the start of a new term. If you missed it you wouldn't be able to catch up.' She let this sink in, but that fact obliged her to mention something else. 'You know the books Miss Mackintosh was kind enough to bring . . . well, you'll hear Gaelic spoken tomorrow besides English. You mustn't mind if it takes a while to understand what some of the other children are saying. It's their language; for them it's the English *we* speak that seems strange. You have to learn their language, they have to learn yours.'

Jamie's attention was at least caught and he now considered something else. 'I asked Brett why *he* didn't sound like us. He said it started off as English but got changed on the way to Australia. I don't see why that should be.'

'Nor do I,' Louise had to admit, aware by now that unless she could give him a convincing answer it was better not to offer one at all.

'I expect Iain will know; I'll ask him,' Jamie decided.

But the following morning when he'd been deposited, white-faced and unhappy, with Elspeth Mackintosh, Louise walked back to the manse to find her father looking perplexed.

'Your face says something's wrong,' she suggested anxiously.

'Something is unexpected, at least.' He put down the newspaper he'd brought back from Armadale, and carefully smoothed out its crumpled front page before he explained, 'Iain Macrae was on the quay, waiting behind Brett and Ellie to board the ferry when it turned round and went back to Mallaig. There was only a moment to talk to him, but he just said he was on his way to Edinburgh too . . . something to do with turning in his hired car. I suppose it means he's leaving as well as our Australian friends.' Andrew looked up from the newspaper to see the shock in his daughter's face. 'It seems strange that he should go so suddenly,' he was forced to add, 'but I suppose it's understandable; we should never have involved him in our affairs.'

'*We* didn't – Tom Hepburn did,' Janet Maitland snapped, 'but having set his hand to the plough he should have gone on. Americans lack staying power, I'm afraid.'

'He's a Canadian,' Louise pointed out mechanically once again. 'Father's right – we've no claim on him at all; the scheme Mr Hepburn embroiled him in was never going to work, and now Sir James Guthrie will win. All the same, it's a very churlish departure, just to drive away. Jamie will be upset . . . I'm not sure why but he seemed to like Iain Macrae even more than Brett.'

She stopped, aware that she felt too close to tears to go on talking. Instead, she stared out of the window but no comfort was visible there. A change of wind-direction overnight had brought the promised change in the weather. Now, beyond the sodden garden, there was a gunmetal coloured Sound, and a backdrop of sombre mountains merging with a grey-black rain-laden sky. Dear God, how grim it all looked, and how entirely joyless life now seemed. Almost submerged in a wave of despair, she still heard Fiona whimper, and saw the child's distress reflected in the adult faces watching her. They were all afraid, she realized – afraid, above all, that it was in her mind, too, to abandon them as Iain Macrae had done.

She forced her stiff mouth to smile at Fiona. 'Jamie's in the classroom – why don't we do some work, too? Let's walk round the house with Grandpa and he can tell us the gaelic name for things.' Then she turned to Janet Maitland. 'My turn to cook supper – we'll have something special to celebrate Jamie's first day at his new school.'

There was nothing to fear after all, her calm voice seemed to say. They were there together, and for as long as they stayed that way nothing bad would happen. Reassured, Janet managed to sound herself again. 'If the dog's going round the house with you, he'll need cleaning up first; the creature's muddy paw marks are all over the lobby floor.'

God was in his heaven, and all was right with their world after all, if Janet was only worried about the lobby floor; Andrew and his granddaughter smiled at Louise, and then at one another, and went to deal with Macgregor. Louise understood the moment of peril they'd just survived,

and realized that she mustn't frighten them again; from
now on, whether they stayed at the manse or had to find
somewhere else to live, their peace of mind somehow
depended on her. She'd spoken glibly to Iain Macrae of
staying because she had to – an audience had made the
heroics feel almost pleasurable. That audience had left
now, and so had her dear friend, Brett; it was time to find
out how well she could manage on her own.

After days of almost continuous rain the swollen clouds
being driven in from the Atlantic at last blew themselves
out over the mainland and left behind a sky the delicate
blue of a blackbird's egg. Released from the house, the children slithered after Macgregor down the path to the beach
and poked happily about among the shells and wrack scat-
tered by the outgoing tide. Louise selected what they could
take back to add to their collection; the rest they solemnly
returned to Father Neptune, agreed to be residing at the
bottom of the Sound.

Reluctantly back indoors and Macgregor towelled dry
again, they sat down to Aunt Janet's tea, while Louise was
warned that she had been invited to dine with Elspeth
Mackintosh.

'I accepted for you,' Andrew said cheerfully, 'so you'll
have to miss tonight's instalment of *The Hobbit.*'

It had become an evening ritual now that he read to the
children when they were bathed and ready for bed, and
because he read so beautifully Louise joined the audience
as well.

'You don't *want* to miss what happens to Gandalf next,
do you?' Jamie asked. 'Can't you say no?' Louise smiled,
aware that he was concerned for her that she shouldn't
miss a treat.

'I could, but I think it would be rather rude, and I expect
Miss Mackintosh wants to tell me how well you're doing.
You'll have to let me know what happens in the morning.'

He looked dissatisfied until Fiona began to sound tearful,
not liking the idea of her aunt going out. Then, with the

sweetness inherited from his dead mother, he promised his sister that there was no need to fuss – Lou-Lou was only going to talk to his head teacher. In Fee's opinion, her brother ranked only just behind the Lord Jesus in the scheme of things; if he said there was no cause for alarm she could safely settle down to listen to the book at bedtime.

Elspeth's cottage, in the next hamlet along the Broadford road, was small but attractive, and sited high enough on its hill to have a splendid view of the Sound.

'I bought the cottage for that,' Elspeth agreed when her guest went to look at it from the sitting-room window. 'But now I love my wee house for its own sake as well.'

'And so you should,' Louise said with a smile, looking round the room. It was simply furnished, but Elspeth had excellent taste, as well as an interesting selection of paintings on her whitewashed walls. She made no apology for serving dinner in the kitchen, the only other room on the ground floor, but did warn her guest that in culinary matters she couldn't match the standards of the manse.

'Why should you – I'm a professional cook,' Louise explained. 'At least I am when I'm not exiled from London!'

She said it lightly, but Elspeth's smile faded. 'I know why that was, of course – Mr Maitland explained about the tragedy . . . those poor bairns. But I'm sorry for you as well; exile must be how it seems.'

Louise regretted using the word, and waved it away. 'Tell me how Jamie is doing, or is it too soon to say? He isn't forthcoming himself, of course, and I don't want to drag information out of him, bit by reluctant bit!'

Elspeth thought for a moment before answering. 'He's still nervous, but that's to be expected. He's also very bright, and I think that means that sooner or later he'll be telling the other children what to do! Just now the gaelic-speaking children can use their language as a weapon if they want to, but they have been asked to show him kindness, and I think they mostly do.'

'Do I need to worry about him?' Louise asked.

Elspeth's shy smile reappeared. 'No, because he's our responsibility at school. We shall take care of him.'

'The children here are fortunate in their head teacher,' Louise said sincerely, but Elspeth disclaimed the compliment.

'I love my job,' she replied simply. 'I suppose I can see why teachers look upon coming here as being the end of their careers, but that's not how Kilchrist seems to me.' She considered Louise for a moment across the table. 'When we listened to you play the other evening I thought you must be a professional musician, not a cook! We have a piper who sometimes comes to give the children demonstrations, but our regular music teacher went back to the mainland, and we haven't been able to replace her. I was wondering if I could persuade you to help.'

'I could teach the piano, of course,' Louise answered after a moment's thought, 'and the history and development of music as well, I suppose, if I did some preparatory work on it. Could you wait until the new school year starts in September? I wouldn't want to leave Fiona at home without me, but by then she'll start school as well.'

'Of course – it will give me time to make the necessary arrangements and include music classes in the timetable for next year.' She smiled ruefully. 'The pay isn't brilliant, I'm afraid.'

'Any pay at all will be welcome,' Louise answered with her usual candour. 'I need to earn some money.'

She helped to eat her share of a dispirited toad-in-the-hole that even Elspeth had looked doubtful about as she brought it to the table. The offer of *cookery* lessons in the school might be more useful, she was thinking, but while she considered how to suggest it tactfully, her hostess spoke again.

'You'll have been sad to see Brett and Ellie leave. I only met them that evening at the manse, but they were the sort of people we'd do well to persuade to stay here.'

'Brett needed no persuading,' Louise pointed out rather sadly. 'But his life had been planned out, and by the time he got here it was too late to tear up the plan and make a new one.' She brushed aside the memory of his unhappiness and managed a smile. 'We've lost our other visitor from foreign parts as well – Iain Macrae left the same day as Brett and Ellie.'

'But not for long,' Elspeth corrected her with a note of contentment in her voice. 'He'll be back soon, I'm sure. He's buying Donald Mackinnon's croft, you know.'

Oh, dear God, Louise thought, it was exactly what she didn't know, because it wasn't true; so much for Tom Hepburn's scheme and Iain Macrae's ridiculous connivance in it. Now, a mixture of guesswork and rumour in a small community had landed them in this appalling muddle.

'I heard some gossip,' she said slowly, picking her words with care. 'But I'm afraid it isn't true – Iain Macrae is only waiting to get fit again, then he'll go back to Africa. That's where his work lies.'

Elspeth shook her head. 'It's not gossip,' she insisted with gentle firmness. 'I had it from Mary Mackinnon herself . . . she's a distant cousin of mine; in fact it was she who led me to come here at all. Donald hates the thought of leaving the island but Mary is in poor health and they're going to live with their son in Ayrshire. It's all settled now.'

'It must be, if Mrs Mackinnon says so,' Louise had to agree, 'but I understood that someone else was involved. Perhaps she's mistaken in the name of the buyer – it was to have been a man called Sir James Guthrie.'

'It isn't now,' Elspeth corrected her, happy to be sharing the good news. 'Iain Macrae has agreed to buy the croft . . . if he's not here now it will be because he has things to see to. We shall all be happy to have him back.'

There was no doubt, at least, of Elspeth's pleasure, Louise thought distractedly, it shone in the girl's smile as she spoke of him, and that would be another betrayal of trust to add to the Mackinnons' when the truth came out. She stayed at the cottage for as long as courtesy demanded before she could say goodnight, and then drove home, to find her father in the garden, staring at a star-studded night sky.

'No clouds for once,' he said smiling at her. 'Look, there's Orion, clear as anything . . . and Betelgeuse . . . and over to the left . . .'

'Pa dear, stop stargazing, please. I need to talk to you,' Louise said urgently. 'The Mackinnons think they've sold their croft to Iain Macrae. How *could* he have allowed them to believe that he was serious about wanting it? I told Elspeth – at least I tried to tell her – that he'd left the island, but she's convinced that he's only gone to settle up his affairs. When he doesn't come back the Mackinnons will have lost the chance of leaving, which they badly need to do, and they will have been criminally misused.'

Her voice trembled between anger and distress and he could hear that she was close to tears. It was understandable, of course, but Andrew suspected that she also felt personally betrayed in some way by a man she hadn't seemed to like. More than concern for a couple she didn't know lay beneath her present unhappiness. His own reaction to events was very different from hers, but it was equally troubling.

'Guthrie has been too clever for Tom Hepburn,' he said gravely. 'I think he probably changed his mind about coming to Skye . . . decided that it wasn't the site he wanted after all; but he's seen to it that Iain Macrae is left with a failing croft that he had no real intention of buying. Yes . . . I think that would appeal to the sort of man we know Guthrie to be.'

Louise stared in astonishment at her father's anxious face, clearly visible in the bright starlight. 'You mean you really think Iain Macrae has bought what he was only pretending to buy? That's impossible – he's waiting to go back to Africa or . . . or anywhere else where he can tell other people how to run their lives.'

Andrew almost smiled at that, but shook his head. 'He may not have meant to, but I think the delaying tactic went horribly wrong. Donald Mackinnon loves his land,

and probably hated the idea of what Guthrie was going to do with it. Tom Hepburn didn't know that, and nor did Iain. The last thing they expected was for Donald to turn Guthrie down, but that is obviously what has happened, I feel very responsible – Tom was trying to help us and so, I think, was Iain Macrae. I'm rather sorry you have such a poor opinion of him.'

Trying to come to terms with her father's view of the man, Louise still couldn't quite relinquish her own. 'Wrong chemistry, I expect – my fault as much as his therefore!' she said slowly. 'But he doesn't strike me as the sort of man who would allow himself to be outmanoeuvred, even by the James Guthries of this world. If I'm wrong about him and he *is* buying the croft in good faith, then presumably he'll find someone to work it for him. The Mackinnons won't suffer, which is something to be thankful for, but I'm afraid Elspeth's trust in him will be sadly shaken. She doesn't know it, but even her voice alters when she talks about him.'

There was a little silence before Andrew Maitland spoke again, rather sadly, 'I'll talk to Tom Hepburn in the morning. Meanwhile bright Orion has disappeared and it's time we went indoors.'

She kissed him goodnight and climbed the stairs, aware that neither of them had mentioned what they were both thinking: Guthrie's offer had included the church and the manse as well. Whatever Iain Macrae did with the croft only concerned him, but their own future still looked as worryingly uncertain as before.

Eighteen

Andrew knew the habits of his friend in Edinburgh very well – by 9.30 a.m. precisely he would be at his desk, with Miss Morrison allowed to make no client appointments before 10 a.m., his number could be safely rung at 9.35 a.m.

Their conversation began as usual with an exchange of family news: Jane Hepburn's poor health; the children and their progress in settling down on Skye. But finally Andrew could come to the main purpose of his call – his concern about Iain Macrae.

'I assume you've seen him, Tom, since he went back to Edinburgh. On our account, though, not on Donald Mackinnon's of course. I should be deeply relieved if you could confirm for me that we're misinformed about his buying the croft.'

'To begin with, he isn't here,' Tom Hepburn said. 'He crossed the Atlantic two days ago.' A muffled groan at the other end of the line made him hurry on. 'But there's no mistake about your information. He *is* buying Mackinnon's croft – house *and* land, that is to say – and I might as well confirm that his offer for the land belonging to the Church of Scotland has also been accepted. He's only returned home to sort out his affairs.'

Silence at the other end of the line made him go on. 'I felt quite as badly about it as you clearly do – worse, in fact, because it was all my idea. But I can tell you this, Andrew: it's true that Iain Macrae felt an obligation to Mackinnon, but he was most emphatically *not* looking for a way out of the entanglement I had got him into. He assured me, and I believe him, that he was looking for a challenge which he has found – to prove that crofting can become a viable occupation again. He is going to do the work himself, what's more, at least until he has to return to his UN relief agency.'

Inclined not to be comforted, Andrew did then remember something that the Canadian had said about crofting being difficult but not impossible. 'It's extraordinary all the same,' he commented, 'that a small corner of Skye should seem interesting enough to make him invest a considerable amount of money and time in it. Louise won't know what to make of him – she was inclined to believe that he'd ducked out of whatever agreement he'd reached with Donald and gone home. She doesn't like Iain Macrae, for some reason I don't quite understand . . .' He hesitated for a moment, then went on. 'You mentioned the glebe land, but not the kirk itself or the manse . . .?'

'Not included in the agreement,' Tom said briskly. 'But Mr Macrae did strongly ask for the church building not to be allowed to fall into ruin, and for you to continue to rent the manse. I can't *promise* that will happen, Andrew, but I'm fairly confident. If the Church authorities should ever change their minds about it we'd have to find a way of dealing with that problem.'

Slightly nervous now of his friend's imaginative way of dealing with problems, Andrew thanked him for all his help, sent Janet's and his own love to Jane Hepburn, and rang off. Then he went in search of Louise, and found her trying out an experimental music lesson on her niece.

'I forgot to mention last night that Elspeth is going to give me a job,' she explained with a smile. 'I can manage the music side of it, but I might need help with the teaching bit!' She left Fiona happily pressing down different keys on the piano, and went to stand beside her father at the window. 'You've spoken to Tom Hepburn, I can see; you're looking relieved.'

Andrew recounted the conversation he'd just had. 'I know it seems very strange,' he finished up, with what she reckoned was a magnificent understatement, 'but there's no doubt about any of it, except perhaps what the church authorities finally decide to do with us; but Tom seemed fairly sure even of that – he thinks we'll be left here in peace.'

Louise gave his hand an affectionate little pat. 'It's certainly what you deserve, not to mention being one in the eye for would-be developers and all such barbarians!'

'Very elegantly put,' Andrew suggested with a straight face. 'Now I'd better go and tell Janet while you get on with Fee's music lesson. There's not a moment to lose if she'd going to be a virtuoso by the time she's fifteen.'

Louise gravely agreed, aware of one of the compensations of her new life: her own sense of humour, not always in tune with other people's, was certainly shared by her father – in fact, had probably been inherited from him – and it made for a very satisfactory relationship. Then her thoughts returned to the news he'd given her.

'Elspeth was right after all about Iain Macrae,' she said at last. 'I'm glad about that. She's too nice to have her trust in human nature shaken, and she's inclined, I think, to offer him all the trust she's got.' Then a different thought occurred to her. 'Can he make a success of it? Don't today's crofters have to survive by doing other part-time jobs?'

'In the main they do,' her father admitted, 'but he'll have too much work on his hands for that. I pray that he will succeed, knowing that he wouldn't have come here at all but for Tom's lamentable scheming.'

Louise smiled at him. 'All right – feel a little bit responsible if you must, but I still think that Iain Macrae does at all times what he chooses to do; for the moment it seems to amuse him to choose Skye. I expect it makes a change from Africa!'

'Certainly that,' her father agreed, not saying as he left the room that he wished she could think more generously of Iain Macrae. One day he would ask why she didn't, because, in general, she was tolerant and not judgemental of other people; she'd suggested a lack of chemistry, but he scarcely knew what she meant by that.

Louise didn't immediately go back to her music lesson, instead she sat down by the window to think about the very antipathy that she was uncomfortably aware of in herself; because it had to be dealt with if she and he were going to be neighbours, even if only temporarily. In the first place she resented on her father's behalf the Canadian's failure to let him know about his change of mind; after all, whatever else it might lead to, his purchase of the croft couldn't help but affect the manse as well. But that carelessness confirmed what she disliked about him. He was committed to saving situations, as in a way he was doing here; that was his job, and she could believe that he did it unsparingly and well. But his heart wasn't committed, only his physical strength and formidable intelligence. She wanted him to save Donald's croft, protect Kilchrist kirk and keep the Maitland family in the manse out of love, not out of a professional curiosity to prove that he could.

She knew what her father would have said – that she was being wildly unreasonable. But the occasional glimpses of warmth and kindness she'd seen in him weren't enough; she needed him to unconditionally jump in and sink or swim with the rest of the human race, not stand watching from the bank, wondering why they always made such a mess of things. Perhaps something had happened in his life to make him the way he was; some great unhappiness, maybe, had turned him into the clinically detached observer he now mostly was. But, on the whole, she thought not; he'd been born self-sufficient, and he was solitary from choice.

Unaware that he'd been thought about hours earlier and four thousand miles away, the man himself sat calmly with James Hollister in Ottawa, about to discuss his future life. He looked, the lawyer thought, better than when he'd seen him last. Not that Iain had put on any weight – he was still skin and bone, as the saying went – but there was an air of purpose about him now that had been missing before, and an air almost of serenity.

'The trip across the ocean seems to have done some good,' his host said approvingly. 'At least I think you found it interesting to pick up William's trail in Edinburgh.'

'Oh, I did rather more than that,' Iain admitted with a slightly rueful smile. 'I met the man who'd written to my father, of course, but that was only the beginning of my adventures. I'd no sooner done telling Tom Hepburn that I'd no interest in my Scottish antecedents than I was plunged up to my neck in the present-day affairs of the family he's related to by marriage. They sent me chasing across Scotland to the Hebridean island of Skye, and I finished up in the very place the Macraes set out from a hundred and fifty years ago.'

'Extraordinary,' James Hollister said, unable to find a more adequate comment. 'Am I to hear the whole story – I feel sure there is one.'

'Better not, I think – it's long and confusing, and without knowing the people involved you'll think I've run mad . . . because it's the people, you see, who make the story.' There was time for James Hollister to marvel that he should hear that from the man in front of him before Iain went on with what he was obliged to confess.

'The upshot of it is that I'm buying the land my great-great-grandfather sailed away from; on one edge of it is the very kirk whose roster of ministers still bears his name.'

There was a moment's astonished silence; James couldn't even manage another 'extraordinary'.

'A sentimental purchase?' he at last hazarded doubtfully. It seemed so unlikely that he wasn't surprised when Iain denied the idea very firmly.

'There's nothing sentimental about it. I have a professional interest in making land that has been abused by generations properly productive again.'

'Very well – I accept that; but I don't need to remind you that it's scarcely practical to own land on Skye and spend your working life in Africa!'

Iain's gesture with his hands admitted the truth of that,
but he made an effort to explain. 'My plan for as long as
I'm on sick leave was to try to farm it myself . . . make it
viable again. If that worked, I'd find someone to take it
on when I had to leave; if it failed, I'd cut my losses and
forget about Skye.'

'Your plan "was", you said,' James Hollister pointed
out. 'You mean you've decided already that it's not a . . .
a very good idea?'

Iain acknowledged the tactful phrase with a smile. 'No,
I hadn't decided that; my mind was changed for me by
the doctor I saw in New York on my way up here. He
was quite definite about it: if I went back to Africa it
wouldn't be for long – a return of the malaria would soon
put an end to me. From what he knew of Skye, however,
he thought I might live there to a ripe old age!' Iain saw
the shock in his friend's face, but shook his head. 'Don't
be upset on my account. I admit that it's a blow – despite
Africa's appalling problems it's a continent that gets a
hold on anyone who goes there, and I shall miss it very
much, but the doctor's report means that the agency won't
send me out again. They'll probably reckon it isn't a good
investment to send me anywhere at all, so I shall retire
gracefully to Skye and become a Hebridean!'

'For good . . . permanently?' James Hollister asked
anxiously. 'My dear Iain, think about it some more, please . . .
consider what life there will be like. Maybe you've just
seen it in fine weather – I believe it's beautiful then; but
God knows how it is for most of the year; think how cut-
off you'll be . . . how bored and lonely.'

Iain's rare smile appeared and again the lawyer registered the change in him. 'I've been in much lonelier places,'
he said gently, 'and much harsher places. And the truth is
that I don't expect to be bored – the people I mentioned
will see to that! But the move has to be permanent now,
because I shall have no other job. I'll have to realize everything I possess here – sell up, in short – because I must
invest in equipment and stock. So I need to know what

I'm worth, and I count on you to help me with that! The crofter I'm buying from is anxious to leave, and I don't want the summer to pass before I get started. Speed things along, please, James, in any way you can.'

The lawyer stared at him for a long moment, then held out his hands in a little gesture of defeat. 'All right – I give in. I don't recollect that you've listened to advice since you were about ten; why would you be likely to start now? I'll be as expeditious as I can.' He stopped speaking for a moment, then risked reminding Iain Macrae of something he might prefer to forget. 'So much for your dream of going to the Canadian north to look for . . . what was it? . . . the place that isn't on the map – Sick Heart River?'

Even that seemed not to disturb the man who sat facing him. 'I would have been looking in the wrong direction,' Iain answered quietly. 'I know Buchan's hero found fulfilment up there, but I think I might be going to find my own Sick Heart River on Skye.'

The lawyer digested that in silence, then thought of something else. 'I hope you're going to let your step-mother know? I have her address.'

Pure amusement now touched Iain's face for a moment. 'Yes, I'll write, of course. She'll be more forthright than you've been and tell me in plain New Yorker terms that, as she'd long suspected, I need the services of a reliable analyst! She may be right, of course, and perhaps I *am* making the mistake of my life. But it feels right, James, and nothing else has for a long time.'

The lawyer nodded, aware of the sadness and the truth contained in that last remark. 'You spoke of the people concerned in the story you didn't tell me. When Jean hears what you're going to do she'll want to know who the characters are.'

Iain considered this for a moment, then counted them off on his fingers. 'There's a retired schoolmaster who is also a Gaelic scholar; his spinster sister – a stern Presbyterian lady who disapproves of men in general and me in particular; the schoolmaster's recently orphaned grandson and daughter, and the small boy's dog, a mixed-up hound called Macgregor; then comes a shady lawyer and the villainous millionaire who wanted to knock down the manse they live in and "develop" the land I've bought . . .'

'That's enough,' James Hollister said, throwing up his hands, 'and I'm not sure you aren't making them up!'

'Come and meet them for yourself one day,' Iain suggested. 'Bring Jean for a holiday. I can't promise that you'll fall under Skye's spell, but I *can* promise that you won't forget it. Now I've got things to see to and I must let you get on with all the work I'm burdening you with. I'm grateful . . . very grateful, James. Call me when you need me to sign papers.'

The lawyer promised that he would, saw the door close behind his visitor, and then sat for a moment wondering what his old friend, Tom Macrae, would have made of his son's extraordinary move. Well, he was to blame for it in a way; if he'd simply torn up his correspondence with the lawyer in Edinburgh, Iain would be safely in the far north by now. James spared another moment to guess what Jean would say when he took the story home – probably that there must be a woman in it somewhere. But, except for an elderly Presbyterian spinster, there wasn't one. Nor was it the doctor's report that had shocked Iain into this foolishness – he'd bought the land even before he flew to New York. The simple truth seemed to be that he'd fallen in love at last – with a small, remote island that still held for him the ghost of his great-great-grandfather. Jean wouldn't believe it, of course, and he really couldn't blame her. Only Iain's instructions on the papers in front of him made him believe it himself.

Nineteen

A quiet week with no disturbing news from Edinburgh and no domestic stress encouraged Andrew Maitland to think that his family could begin to settle down. Perhaps they weren't going to be evicted after all. Jamie was setting off for school at least without complaint, and even Janet had been heard to say that they must bide their time before judging the man who was to be their new neighbour. He couldn't, she said unarguably, be worse than the dreadful Guthrie man who for once in his life had been outwitted. It was reassuring to know that the Devil didn't always take care of his own.

Andrew's heart still had misgivings at the thought of his daughter; but whatever inner struggle was required, she managed to seem content with the life she was leading at the manse. Both she and Fiona were now enrolled as pupils in absentia at Kilchrist school. Each day Jamie brought home new Gaelic phrases and, mindful that September wasn't far away, they both struggled to keep up with him. His mentor was a shy, gap-toothed child called Rory, who turned out to belong to Donald Mackinnon's younger sister. The island was full of such webs of kinship, and Louise realized that it behoved them to learn not only who they talked to but who these people were related to. Altogether, there was a great deal more to life on Skye than she'd been even remotely aware of. Before long she must dip into her father's treasure-house of Gaelic poetry and music; but for now she needed to be able to greet and meet children who thought of English as a foreign language.

Another ordeal loomed as well. Elspeth Mackintosh, whose offer to introduce her to the hills Louise devoutly hoped had been forgotten, telephoned one evening. The forecast for the coming weekend looked favourable; all Louise had to do was to go to Broadford and buy a pair of decent walking boots. Unable to think of an adequate excuse, she heard herself weakly agree.

'I must be mad,' she said, putting down the telephone. 'I'm terrified of heights, and to want to climb a mountain "just because it's there" seems to me to be the ambition of a lunatic.'

Andrew's sympathetic smile agreed, but Janet Maitland answered in a voice that for once sounded nearly wistful.

'I always wanted to try,' she said astonishingly. 'I knew someone who promised to teach me – he was a very fine climber. Then . . . things changed and I had to give the chance up. But I should dearly have loved to stand on a mountain top.'

In the silence that followed that little speech Louise was aware of several things, and shocked to realize how long it had taken her to learn them. 'Things changed' had meant Janet Maitland giving up her own life to help take care of Angus, and, in doing so, she'd given up the hope of love, marriage and children of her own. With Angus dead so untimely what a bitter waste it must all have seemed. Why should she not have hated Drusilla Maitland and distrusted Drusilla's English daughter?

Louise shook the thought away and smiled at her aunt. 'Now I'm shamed into having a go, but don't expect me to make it to the top!'

'Never look down,' Janet suggested. 'That's what Kenneth used to say – just keep your eyes on what's ahead of you.'

Louise repeated this advice to her guide when they set out the following Saturday afternoon, and Elspeth agreed that it was sound.

'Not that we're going climbing, though, today. You're a townie still; your feet have got to get used to the feel of boots, and you're probably needing to learn to breathe

properly as well.' She looked at her companion's pale face
and spoke more gently. 'If you really hate it you need
never climb at all; it's not obligatory even if you do now
live on Skye and have the Cuillin at your back door!'

Louise shook her head. 'It's not the mountains . . . it's
being afraid of them; that's what I have to beat. You look
a different person out here – liberated from everyday
worries, at home in this landscape that still intimidates me.'

'It won't when you've learned what to do,' Elspeth said,
'which includes what not to do: never climb on your own
or in bad weather, and always take with you warm, water-
proof clothing, some food, and a compass. Otherwise you'll
get into difficulties and need rescuing, which is tiresome
for the people concerned.'

'I shall try not to trouble them,' Louise agreed solemnly.
'Now, lead on, Macduff!'

It was only a hill walk, but a strenuous one, and when
they reached the point at which Elspeth said they would
turn back, Louise was glad of the chance to sit down and
recover her breath.

'All right so far?' her guide enquired.

'Right as rain, whatever that means.' Louise accepted
the piece of chocolate she was handed, content just to look
at the landscape spread out around and below them. But
her companion had information to share.

'Iain Macrae is a climber – he mentioned it to Donald
Mackinnon the day they spent together; out of practice,
he said, and not fit, but of course he soon will be.'

The lilt of pleasure in her soft voice forced Louise to
frame some hint of warning. 'Will there be time for that?
He's got to do a lot of hard work, surely, and it isn't as
if he's here for good. He has a job to go back to.'

Elspeth shook her head very firmly. 'Not according to
Mary Mackinnon. Iain is still in Canada, but Donald is in
touch with him, and they've agreed that he's going to stay
on here for a wee while once he's got Mary settled in
Ayrshire. Iain will live in the croft, and Donald will bide
with his sister for a few months.'

'Does Mary mind that arrangement?' Louise asked.

'Och, no, she'll be with their son and daughter-in-law, and she knows how much Donald wants to help Iain . . . there's too much work for one man to do on his own.'

It left unconfirmed, Louise thought, the length of time that Iain Macrae could stay on Skye, but Elspeth would believe what she wanted to believe, and no doubt saw in her mind's eye a future of mountain walks shared with him instead of a nervous, weak-kneed townie.

Safely back at the manse an hour later, she told her father what Elspeth had said and found him absent-mindedly inclined to share her own view that the Mackinnons had misunderstood Iain Macrae's intentions.

'Speaking of intentions,' Andrew said with an abrupt change of tone, 'your mother telephoned while you were out. For the first time in years we had a long conversation. She's worried about you, and so am I. You didn't tell me that you'd asked her to sell your flat – it was to be a bolt hole you could always go back to.'

'I don't need a bolt hole,' Louise explained with a smile. 'Under Elspeth's tuition I'm going to learn how to love mountains!' But her father's unhappy expression didn't change and when she spoke again her voice was serious. 'It's all right, really it is. I've accepted that I'm never going back to London, so what's the point of saddling Drusilla with the job of renting out the flat? Far simpler just to sell it now.' She didn't give him time to argue, but brushed the subject aside as being unimportant and hurried on. 'What else did Drusilla say . . . how did she sound?'

The question made him pause for a moment. 'Unchanged,' he finally answered. 'I even had the feeling that if I could see her she would still look the same as she did – beautiful and unsettling! She promised to pay us a visit one of these days, but perhaps I wasn't meant to take that seriously, but I was to tell you that she's putting your furniture into store for the moment. Everything else – clothes, books, music – should arrive here soon. She's been very busy on your behalf.'

'I know, and I'm grateful. But it's been good for her to have something to do – she still misses my stepfather.' Aware of aching legs, Louise bent down to rub them. 'I need a hot bath, I think, but first I'd better see what the children are doing.'

'No need – Janet is teaching Fiona how to make scones in the kitchen; Jamie and Macgregor are waiting to see what emerges from the oven as a result. Go and enjoy a long, hot soak or you'll be stiff in the morning.'

He watched her walk away, and picked up the last page of the article he'd been writing for the *West Highland Free Press*; then he put it down again, to think about what hadn't been said in that conversation with his daughter. He knew as certainly as if she'd put it into words that the sale of her flat was to provide the capital they might need to buy the manse if the church authorities decided to dispose of it. Tom Hepburn's solution would probably have been to break the trust set up for the children – a choice between Scylla and Charybdis, it seemed to Andrew, both equally uninviting. He put the problem aside with a sigh, and thought of something else.

Iain Macrae was coming to Skye to work purely as a professional experiment a croft that Donald, because of his wife's illness, had to be exiled from. Louise was giving up her home and her life in London because she felt obliged to stay here, while Brett Macdonald, who asked nothing better than to stay, had had to go back to Australia. He knew what Janet would say: their affairs were in the hands of God Almighty who in His infinite wisdom understood better than they did what was good for them. But Andrew's own opinion, which he wouldn't share with her, was that Will Shakespeare was right as usual: 'As flies to wanton boys, are we to the gods; They kill us for their sport.' Yes, that was nearer the mark, that old, pagan view of things.

A week later, walking back from the Gaelic College one evening, he heard someone pull up beside him. The Land

Rover was unfamiliar but it was Iain Macrae driving it, and leaning over to open the door and offer him a lift.

'I know you're nearly home, but why trudge when you can have a ride?' he suggested.

'The car's being fixed in Broadford,' Andrew explained as he climbed in. 'Welcome back! We've heard from various sources that you hadn't left Skye for good, but gossip abounds in small communities – it's hard to know what to believe.'

Iain heard the slight reproach in what had just been said. 'I should have let you know but I'm sorry – I left in a hurry, with a lot to do and some questions to find the answers to. Now I know for sure what's happening.'

He turned into the manse drive, and Andrew remarked that Louise's car was still missing. 'She and the children have driven my sister to Portree. They won't be back for a while, so come in for a drink, unless you're required to be somewhere else.'

Settled in the kitchen, with whisky and glasses on the table, Andrew looked at his guest. 'I know from Tom Hepburn that you're buying the croft. He's tried hard to convince me that it's not because you were left by James Guthrie with something you didn't want.'

'More accurately, Guthrie was deprived by Donald Mackinnon of something he *did* want. In the process it fell into my lap instead.'

'Now my "gossip" becomes more speculative,' Andrew admitted. '*Is* Donald going to stay and help you remodel the croft until you have to leave? That's our third-hand information.'

Iain sipped his whisky before answering. 'The information is correct but not quite up-to-date. I'm here to stay; in New York last week I resigned from the agency. Well, I was released, let's say, from further service. It seemed the moment to find myself a new career and I've fortuitously picked the right time to do it – the regeneration of crofting in the Highlands and Islands is now being given high priority.'

He smiled at the expression on Andrew's face. 'I know what you're thinking, even if you're too tactful to put it into words. There's more to life than a career and a burning desire to prove that my farming theories are right! Well, in Donald's croft I shall be housed more comfortably than I've been for years. I shall have neighbours, make friends, become part of a community, I hope – in fact, I might even rejoin the human race, something my stepmother has been waiting for me to do for years!'

Andrew's smile acknowledged the wry humour, but made no comment on it; instead, he had one final question to ask. 'And Donald – *is* he staying for a while?'

Iain nodded. 'I merely hinted at the idea and he jumped at it. He'd stay for ever if he could, but he'll be around long enough to help with things I can't do on my own – tree-planting, for instance; windbreaks are needed that can be coppiced later on. There'll be hedges needed to keep in the new livestock, and winter-housing for the beasts; and ground to be got ready for sowing corn and oats . . . the list is endless.'

'And farewell to the Great Cheviot?' Andrew asked. 'The accursed animal that drove the crofters out, according to the history books.'

'Not entirely; there's nothing else to do with really marginal land except run sheep on it; but they're the ruination of good land. I shall keep a few of Donald's breeding ewes.'

Iain glanced at his watch, then stood up. 'Thank you for the drink, but now I must get on – I'm invited to share the Mackinnons' evening meal, and there's a lot to talk about with Donald afterwards. I know what I want to do – he'll know whether it's possible or not!'

'Talking of which, let me lend you a book that you'll find interesting.' Andrew left the kitchen and returned a moment later with the volume in question. 'It's *The Past and Present Condition of the Skye Crofters*, published in 1886, and long out of print!'

Then he walked with his guest out to the Land Rover,

but before Iain could climb in, he held out his hand. 'We do realize what would have happened if Guthrie had won – we would have been looking for a new home, but much more was at stake than that. I hope this corner of Skye will feel as indebted to you as I do, Iain. As Louise would say, it's also one in the eye for the barbarians, and how heart-lifting that is!'

The man in front of him smiled, but waved it aside. 'How's Jamie getting on?'

'He's started school and, according to Elspeth Mackintosh, there aren't any real problems except his lack of Gaelic, but we'll overcome that in time.'

'And Macgregor and Miss Maitland?'

'Learning to live with one another,' Andrew said solemnly. 'Progress is slow but sure.'

'The very best kind,' Iain agreed, then turned the Land Rover and drove away.

Half an hour later when the rest of the family returned, Jamie was put out to have missed his friend, and disinclined to believe that Iain Macrae was going to be their nearest neighbour. 'He *said* he was only visiting,' he insisted, 'just like Brett.'

'He was, but now he isn't going back to Africa. This is going to be his home.' Jamie didn't reply to this, but when he'd examined his grandfather's face carefully he gave a little pleased nod.

Janet Maitland's contribution to the discussion was typical. 'He'll need someone to keep the croft clean for him. I wonder who I could suggest for that. I shall have to think, Andrew.'

It was only when the children were in bed and Janet had retired as well after supper that he returned to the subject of their neighbour-to-be.

'You didn't say anything about Iain. Does that mean you disapprove? I know you don't like him very much, but I can't guess what the reason is for that.'

Louise held up her hands. 'Does there have to be a reason? We can't like everyone we meet. He and I haven't hit it off since the first time we met – on the train from London to Edinburgh! I suppose I now feel that we're under some kind of obligation to him, which doesn't help either, but it doesn't matter. We're busy, and so will he be – our paths will scarcely cross.'

Andrew held his peace about this, seeing no need to point out that Janet wouldn't rest unless she knew that Mary Mackinnon's house was being properly looked after, and that Jamie would insist on watching and, if possible, sharing in whatever labour was going on at the croft.

'The poor man can't be busy all the time,' he finally suggested. 'Do we ignore him when he isn't working?'

'We leave him to Elspeth Mackintosh,' Louise answered. 'They can climb every one of Cuillin's blasted peaks together, and I can safely put my boots away.'

Twenty

On his way back from Armadale as usual, Andrew loitered in the garden before going indoors. The overnight rain had cleared away, leaving behind it the crystal-clear visibility that allowed him to pick out every seam and crevice in the mountains across the Sound. Close at hand sunlight glinted on the raindrops still clinging to each leaf and twig and, across the now neatly-mown lawn, the old stone house sat with solid grace among its sheltering trees. It was a moment to thank God, he thought, for the sheer beauty of the world, but there was still more to be grateful for than that.

There was no question about it: the arrival of two small children and one large dog had transformed the manse into a home again. Janet still tried to preserve order intact but she was slowly giving ground, and even the primness of her drawing room was going down defeated in the face of his daughter's habit of bringing in from the garden anything that bloomed. Janet had accepted another alteration, too, which he still marvelled at. She remained in charge of the kitchen until supper-time approached, but from then on it was Louise, now, who took over. Janet never enquired about what they ate, but although Andrew suspected that wine often contributed to its delicious flavour, he noticed with amusement that nothing was ever refused or left on her plate.

Life wasn't entirely serene. There'd been, for instance, the moment when a muddy-pawed Macgregor brought into her shining kitchen the rabbit he'd caught devouring his master's lettuces in the vegetable garden. The dog's mouth was gentle and they'd been able to return the creature, terrified but still alive, to a neighbouring field. Told about it when he got back from school, Jamie had explained that Macgregor thought he was doing his best for them. Janet had considered this and finally agreed, not mentioning that the kitchen floor had had to be cleaned again.

And only yesterday there'd been another episode that promised to alter life at the manse – much more significantly. Back from Sunday morning church – where Louise was still filling in for the missing organist – the children were left playing ball with Macgregor in the garden. But Jamie suddenly streaked into the house and fled upstairs to his bedroom. Fiona trotted indoors behind him, lisping – because of a missing front tooth – that 'it wath the cuckoo' that had upset her brother.

'Fee darling, it couldn't have been,' Louise said anxiously.

'It wath . . . it *wath*,' Fiona insisted, now beginning to weep because Lou-Lou didn't understand what she couldn't explain; and there certainly *was* a cuckoo – Louise could hear its reedy, two-tone song even inside the house.

She ran upstairs, knocked on Jamie's door, and then went in. He was sitting by the window, his thin body wracked with sobs. She was afraid even now that comfort would be rejected but it couldn't not be offered. With her arms tightly around him, she felt him stiffen for a moment and then suddenly bury his face against her. At last, at long last, the battle to keep grief and anger locked up inside him was over.

She waited for the storm of weeping to pass, then mopped his wet face. 'Tell me what that was all about,' she said gently when he was almost calm again. 'Fee thought the cuckoo upset you – was it really that?'

Jamie nodded. 'I 'spect she remembered . . .' A last, hiccuping sob had to be swallowed before he went on. 'We always played a game – who would hear the cuckoo first. Mummy always won, no matter how hard we tried.' He looked at Louise with such desolation in his face that her own eyes filled with tears. 'I miss her and Daddy all the time.'

'I know, Jamie,' she said brokenly, 'and there's nothing the rest of us can do to take the hurt away except love you, as they would if they were here. I can't explain why things happen as they do, or why we can't stop them happening. If you watch someone weaving a piece of cloth you can see only the part of the pattern that's been completed; eventually, at last, the pattern makes sense. I think life's a bit like that . . . it *will* make sense to you, but not yet; I'm afraid you've got to grow up first.'

She wouldn't have blamed him if he'd pointed out, with his customary forthrightness, that what she'd just said made no sense either; but his mouth only trembled for a moment. 'I thought you'd say that – about having to wait to grow up. Daddy said it too whenever he didn't know the answer.'

The mention of his father threatened more tears but Jamie knuckled his eyes and gave a little sniff instead.

'Remembering hurts now, love,' Louise had to agree, 'but later on you'll be glad that you *can* remember the lovely times you had at Scarsdale. But life isn't over for you and Fee – it's just beginning, only differently.'

He nodded and managed to speak almost normally. 'It's Macgregor's grooming day – I think I'd better go and see to him.'

'Talk to Fiona too, please,' Louise suggested gently. 'She's unhappy when she knows you're upset.'

They went downstairs together and he explained to his white-faced sister that she was needed to help brush Macgregor. When the children had gone outside Louise smiled unsteadily at the anxious couple watching her. She recounted what had happened upstairs and finished up regretfully by saying, 'I wasn't any real help at all, I'm afraid. But I bless that noisy cuckoo.'

Now, remembering it in the quietness of the garden Andrew realized that it hadn't only released a child from private, locked-in grief. Almost the most astonishing moment had come at the end when he'd looked at his

sister and found her unable to speak for the tears pouring
down her face. He'd not known what to do, but Louise
had; she'd simply folded Janet in her arms and let her
weep, while he, not needed, had left them together. When
he came back an hour later normality had returned. Janet
was working bread-dough and sounded just as usual.

'Louise has taken the children down to the beach. They'll
all be grubby again, and Macgregor will drip sea-water
over my clean floor.' But she'd smiled as she said it – and
things were not just as usual at all.

It was time to go indoors because he'd finally remembered that he was driving Janet and Fiona to Broadford
to shop. Louise had offered to stay and see that Macgregor
didn't get lonely while Jamie was at school. He could hear
her playing the piano in the drawing room; she'd taken to
practising regularly again for her coming new role as a
music teacher.

But after they'd driven away it wasn't long before she
closed the piano lid; it was no morning to be indoors, and
she was intent on reclaiming an overgrown bed in the
garden that, in her mind's eye, was already a beautiful
herbaceous border.

She was struggling to dig out the roots of an old,
exhausted honeysuckle when a voice spoke behind her.

'I could lend a hand – you don't seem to be winning
on your own.'

Aware that she was hot, grubby and not looking her
best, she turned to find Iain Macrae standing ten feet away.
It was disconcerting to think, since she hadn't heard him
arrive, that he might have been watching for some time,
listening to her swearing at the honeysuckle.

'Brute force *would* help,' she agreed. 'It doesn't seem
to respond to the subtle female approach.'

She handed over her spade and prepared to watch in
her turn. It was interesting to see that he didn't immediately do anything at all except consider the problem;
no impetuous leap into action for this man – the way to
deal with a task was to think about it first. Here, she

reckoned, was the calmly logical way he ran his entire life. Only it wasn't logic, surely, that had sent him to Fort William to look for a child he didn't know, and it certainly wasn't logic that had kept him embroiled with the Maitlands ever since. He was still a puzzle she couldn't solve.

But he *did* have a winning way with honeysuckle roots; in no time at all the knotted mass had been disinterred and deposited in her wheelbarrow. She thanked him for his help and explained that her father was on the way to Broadford; no one was in the house.

'I only came to return a history of crofting that he lent me,' Iain explained, pulling it out of his jacket pocket. 'It made interesting but depressing reading.'

She glanced at the title. 'Out of date, though; things have improved since then, my father says.' It was the moment, she realized, to say something about his own imminent plunge into the island's traditional way of life. But while she worked out what it would be safe to say he brushed the subject aside.

'What exactly are you doing out here apart from trying to break your back?'

'I'm making an herbaceous border,' she said firmly. 'I expect Jamie, and you too, will tell me that the plants I want to fill it with won't grow in this sea-rimmed part of the world, but I shan't know until I try.'

'It's called learning the hard way,' he pointed out with the indifferent air that still irritated her.

If he'd said reasonably, wasn't it a waste of good plants that would promptly die in a coastal region, she would probably have listened; as it was she'd implore Jamie to help her keep them alive somehow.

They'd disposed of the border as a subject of conversation and she still hadn't found a way of welcoming him to life at Kilchrist when there came an almost welcome diversion in the shape of a small insect that flew into her eye, and she pulled off her gardening gloves to try to deal with it.

'You've got grubby hands – you'd better let me,' he said, coming to stand beside her.

She felt his hands on her face – a gentle, impersonal touch that shouldn't have made her skin tingle, but it did. Then he showed her the tiny fly he'd removed with the tip of his handkerchief, and she blinked hard because her eye was watering. But he didn't move away and she stepped back herself, to put a little more space between them.

'Unusual eyes you have,' he commented casually. 'Rather beautiful ones in fact.'

She managed to sound calm, she thought. '"Item, two grey eyes with lids to them".' But he knew the quotation as well as she did.

'"Item, two lips indifferent red"?' he added, making a question of it. 'No, I don't think so,' and, even before she could guess what was coming, he leaned forward to kiss her mouth.

Released at last, but bereft of words for the moment, she could only stare at him.

'Neglect not thy opportunities,' he said unsteadily. 'A useful motto I picked up somewhere, and I doubt if that particular opportunity will come again. But at least I proved that the lips were *not* indifferent.'

She forced herself to smile – dammit, she could do 'careless' too. She was a sophisticated thirty-one-year-old, not an inexperienced teenager; tolerant amusement at his mannish moment was the emotion to show.

'I didn't know you had the Shakespeare quotation habit – it's obligatory for anyone who lives with my father.' Having got that far she found that she could go on. 'We know about the croft, of course. Is this the moment to wish you well? If Jamie turns up too often you'll have to shoo him back here.' Now, of course, she was talking too much. She would pick up the book he'd left on the garden seat and take it indoors. It made for a rather abrupt departure, but after all that was how he usually left himself.

He watched her walk away, then knew between one moment and the next, more clearly than he'd known anything in his life, that what she was doing was entirely wrong – she should have been coming towards him, not going away. There was no arguing with the discovery – he knew it, and that was that.

He was still standing where she'd left him when she came out again from the house. For a dazzling moment he thought she'd made the same discovery too, but she picked up the spade and then stood leaning on it while she spoke to him.

'I need to ask you something,' she said in a low, firm voice. 'It's worrying not to know why people do the things they do.'

'Then ask,' he suggested, aware that in what remained of his rational mind he could guess what was coming next.

'I don't know much about malaria,' she began, 'but enough to guess why you're not going back to Africa. Perhaps your UN work has had to come to an end altogether and you're looking for something else to do. But you could stay in Canada or go anywhere else in the world – why come here?' When he didn't answer at once she went on herself, more hesitantly now.

'I don't quite know how it's happened but I'm afraid you've been made to feel responsible for us. Tom Hepburn, Guthrie, even the children, seem to have . . . entangled you, and because you're programmed to sort out people who're making a muddle of things, you haven't just walked away. Am I right?'

'Almost totally wrong,' he answered, able to speak calmly now. 'It *is* true that I have to find a new career, but I've chosen it for reasons that have nothing to do with the Maitland family. You can manage your affairs without any help from me.' She looked so unconvinced that he decided to amend what he'd just said. 'It's true that Jamie concerns me. I was twice his age when my mother died, so perhaps twice as angry, but *he* lost his father as well; mine only remarried a woman I didn't like. Does it put you under such an unbearable obligation if I take an interest in him?'

Put like that, unfairly he knew, she could only shake

her head. But because she didn't argue he suddenly wanted to make her understand.

'I've no home in Canada, no ties except for some good friends there that I shall keep in touch with – so why *not* here? If you haven't lived on great masses of land you won't realize the attraction of a place that is small, but complete in itself, soaked in its own remarkable past history but still intensely alive. It's true that when I went to meet Tom Hepburn I hadn't the slightest intention of even visiting Skye, but I'm thankful I did. I'm sure your aunt would tell us that God works in a mysterious way His wonders to perform!' He said it lightly, but she knew that she had to believe him. The truth was that he *was* content to be there; it wasn't their or anyone else's unfair pressure on him – Skye itself was recognized now as the place where a man who'd been homeless found that he belonged.

She thought of one last question to ask. 'Donald Mackinnon is taking his wife to Ayrshire this weekend. What happens after that?'

'I take possession of the croft, furnish it, and live in it from then on. Donald will come back to lend me a hand for a few months with all the work there is to do outside.' She saw him smile, and sensed again the change in him – she could swear that he was happy at last. 'Perhaps you'd feel duty-bound to lend me your advice indoors?'

She thought about this for a moment, then shook her head. 'You won't need advice from me . . . not with Aunt Janet and Elspeth on hand, and I dare say every other unattached maiden on the island will be beating a path to your door as soon as they know you're here.'

Pleased with this prediction, she said a cheerful goodbye and trundled her wheelbarrow further along the path. Conversation was over, the gesture said; she had more important things to do. He accepted his dismissal with equal cheerfulness and walked back along the drive. Honours were roughly even, he reckoned; match temporarily drawn and still to be fought to a finish, but he wished he could be certain how it would end.

Twenty-One

The talk was all of the new owner of the Mackinnon croft. Eavesdropping in the general store, Andrew went home to report that local opinion favoured making the newcomer welcome. Rumour had gone round about the proposed luxury hotel, but so had Chrissy Macdonald's verdict on Sir James Guthrie: 'Och no, he wouldn't do for Kilchrist; better the nice Canadian that Donald thought so well of.'

A few people aired the view that Guthrie's scheme would have brought in money and provided jobs, but this was knowledgeably demolished in the bar of the Ardvasar: who would benefit when everything was flown in from the mainland, and who wanted the job of waiting on rich southerners, well-known for being arrogant and contemptuous of any culture different from their own?

Andrew recounted all this when he went to pay Iain a neighbourly visit the day after he arrived, taking with him a gift of whisky and some of Janet's freshly-baked bread.

'I hope you realize that everyone will be watching what you do,' he said with a smile. 'You're a godsend to a small community – an unknown quantity, therefore providing much enjoyable speculation!'

'I'll try not to be the fool who rushes in,' Iain promised. 'Your own softly, softly approach seems to have worked very well – I shall copy it if I can.'

Andrew looked round the still disordered room. 'How can we help you settle in? We'd like to be of use. Janet will find someone to clean for you – she's not convinced that any man can properly look after a house – and Jamie

offers the services of himself and Macgregor to herd your
sheep, at least until Donald returns!'

Iain unearthed glasses from a box on the draining board,
and opened the bottle Andrew had brought. 'Thank you
for this, and thank Miss Maitland, too – I'd be glad to
accept her offer. Jamie is welcome to come anytime. I
suspect he may know more about sheep than I do at the
moment. I've got a week before Donald comes back to
sort out the house, and plan the order of work outside.
There's an immense amount to do while the summer lasts,
but reinforcements are arriving rather unexpectedly. Brett
Macdonald telephoned yesterday evening.'

'To tell you about the wedding?' Andrew asked. 'Louise
had a letter from Ellie sounding very excited and happy.'

'Brett didn't mention that. I'd written to him from
Canada because the day we left for Mallaig he made me
promise that I would – he's anxious about the Maitlands!
Now he wants to "lend" me his younger brother who,
according to their father, is lounging about with not nearly
enough to do. The plan is for Liam Macdonald to come
as soon as possible.'

'Someone you don't know?' Andrew sounded scep-
tical. 'Suppose he isn't useful, or congenial to you and
Donald?'

'Then I shall ship him back to Oz,' Iain said cheerfully.
'Brett knows that. But with so much work to do the prospect
of another pair of hands is welcome, and I'm very grateful
for the offer.' A smile touched Iain's mouth for a moment.
'I'm providing someone else for the island's unattached
maidens, not being in the market myself; your daughter
might like to know that!' But Andrew's serious expression didn't change. 'Something bothering you?' Iain asked
the man in a different tone of voice.

'I'm bemused, not bothered.' Andrew confessed. 'A
month or two ago Janet and I were a sad, rather lonely
brother and sister living in a spotless but gloomy house
that we were threatened with having to leave. Our grief
at losing Angus and Ailsa remains, and always will, but

everything else has changed. It's like recovering from frostbite – painful at first, but worth it!'

Iain smiled at the comparison, but his next question was still serious. 'What about Louise – is it worth it for her?'

'Oh, I do pray so,' Andrew said earnestly, 'because it's she who has worked the magic for us.' He glanced at his watch and then stood up. 'I must go – come and share our supper whenever you can. It's cooked now by our resident professional, and she could even give Lady MacDonald a run for her money!'

He said goodnight, and set off home across the fields, but he walked slowly, deep in thought.

It was Brett, that so likable Australian, who concerned him, not the unknown brother who was coming to Skye. The openness that was Brett's defining trait had given him away whenever he'd looked at Louise. Now he was required to stay behind to marry someone else, and do it cheerfully what was more. Andrew saw it as his own experience in reverse – he'd had to free Drusilla to marry someone else and been left behind himself. Janet, too, had given up her climber to stay with him and his small son. The lost chances of happiness were surely the saddest thing in the world.

Back at the manse at last, he reported the news about Liam Macdonald.

'Extraordinary,' Janet commented, not displeased by this new excitement; she thought she was getting quite used to not knowing what was likely to happen next.

'It's Brett's way of helping,' Louise pointed out. 'He must realize that Iain Macrae still isn't very fit. Liam Macdonald will turn out to be a tough, young giant who can move mountains with his bare hands!'

Andrew smiled but added another guess. 'I think Brett wants his brother to have the Skye experience in return for helping Iain – something to remember when he goes back to Australia.'

'You're right,' Louise agreed more seriously. 'It's exactly

what Brett would want.' She was silent for a moment, then
spoke in a voice she struggled to make cheerful. 'Now . . .
what are we going to send him and Ellie in the way of
wedding-day greetings . . . suggestions, please.'

A week later, with Donald Mackinnon back on the island
and installed with his sister, Kirsty MacNeish, the work
of transforming the sheep-holding into another man's
vision of an almost self-sufficient farm could begin.
Jamie returned from a visit with Macgregor to report
that a large map now adorned one wall of the kitchen.
On it Iain had drawn his plan: livestock here, corn and
oats there, the new hedges that must be planted, the
necessary wind-breaks of trees, the sheep in future
confined to the hilly ground where the soil was thin and
poor . . . Andrew couldn't help wondering what Donald
made of it all, but when he met the Highlander at
Armadale quay one morning, come to collect something
off the ferry, he could detect only satisfaction in Donald's
calm opinion that what he and Iain were embarking on
was very good; just how crofting must be in the future
if it was to survive – large enough in scale to be viable,
adequately financed, and professionally managed. 'But
for now,' he said happily in his soft voice, 'there *iss* a
great deal of work to do.'
    Louise remembered this when she was with Elspeth
Mackintosh one afternoon on the hills above Glen Brittle
that gave them a different view of the Cuillins. While they
took their usual breather, Elspeth named the peaks they
could see, then suddenly abandoned the subject of mountains for one that was much more on her mind.
    'Iain called on me one evening the other day,' she said
softly, 'to ask who's in charge of the schools in Broadford
and Portree. He thinks school-leavers should be encouraged to think of crofting as a career again, and landowners
like him should be ready to take in young students and
begin training them. It's a wonderful idea.' But she
sounded wistful, nevertheless, for the reason that came

out next. 'He's so very busy, though, poor man, too busy to come walking; and lonely too, I expect, living in the croft alone.'

'Busy certainly,' Louise agreed, 'but I doubt if you need worry about him being lonely – he's a very self-sufficient man. In any case, he won't be alone much longer. Brett Macdonald's young brother will be turning up any day to stay and help for a few months.'

'He didn't mention that,' Elspeth said, frowning over an idea she didn't entirely like. But aware of Louise looking at her, she managed a faint smile. 'Well, I think he'll be glad of the company . . . men aren't very good as a rule at living on their own.'

Louise didn't argue the point, aware that her own and Elspeth's view of Iain Macrae was likely to differ in almost every particular. Instead, she pointed to what Elspeth had identified as Sgurr na Bhairnich, now beautifully catching the afternoon sun, and then it was time to start the downward trek home.

She didn't see Elspeth again before Iain arrived at the manse one morning to introduce his guest and new recruit, who turned out in fact to be the giant she'd predicted. He even towered over Andrew Maitland, and Louise had to stand on tiptoe to kiss his cheek.

'Welcome to the family,' she said, smiling at him.

Liam Macdonald looked surprised as well as pleased, but rose rather well to the occasion, Iain reckoned. 'Brett promised me I'd like Skye and fall in love with you,' he said with a broad grin. 'He's usually right, too.'

'Not this time,' she answered, immediately at home with a younger, larger version of Brett. 'I'm afraid I'm much too old for you.' But Iain's bland gaze brought colour to her cheeks, and she was glad of the diversion that came next. Liam opened the bag of gifts his brother had asked him to deliver and began to hand them out: a cuddly Koala bear for Fee, a little mouth organ that left Jamie speechless with pleasure, a soft leather purse for Janet, and a history of the Aborigines for Andrew. Louise's gift came last – a small painting of the lighthouse at Isle Ornsay, simply signed Brett.

'He said you wouldn't mind that he isn't much of an artist,' Liam suggested hopefully.

'I don't mind at all,' she answered in a voice she struggled to hold steady. 'In any case, it seems that painting is another light that Brett hides under a bushel, like his playing of the mouth organ.' Aware that Iain was still watching, she was obliged to put the little picture down on the table beside her.

Then there were wedding photographs to be handed round – Ellie looking beautiful, Brett serious but proud.

'He seems older than I remember,' Janet Maitland said unexpectedly.

'He acts older than he did, doesn't laugh quite as much,' Liam admitted. 'I guess marriage ages a man.'

Iain agreed solemnly that this was true and then suggested that their visit had lasted long enough – there was too much work to do to allow his assistant to linger over morning calls. But the kindness that was in Brett was in Liam too, and Jamie's enchantment with his mouth organ hadn't gone unnoticed.

'I'm not the wizard that my brother is,' he said to the small boy, 'but I know roughly what to do with it. When I'm allowed off the hook by Iain we'll have lesson number one – OK?'

'OK,' Jamie agreed, beginning to grin.

Then, with an invitation from Janet to come to supper the following evening accepted, the visitors went away. Andrew smiled at the rest of them.

'I was worried that Brett's kind idea wasn't going to work; but of course it is. Iain will know exactly how to handle that nice young man.'

Louise, already contemplating what the following evening's supper might consist of, absent-mindedly agreed, and then suggested that Elspeth should be invited as well to even up the numbers. Janet calmly accepted the idea of another guest, and Andrew once again acknowledged to himself the extent to which their lives had changed – they were becoming positively social, and how enjoyable it all now was.

Out in the garden the following evening, gathering last-minute herbs for the Niçoise salad that was to be the supper-party's first course, Louise registered the fact that spring was sliding into summer. She'd given up counting how long ago it was that she and the children had set out from London, and accidentally met on the train the very man who was now their near neighbour. Both she and he, for different reasons, had come to see the Eilean-a-Cheo as their home. That was extraordinary enough, but even odder was the feeling that she could scarcely remember any other life than the one she was living now. It was as if she'd always been part of this windswept, rain-washed and sometimes miraculously beautiful island.

She couldn't guess whether the children shared this feeling. Fee probably did, because she was too young for memories of the Cheviot Hills not to fade; but Jamie, she thought, *did* still measure his present life against the one he remembered. It made her the more thankful that settling in at Kilchrist school hadn't been a huge problem after all.

She was still in the garden when the first guest, Elspeth Mackintosh, arrived and was given a smiling welcome.

'I was just calling down blessings on your head,' Louise said cheerfully, 'for all your kindness to Jamie. And Rory MacNeish deserves a little credit too! It just happens that they're two of a kind – not very bookish, bored with computer games, and enchanted with the great outdoors – animals, birds, trees, plants – and of course fascinated with everything that's going on at Iain Macrae's croft! If they're the nuisance I suspect, he's managing very well not to say so.'

'He won't discourage them,' Elspeth said with absolute conviction. 'The children are fortunate to have him there – we all are.'

Louise agreed, but couldn't help feeling anxious. Her friend was well on the way to giving her loyal, loving heart into Iain Macrae's keeping, if only he would ever find the time or the inclination to accept it. But despite the change she was aware of in the Canadian-turned-Skyeman, it still seemed likely that Elspeth might be disappointed.

'I must put the finishing touches in the kitchen,' she said, 'and you must be longing for a drink.'

She led the way into the drawing room and left Elspeth with her father and Aunt Janet. Back in the kitchen, a ring on the doorbell announced the arrival of the two other guests, but although there was very little left to do to the salad, the poached salmon or the lemon mousse, she was in no hurry to leave her present haven; here, she wasn't under the observant, appraising gaze of Iain Macrae – she need neither school her expression nor guard her tongue.

But at last, with a final look at the dining table, she went back to the other room. Liam was already on good terms with both the ladies present, her father and Iain Macrae were talking together about mountains. As Louise approached, Iain bowed good evening and congratulated her – with tongue in cheek, she thought – on her progress on the hills. Elspeth had reported that she was doing very well.

'Perhaps she hasn't mentioned that I shan't ever progress from walking to climbing,' Louise pointed out calmly.

'No head for heights?'

'None at all, but even if I had the sure-footedness of a mountain goat I'd still rather look at the Cuillin from a distance than scramble to the top of them.'

His lifted eyebrow warned her what was coming next. 'I see – an aesthetic preference . . . you think the world's great hills should remain inviolate, not be strewn with the rubbish that climbers leave behind?'

She suspected him of laughing at her, but answered seriously. 'Admit that we do seem to despoil whatever we touch. I'd rather we resisted these so-called challenges instead of debasing or destroying them.'

'I agree with you, my dear,' Andrew Maitland put in, 'but you mustn't expect a climber to.'

Iain looked suddenly regretful. 'I'm torn, as a matter of fact. We only make discoveries by accepting challenges, but what Louise says is also true, I'm afraid, and not only careless climbers are at fault; people at large treat our planet very badly.'

He smiled at her then, with such grave sweetness that she was disorientated for a moment. His tolerant amusement, indifference even, she could handle easily enough; he had no right, though, to disarm her in this treacherous way. Aunt Janet came to her rescue by suggesting that it was time they moved into the dining room. Sitting safely between her father and Liam Macdonald she could recover from that brief light-headedness and even pretend that she'd imagined it. But her attention occasionally wandered from the men beside her to the one who sat opposite, listening attentively to something that Elspeth was saying. The conundrum that was Iain Macrae she still needed to solve, then she could forget about him. A straight question put to Liam might help.

'I know you've only been here five minutes,' she said to him, 'but first impressions are usually reliable – are you going to enjoy working with Iain?'

'I'm not supposed to be here to enjoy myself!' But his effort to look solemn made her smile, and he gave up trying and grinned back. 'Learning from an expert is what it's all about, and working hard and making myself useful! Well, I'll have a good go at those things, but I'm certain already that I'll enjoy being at the croft as I've not enjoyed anything before that I can remember.'

'Because you like the work so much?' she queried.

'Mostly because I like Iain Macrae,' Liam said frankly. 'I just hope he can put up with me at fairly close quarters. Brett warned me that he's a . . . a private sort of man . . . so I'm treading carefully!'

Louise smiled at the image of this large, likable creature walking round the croft on tiptoe, but his testimony had been seriously given and she must accept it seriously. Then Janet Maitland claimed his attention, and Louise was free to revert to the role of waitress-cum-kitchen-maid.

But when the delicious meal was over, and they were back in the drawing room, with coffee poured, it was Aunt Janet who spoke of the evening when Brett and Ellie had played for them.

'The mouth organ was just what street urchins had, I thought,' she said, almost apologetically. 'But listening to Brett was like hearing a piper play the "Great Music" – the "Ceol Mòr". It was just as sad and just as haunting.'

Iain broke the little silence that followed what she'd said. 'No mouth organ tonight, Miss Maitland, but we have another weaver of magic here.' Then as Brett had done, he went to open the lid of the piano. 'Will you play for us?' he asked, looking at Louise.

She nodded, moved to the piano stool, and hesitated with her hands resting on the keys. What to play this time? Then a soft cascade of sound introduced her favourite Chopin nocturne. She played two more after that, then turned round to smile at them, deliberately breaking the spell.

'That's enough. I can't help thinking of Mr Bennett in *Pride and Prejudice* telling his unfortunate daughter Mary, who was always reluctant to stop, that she'd "delighted them long enough"!'

Andrew smiled but shook his head. 'We're enchanted, not "delighted". Won't you go on?'

But Louise shook her head, aware that what she wanted now was for the evening to end. It had been successful: Liam had been made to feel at home, Elspeth had spent a happy hour or two in Iain Macrae's company; but now, please God, let them all decide to go home. She wanted to crawl upstairs and lie in bed watching the stars move across the black velvet backdrop of the sky – thanks to her father, she could identify some of them now. She might have said to Iain that she didn't want the moon or any other planet tampered with, any more than she wanted Mount Everest diminished by a stream of climbers claiming that they'd 'tamed' it; those unimaginably distant stars were best left unvisited, but watching them across great voids of space was as good a way as any of passing a wakeful night. What she most wanted *not* to do was leave her mind free to think about Iain Macrae, because with *that* would come the knowledge of something very important missed and the prospect of a long and lonely future. No, much better not to think of that.

Twenty-Two

L ife at the manse now rearranged itself to take account of the new neighbours at the croft. Janet Maitland kept a sharp eye on two men whose aptitude for housewifery she strongly doubted. Andrew often strolled across the fields to share an evening dram with Iain and Liam, and Jamie found it necessary to visit them whenever he'd been released from school. Macgregor needed exercise, he explained, if Louise suggested that he went too often. It was less important, but still necessary, of course, to watch Iain's plan on the kitchen wall begin to take shape out-of-doors; and there was also the little matter of the mouth organ – for as long as Liam was there his knowledge of how to play it had to be tapped.

The only manse inmate who didn't visit the croft was Louise, even though she knew that Liam's friendly companionship would have been welcome. She didn't examine very closely her reasons for staying away – Elspeth's devoted concern for Iain Macrae came into it, but a sense of their own obligation to him remained to fret her; and in any case, she told herself, since she never felt at ease with him, the answer was simply to stay away. He didn't, apparently, have time to call at the manse, so whatever reservations she had, he seemed to have also.

It was how matters stood at the start of the school summer holiday, which coincided with news from Edinburgh. Tom Hepburn's ailing wife, Jane, had finally died, and that meant that Andrew and Janet must set off to attend her funeral.

Left alone with the children at the manse, Louise found

herself lonely when their bedtime came, and was glad, when the telephone rang, to hear her mother's voice at the other end of the line. The good news was that her London flat had now been sold, but Drusilla sounded mournful about it.

'I still think it's a mistake,' she insisted. 'It's not as if you're anything but city-bred; what can you find to do on a remote island where half the population speak a foreign tongue and the cultural high-spot of the week is a visit to the Presbyterian kirk? You'll go mad with boredom.'

'Boredom is not having enough to do,' Louise answered firmly, 'that's not my problem; and you're forgetting the bonus for living up here: unpolluted air, uncrowded roads, a pace of life that keeps people sane enough to be aware of one another, and wonderful scenic beauty.'

'In mid-summer, maybe,' Drusilla commented on this last point. 'What happens when winter sets in and you can't see the "wonderful" landscape for mist or driving rain for days at a time. Your father took me to Skye once soon after we married – it didn't stop raining the whole time.'

'So you won't come again,' Louise suggested. 'I thought you hinted that you *might* venture across now that you don't have to arrive by boat.'

'I expect I was trying to make Andrew nervous at the thought of his sister and his ex-wife coming face to face again. But if I'm never going to see you unless I *do* come, I may have to risk it. It's rather lonely down here on my own.'

Louise heard the ring of sad truth in that – her mother wasn't cut out for a single life, happiness depended on having a companion close at hand. She was easily capable of attracting a new lover or husband, but Miles' death was still too recent; she wasn't ready yet to make a fresh start.

'If you can bear the thought of Scotland at all, *please* risk it,' Louise urged. 'There's a comfortable hotel nearby called Toravaig House, and winter won't set in for months yet.' It was as far as she dared go in persuading her mother

to visit them. There was still a strong chance that no good
would come of it, but she suddenly wanted two 'no-longer-
young' women to put the troubled past behind them and
discover that they could at least accept, if not like, one
another.

Drusilla promised to think about it and rang off, but
her conversation had left pessimism behind. Louise put
down the telephone suddenly assailed by loneliness, and
a wave of misery that threatened to close over her head.
It was pointless when she couldn't change anything, and it
was shaming at her age to react like a spoiled adolescent
rebelling against the only future she could see – long
years of service, first to children who weren't hers and,
by the time they'd become self-reliant, to a father and
aunt who would then need her to take care of *them*. It
was a nadir moment of despair, and she recognized it as
such, thanking God no one else was there because, with
very little encouragement, she'd become maudlin with
self-pity.

It was time to pull herself together, and from force of
habit she went to the piano. Something loud and defiant,
safely played con brio because it couldn't wake the children sleeping two floors above, was what she needed.

With the storming conclusion of Chopin's 'Revolutionary
Study' finally reached, she sat for a moment, drained but
calm again; the future hadn't changed, and there'd be other
bad moments still to live through, but at least she knew
now that she could learn to surf her way through the waves
of despair and not be drowned by them.

She got up and walked to the open French windows;
for once the evening was windless and the sunset sky so
beautiful that she stepped outside to look at it. Then, heart
suddenly in her mouth, she saw the shadow of a man
thrown on the grass as he got up from where he'd been
sitting on the garden bench. Fear died as she turned and
recognized Iain Macrae, but it left the tremble of anger in
her voice.

'Unkind of you to startle me – you nearly frightened

me to death,' she said unsteadily, keeping a safe distance between them.

'I'm sorry . . . very sorry about that,' he answered after a moment. 'I heard you playing as I arrived . . . couldn't interrupt . . . I was going to go round to the front door when you stopped.' The words came jerkily because he was still off-balance himself, shaken by the music's torrent of emotion, and by the way it had been played – even passion generated by notes on a page shone a new light on the girl who stood so warily in front of him. Cool and composed Louise Maitland undoubtedly was, but not all the time, and certainly it wasn't how she'd been a few moments ago.

'You weren't just playing that music, very beautifully,' he suddenly went on, 'you were living it as well.'

'I was enjoying myself, maltreating my grandmother's piano,' she agreed in a calmer voice. 'I just felt like letting rip.' Her hands brushed the subject aside. 'My father and Aunt Janet aren't here – they went to Edinburgh this morning for Jane Hepburn's funeral.'

'I know – Andrew mentioned that they'd be going. I didn't come to see them. Liam's at a ceilidh at the Ardvasar – it seemed a good moment to stroll over and enquire why *you* never visit the croft with the rest of your family.'

'Probably because they visit you too often,' she said, trying to sound casual about it. 'Jamie especially, of course, and if you don't want him to haunt you for the entire school holiday you'll have to be firm about sending him away. He's got a list of excuses, whatever I say to him, I'm afraid.'

To her surprise the comment was dealt with seriously. 'Do you *mind* his coming . . . want me to discourage him?'

'How could I?' she answered, serious now in her turn. 'From being a silent, haunted ghost, he's slowly becoming a normal boy – still thin, but not painfully so, still no chatterbox but now in communication with the rest of us, because life's become interesting again. I'm very grateful to you for being so patient with him, but you mustn't let him get in the way.'

That, she thought, dealt adequately with the subject of her nephew. It left ignored the comment about herself, but she hoped that it had been forgotten now. Her own absence from the croft had been an excuse for his visit now, of course; more probably he'd come to make sure that she was managing in her father's absence; some might call it neighbourly concern, but it was irritating nevertheless – he could just as well shout his opinion from the house-tops that Louise Maitland needed city pavements under her feet and a string of minders standing by to help her over life's hurdles. His next words proved it.

'To go back to where we began,' he said, 'I think you played that music because you needed to release whatever emotion is inside you – anger, grief, loneliness, boredom. Am I right?'

He had the tenacity of a terrier at a rabbit hole, she thought, and a total disregard of what constituted the normal small talk of polite society. As well to try to swat an intrusive fly that disturbed the peace of a room on a warm, sleepy afternoon. Chase him away in one direction and he'd find another to attack from.

She held up her hands in a little gesture of defeat. 'I'd just been talking to my mother in London. Without being able to tell me what else I could have done, she persists in believing that I shan't be able to stay here without going mad. I suppose she can't help remembering that she gave up her own life to share my father's and it was spectac-ularly unsuccessful. If I gave up too she'd feel exonerated in some way. I shan't give up, of course, but just for a moment when our conversation ended I looked at a future that seemed rather bleak – hence the pyrotechnics at the piano; I was casting out self-pity!'

She wondered what he would offer next – a bracing instruction to do better, a little sympathy, a curt goodnight? None of those things broke the silence between them; instead, he finally said something that took her breath away.

'If the future looks as bleak as all that, you could always marry me . . . I'd like to help with the children.'

The words seemed to echo round the quiet garden, probably sounding like an insult, he thought, to the white-faced girl who stood watching him. What was she – angry, shocked, or justifiably afraid that he'd suddenly run mad? Had there ever been a more cretinously offensive proposal than the one he'd just delivered? With all the richness of the English language to draw on, he'd come up with *that*, and what in God's name could he say now that wouldn't make matters worse?

But she spoke before he did. 'Any port in a storm for me?' she managed to enquire, 'and a surrogate family for you without the bother of begetting it? I think not!' Then she forced her mouth to smile. 'Not, of course, that you were serious, even if it *is* getting to be a habit with you to feel responsible for the Maitland tribe. There's no need; we're in calm water now. It's time I went indoors – Fee or Jamie might wake up and find themselves in an empty house.'

He closed the gap between them and spoke before she could close the French windows and escape. In control of himself again now, his voice sounded almost normal.

'Accepted that it wasn't a serious offer . . . but if it had been, would you at least have considered it seriously?'

'I expect so,' she said after a moment's thought. 'It would have been unkind not to!'

She achieved a more natural smile this time, gave him a little farewell nod, and closed the door. In what remained of her functioning mind she realized that she still hadn't explained why she didn't visit the croft, but he probably knew the reason already – apart, they could think quite well of each other; propinquity seemed to make of it an altogether different matter.

Iain watched the door close, remembered how he'd come there, on foot across the fields, and began to walk slowly back to the croft, but he went mechanically, leaving his feet to find the way; his mind and heart had more difficult work to do. It meant going back to the very beginning in James Hollister's office. The room had still held for him the essence of his father, and perhaps that was why the correspondence with Thomas Hepburn in Edinburgh had brought him across the Atlantic to meet the man himself. From that first step everything else seemed, looking back, to have been a sequence of inevitable events that he'd refused to recognize until now. How many people had he told that he'd set out from Canada for no better reason than boredom or idle curiosity? How many times had he pretended that no inherited legacy from generations past had led him, step by step, to Kilchrist – his home now, his occupation, and his life? Last of all, how often had he repeated to Louise Maitland the silly lie that he'd involved himself with her family because, being at a loose end, he couldn't think of anything better to do.

'There's a divinity that shapes our ends, Rough-hew them how we will' – Shakespeare again, of course; no doubt a habit caught from the Maitlands. She should at least be pleased with him for that. Louise . . . with the thought of her he'd finally reached the heart of the matter. Since that anxious rain-sodden day in Fort William, he'd used the children as his reason for staying close to her. Odd that he hadn't recognized the truth there and then, or perhaps not odd at all; concern for Jamie had been easily explainable; his own need of Louise would change his life. It wasn't until she'd walked away from him that day in the manse garden that he'd admitted once and for all what was wrong – for her to come towards him was now his only necessity.

But had he said so? Of course not. Instead, this evening's performance had been inept enough to make the angels weep – so clumsy that Louise had been right to dismiss it as a joke, but he could see it now for what it really was – the last, despairing attempt of the man he'd been to remain as he once was – solitary, self-sufficient and defiantly unattached.

The other steps had been taken easily: he didn't for a moment regret buying the croft; he could even admit that it already felt like home to a previously rootless wanderer.

But knowing in his heart that the days of being uninvolved were over, he hadn't brought himself to make that confession to Louise; instead, he'd offered her an insultingly casual proposal that she was certain to refuse. It left him in theory still free and unattached . . . but, face it now at least, almost unbearably lonely. Either the inevitable sequence of events had come to a suddenly unscripted end or Louise's firm 'no' had been part of the sequence all along – his proper reward for being the bloody insensitive fool that he was.

It was no comfort to take that thought with him as he reached the croft, to find Liam approaching from the outbuilding where he'd left his car.

'Good evening?' he managed to ask.

'Great,' Liam answered with a happy smile. 'You should have come. I met a lovely girl there, and we got on like a house on fire.'

A strange smile touched Iain's mouth for a moment. 'I also met a lovely girl, I even asked her to marry me . . . jokingly, of course . . . but fortunately she turned me down! Goodnight, Liam – see you in the morning; as usual there's a lot of work to do.'

He went into the house and up the stairs to his bedroom, leaving Liam on the doorstep still watching him; had he been meant to laugh at what Iain had just said? No, he thought not; what he'd just glimpsed in his friend's face had surely been desolation, not laughter.

Twenty-Three

The fine summer weather was due, Andrew explained when he and Janet returned from Edinburgh, to a high-pressure system obligingly sitting to the north-east of them. The children, with Rory MacNeish in daily attendance now, didn't care whence it came – the result was occasional swimming lessons with Liam, picnics on the beach, and the carefree, vagabond atmosphere of long hours spent in the open air.

'Nothing new to you, of course,' Louise said to Liam one day when lunch was over and the children were absorbed in their hunt for shells. 'But to us it's a matter for wonder to get even a week of fine days in a row!'

'I like the way it changes,' he confessed, smiling at her, 'and the not knowing what's going to happen next.' He stared out across the Sound, sapphire-blue today and mirror-smooth, and all she could see of his face was a brown cheek and a jaw that reminded her of Brett. 'I'd like to stay for good,' he went on quietly. 'Iain knows that but he reckons I'll change my mind.'

'Your brother would have stayed if he could,' Louise decided that it was safe to say. 'Perhaps he told you that? He delved into the history of this place and I think he wanted a Macdonald to give back something in return for what earlier Macdonalds took away. Is that your idea too?'

Liam shook his fair head. 'I'm not much like Brett – he's not your average Australian sheep-man; in fact he's an odd sort of cove altogether! My reason for staying would be to help Iain. There's too much work for one man to do, and it won't be long before Donald Mackinnon has to go back to the mainland – his wife misses him, I think; otherwise he'd stay too.'

'What about your family?' Louise ventured, 'your parents, I suppose I mean. Could they and Brett manage without you?'

'Be glad to, I reckon,' Liam said simply. 'I've got a married sister, and two younger brothers – they aren't exactly short of help; but Iain is.' He turned to face Louise, smiling again. 'There's Jamie coming along, of course, and he tells Iain every day he's growing as fast as he can; all the same it'll be a few years yet before he's ready to sign on!'

Louise hesitated over what to say next. How to point out without hurt that Iain might not be prepared for a visit to extend itself indefinitely? What if he wanted the croft to himself, or to share it with someone else? But Liam had also thought of this.

'Of course I'd need to find somewhere else to live – or Iain might move out! He's got it into his head that he'd like to buy the church when it's closed down and turn it into a house – better than having it fall into ruin, he says; but I think there's another reason. He wants to live in what was his great-great-grandfather's place.'

Louise saw the building in her mind's eye – spacious, light-filled and serene. Yes, it would make an interesting if eccentric house to live in, and who better to transform it than the eccentric Canadian that Iain Macrae was.

'It sounds intriguing,' she agreed at last. Then because the memory of their last conversation still haunted her, she spoke of him again. 'Jamie only talks of livestock, and ploughing, and re-seeding grass when he comes back from the croft, so I don't get news of Iain. If he's filling every unforgiving minute with hard work he'll surely fall ill again.'

'No, he's better,' Liam said definitely. 'He slaves away all right, but this climate suits him – no malaria trouble since he came to Skye. This afternoon he isn't working – he and Elspeth Mackintosh have gone climbing. He's

joined the Mountain Rescue Service and needs to get in
trim again.'

'Nice for Elspeth,' Louise commented, trying to sound
sincere. 'She puts up with a rabbit like me, but I'm no
substitute for a proper climbing companion.'

Liam smiled kindly at her. 'Not a rabbit,' he suggested,
'more of an elegant Afghan hound, I'd say, with silky hair
and lovely long legs!' Then he grew serious again. 'I'm
glad he and Elspeth set off all smiles. I think something
went wrong a little while ago, because he went very quiet,
but they're all right now.'

Louise was silent for a moment, selecting from the
thoughts seething in her head what could safely be said.
At last she came up with it. 'You're fond of him, I think . . .
want him to be happy.'

Liam nodded, wondering why it had taken her so long
to ask the question, if that was what it was.

'I like him a lot. Seems to me he's lonely – no family
at all to speak of. I can't imagine how that feels, but I
know I wouldn't like it.'

'You might miss your own family more than you think,'
she suggested gently.

'I surely would, but there are things called aeroplanes that
fly from there to here!' Then his expression changed. 'The
truth is that I've got another reason for wanting to stay –
she's called Kate and she's Rory MacNeish's big sister.'

There was another small silence. 'She's a very pretty
reason not to leave,' Louise finally agreed. 'I've met her
at Jamie's school. She looks after the smallest children
and they're as good as gold with her – infallible sign, I
think, of goodness in her.'

But all the same, it seemed necessary to remind him of
how little he knew about her and about the island that was
her natural habitat but not his. She pointed at the sparkling
stretch of water and the mountains beyond, capped today
by small puffs of white cloud instead of snow.

'I know how beautiful it looks now, but will you try to
remember that it isn't always like this? There can be not

just days but weeks of mist or rain or gales driving in from the Atlantic. In winter it's scarcely light before ten in the morning, and dark again by four. The history of people leaving the island isn't only that they were driven out by rapacious landlords; they went because their life was too monotonously hard and unrewarding.' She smiled ruefully and shook her head. 'Now I sound exactly like my mother trying to persuade *me* to go back to London! But it's what your own mother would say if she were here. Pretend I'm in *loco parentis* for the time being.'

'I know,' Liam agreed slowly. 'Iain's done his best to put me off as well, and it's not at all certain that he'll let me go on working for him. If not, I'll have to find something else. You both think I haven't been here long enough to know my own mind. Well, I'm sure about Kate – I knew that right away. Don't you think it can happen like that?'

'I'm sure it can,' Louïse had to agree. 'It's what the French call a *coup de foudre* – a flash of lightning, not to be argued with!'

He nodded and went on. 'I think Kate would go back to Australia with me if I asked her, because she's sure too, but that's not what I want. I'd like us to stay here; that's what Skye needs – young, strong people ready to invest their future in the island, not look for a good time somewhere else.' He suddenly looked uncomfortable, embarrassed to have given his feelings away – it wasn't how Australian men were supposed to behave. 'Sorry about the sermon,' he muttered, 'I was talking too much.'

'I'm very glad you did – if that's how you feel I can stop pretending I'm your Dutch aunt! I can't think of anything nicer than having you here for keeps.' She couldn't help wondering, though, what Brett would make of it; but again Liam sensed the anxiety in her mind.

'I know what Skye meant to Brett,' he said quietly. 'He told me it was like coming home. But he's settled now with Ellie . . . settled for keeps. This has become a place he'll dream about occasionally . . . what do they call it? Shangri La.'

'It has a name in Gaelic too – Tir nan Òg – and it's located somewhere west of the Hebrides – a place where Gaels believe the sun sets in ultimate splendour.'

Liam nodded. 'Brett would like that idea, and I think he'd be glad to know one of us was here, helping Iain and helping you – which Macdonald it was wouldn't really matter.'

'And you can't say fairer than that,' Louise acknowledged, touched almost to tears by the kindness and simplicity that seemed to belong to this Australian family.

But there the conversation ended because Fiona trotted up from the water's edge with a dripping handful of shells that her aunt was required to take care of. Liam remembered that it was time he returned to the croft, and when Fee had gone back to join Jamie, Louise was left alone to think about what had been said a few moments ago.

He'd fallen in love very rapidly, but there was no surprise about that – it was exactly how he would do it, diving in boots and all, with no doubts or regrets. It was much harder to believe that his family wouldn't mind losing him to Skye. At the very least they'd surely try to persuade him to take Kate back to Australia.

Then there remained the doubt about Iain Macrae – would he want Liam to stay, could he even afford to pay for permanent help with work he'd reckoned to do himself? If not, what else would Liam find to do?

She clung to this problem, determined not to consider another difficulty; but her mind knew perfectly well what it was being forbidden to contemplate – the image of Iain and Elspeth setting off together, all smiles, Liam had said. Why not, of course, happily deciding what to climb: should it be Sgurr nan Gillean today, or maybe Sgurr Dubh Mor? Then there was the challenge of the climb itself, each of them knowing they could trust the other; and around the whole afternoon would be the glow of pleasure shared and effort jointly understood. Face it, Louise told herself, Elspeth fitted him like a glove.

A small protesting voice tried to make itself heard. He'd

proposed marriage to a different woman. But common-sense could demolish that objection easily enough. He had – heaven alone knew why – some lingering feeling of responsibility for the Maitland family. Correction; she *did* know why. Better than any of them he understood Jamie, and knew what it meant to a child to have his mother die.

The token offer of marriage had stemmed from that. Refused, no doubt to his great relief, he was free to devote himself to Elspeth and those terrifying, bloody mountains they were both so at home on.

The pieces of the puzzle fitted together at last. Thank God she'd had sense enough to see the casual proposal for what it was and not taken it seriously. Looking back, hadn't she handled it rather well? Exited the Maitlands quite neatly from the scene, as Drusilla would have said, and left the stage free for the next act. If it ended with him marrying Elspeth there was no reason at all to feel bereft. She wasn't really hurt by the clear picture in her mind of a man and a woman contentedly descending their chosen hill hand in hand – or was that forbidden? Did some absurd climbing rule insist on them walking one behind the other? It was one of many things she didn't know.

Her hands stung from gripping something sharp too hard; she unclenched them and rediscovered Fee's shells – a reminder that it was time to retrieve two grubby children and one wet dog and make them presentable for their tea indoors.

But as they climbed the path to the house another fragment of Liam's conversation came to the surface of her mind – Iain Macrae's extraordinary ambition to buy the kirk and live in it when it closed at the end of the summer. There was no doubt that it *would* close – Janet was already counting off the weeks that remained before they had to go to Broadford for Sunday worship. But she waited until her aunt had left them alone after supper to mention the subject to her father.

'It's not such a strange idea,' he commented, 'churches are being deconsecrated and converted into homes, instead of being pulled down. Why not ours at Kilchrist?'

'Aunt Janet wouldn't like it, to mention only one member of the congregation – she'd say it was adding insult to the injury of closing it at all.'

Andrew smiled but shook his head. 'I don't think the ghost of the Reverend Macrae would trouble his great-great-grandson for living there, and even Janet might like to know that a long-time wanderer had found a home at last.'

Louise hesitated for a moment, then decided that she could pass on the rest of her news. 'Like Brett before him, Liam wants to stay here . . . make his life on Skye. Perhaps that would have happened anyway, but what clinches it is that he's fallen for the MacNeish's daughter, Kate. It's serious for both of them, apparently, but it means finding a permanent job, and a home for them to live in.' She thought about this for a moment, then stared at her father. 'Do you think that's why Iain wants to try to buy the church – because it would leave the croft farmhouse free for Liam and Kate?'

'I'm sure it's an added reason, but not the main one. He explained to me once that what propelled him into spiking James Guthrie's guns was when the man casually mentioned that the kirk would be pulled down to make room for his new hotel. Iain refused to allow that to happen; the kirk, and this house as well for that matter, stand on what was Macrae land. Guthrie didn't realize it but I think Iain was never going to let him win once he'd seen Tom Macrae's name in the church porch.'

'So – he's got the land back, but he may not get the kirk. What if the church authorities refuse to sell?'

'I don't know any more than you do, but Iain's a quietly persuasive man; and what would be the point of keeping up a building they're never going to be able to use? I think he'll get it if that's what he really wants.'

* * *

Andrew would be proved right or wrong by the time the summer came to an end, but until then Louise had other things on her mind. There was her final performance as Kilchrist's acting organist to prepare for, and she was determined that, music-wise, it should be a service the parishioners would never forget. Then, with early September would come her first appearance as the school's new music teacher, and although Jamie promised that his own class would give her a fair ride, he refused to commit himself as to how the rest of the school would behave.

But more unsettling than either of these events was the imminent arrival of her mother. Drusilla had been persuaded by friends still active in the theatre world to revisit the Edinburgh Festival. There were two productions, they said, that she couldn't miss. One of them was of *As You Like It*, and it had been as Rosalind in that very play that she'd first captivated Andrew Maitland. Clearly it was meant, she explained to her daughter on the telephone – the gods above intended her to pay this one last visit to Scotland, and if to Edinburgh, why not to Skye as well? She genuinely wanted to see her daughter and her grandchildren but curiosity about her ex-husband, although not admitted to, was just as keen. The child she'd raised, however erratically, on her own, wasn't supposed to swap allegiance, but it was obvious that Louise was getting on very well now with the father she'd scarcely known. If she was also learning to like Janet Maitland, Drusilla reckoned that her own maternal cup of bitterness would overflow. She'd go to Skye, though one overnight stay would be quite sufficient.

Louise prepared the Maitlands as tactfully as she could for the ordeal ahead. Her father clearly saw it in those terms, but while Janet pretended to take no interest in the visit whatsoever, she wouldn't – in her niece's considered opinion – miss it for the world. In desperation Andrew suggested inviting their neighbours to dine with them and in the end Louise agreed. Her mother, much preferring the company of men, was always at her best with them; and

Janet would have to behave herself as well if Iain and Liam were there.

Drusilla arrived on time, driving a hired car – no going-astray for her, no sinking into roadside bogs. Despite an air of helpless, fragile beauty always liable to be in distress, she was in fact a very competent woman, Louise reflected with a certain amount of pride. Rather unexpectedly, it was a genuine pleasure to have her there. The children seemed happy to meet her again, and Andrew made her welcome most charmingly – that, Louise reckoned, was as cordial as it was likely to get, since Janet's good intentions couldn't be relied upon.

There came the perilous moment when the two women examined one another, and she could guess what each of them was thinking; Janet seeing even now only the beautiful, selfish actress who'd turned Andrew's world and her own upside down; Drusilla recognizing only the severe, unbending woman who'd helped to ruin her first marriage. But with her daughter's beseeching eye upon her, at least she did her best.

'Thank you for letting me come,' she said simply. 'I miss having Louise in London, but at least I know she's here. I wish I could bring back Angus for you and Andrew.'

Janet accepted this with a little nod, unable to find in it anything she could object to. 'We wish it more for the children than ourselves,' she contented herself with pointing out. 'But at least they're settled here. London was no place for them.'

In agreement with her at least about that, Drusilla refrained from saying that Kilchrist was the place for them only because Louise was there as well. Then, with perfect timing, Jamie invited his grandmother to inspect their kitchen garden, from which his very best vegetables were going to be picked for their supper that evening. She made the right admiring noises, and allowed herself without complaint to be led down the stony path to their beach. With the children now out of earshot, she could speak freely at last.

'They look altogether different from when I saw them in London – but it's your doing, not Janet Maitland's, I swear.'

'Partly mine,' Louise agreed with a smile; 'but this place has had a lot to do with it – it suits them very well – and so has our Canadian neighbour whom you're going to meet this evening. I've told you about him – Tom Hepburn's distant relative. It was he who first got Jamie talking again.'

Drusilla inspected her daughter's thin, tanned face. 'You *look* all right . . . but are you? Your father's a kind and civilized man even if I couldn't stay married to him; but I shall never get on terms with your aunt. God alone knows how you manage to share a house with her.'

'It was uphill work to begin with,' Louise admitted, 'but we're over the worst, and I have to say that she's done her best as well. It was no small thing for her to accept the mess and disruption that the children and Macgregor are bound to cause. Now I think she'd hate it if they weren't here.'

Her mother waved that aside. 'You didn't answer my question – what about you?'

Louise detected real concern, and decided to answer seriously. 'I miss being in my own home. If it becomes certain that the church will do nothing about selling the manse, then I can use the proceeds from the flat to buy a small house up here – not far away; Aunt Janet and my father would miss the children. But for the moment we stay as we are.'

Drusilla knew that it was all the answer she would get, and what more could she expect? 'My moments of truth don't come often, so I must say this now. I can't help feeling that the gods above are making you pay for *my* shortcomings; everything would have been different if I'd lasted the course with Andrew.'

Louise smiled at her with genuine affection. 'Aunt Janet is inclined to think that her Old Testament God is also inclined to punishment; we had our first argument about that! I refuse to have either of you feel guilty, because my own idea is that life arranges itself as it does for reasons we don't understand. What's asked of us is to make the best we can of it. That's all that her God and yours *do* insist on, I think.'

Drusilla considered this for a moment. 'Less breast-beating and hair shirts; more attention paid to the Ten Commandments – is that it?'

'And the Beatitudes as well, maybe,' her daughter agreed with a faint grin. 'Now, it's time we went back – you can admire Aunt Janet's needlework, which *is* very beautiful; I've got dinner for six to think about.'

'Six – has your Canadian neighbour got a wife?'

'Not yet, although there is a nice candidate lined up. He has an Australian friend called Liam Macdonald staying with him. Liam's job at home is sheep-farming but here he's helping Iain reinvent the art and craft of crofting.'

'Just so *not* my scene,' Drusilla mused. 'I wonder what we'll find to talk about.'

'So do I, but bear in mind that we're doing our best to entertain you so please . . .'

'Love thy neighbours as myself?'

'You needn't go quite as far as that,' Louise said firmly. 'Just trying to keep them amused will do.'

Twenty-Four

Supper must be simple and cold, Louise had decided; it wasn't the evening to be toiling over a hot stove while the party in the drawing room congealed into awkwardness. But when she walked in, having put the final touches to the food, Iain was obeying her aunt's instructions to pour sherry for himself and Liam, and so far, at least, there was no tension in the air; Janet was smiling at her guests. Handed sherry in her turn, Louise was admiring Liam's unusually formal rig which even included a school tie, when Drusilla, collected from the hotel by Andrew, made an entrance.

Her black silk dress was simple – only redeemed from plainness by its neckline frill of delicately goffered lace – but Louise heard Liam draw in his breath and she reckoned it to be a proper tribute to her mother's beauty. Andrew proudly made the introductions.

'Gentlemen, may I present Drusilla, the lady who was once my wife – now Lady Glendenning. Drusilla, meet our dear friends and neighbours – Iain Macrae and Liam Macdonald.'

Liam nearest to her, bowed over her hand and kissed it – a gesture that even surprised himself.

Iain smiled at her. 'I can't top that, Lady Glendenning, but I *can* claim something Liam can't. On a visit to London years ago I saw you play Beatrice in *Much Ado About Nothing* – I've never forgotten it.'

Louise decided to stop worrying about the evening – after such a start its success was now assured. She watched her mother take the place that was still natural to her – centre stage – but, perhaps keeping the Beatitudes in mind, she remembered humility and did it with a graceful touch of deference to Janet Maitland. It was safe to leave them and resume the role of cook herself.

She was putting the first course – salmon mousse – on the table in the dining room when Iain Macrae appeared in the doorway.

'Can I help? We seem to allow you to do all the work.'

'Thank you for the offer, but it's pleasure, not hard work. You could tell my aunt that we're ready to sit down.'

'Andrew seemed apprehensive about this evening; are you?'

'Not now,' Louise answered. 'Past history gets in the way of my mother and Aunt Janet liking one another, but a sort of conditional peace seems to have been declared.' She smiled as she said it, and he was struck by the resemblance it gave her to the woman in the room next door. Even in her simple silk shirt and patchwork skirt she had the same effortless style, too.

'You're very like your mother,' he said, 'but you choose not to compete – out of kindness, I suspect.'

Louise shook her head. 'Out of a wish not to be beaten hands down more like! Now, ask my aunt to bring them in, please; everything's ready.'

He nodded and went away, leaving her to wonder whether she would ever be able to have a conversation with him that didn't leave her unsettled in some way. But a moment later Janet led in her guests and supper could get under way.

The mousse was a success, the raised pie that followed stuffed with jellied chicken, veal and ham, pronounced perfection, and Jamie's broad beans made into a delicious purée justly praised. The food led Liam to suggest that Louise's wedding present to him and Kate when the time came might be some cookery lessons. He then explained for Drusilla's benefit.

'I love your daughter, ma'am, but I'm marrying someone else – it's becoming a family tradition!'

Louise smiled at her mother. 'He jests, of course; you don't have to take him seriously.' Then to her relief, the conversation moved on to Drusilla's visit to Edinburgh. She'd dined there with Thomas Hepburn and, knowing that Louise had told her about James Guthrie's failed bid on Skye, he'd mentioned what had happened afterwards – Guthrie had tried to get him debarred for illegal practices.

'He didn't tell me that,' Andrew said worriedly. 'Surely Guthrie didn't succeed?'

'Certainly not – but Tom admitted that his scheme had been the slightest bit unusual!' Drusilla smiled at them round the table. 'It was the merest chance that I should meet the great Sir James at a festival reception afterwards, but by then I had *two* scores to settle. I commiserated with him so sweetly over losing his planned hotel that he almost thought I meant it. Then I reminded him of his visit *here* one day, when he'd failed to recognize in my daughter, Louise, the girl who'd cooked for him at his Highland shooting lodge.'

'It *was* ten years ago – the man can't remember every woman he's ever met,' Louise suggested.

'No, darling, but not many have walked out on him in disgust and torn up his cheque! He deserves to have been trounced by the Maitland family.'

'You're quite right, Drusilla,' Janet put in unexpectedly. 'I don't think we're obliged to be charitable to the likes of Sir James Guthrie.'

'But don't let us forget who actually trounced him – Tom Hepburn and Iain here,' Andrew insisted. 'Without them Guthrie would have won.'

Now it was Iain's turn. 'Without Donald Mackinnon he'd have won. Donald's decision not to sell to Guthrie was what decided matters in the end.'

From there the conversation moved on to the Festival plays and music, prompting Liam to confess to an ambition to learn the pipes.

'Kate's father is going to find me a teacher,' he said

contentedly. 'Apparently the tradition nearly died out after the Stewart rebellion. Think what a loss that would have been!'

Andrew smiled at Drusilla but shook his head, asking her not to offer her opinion of pipe music, and it was Iain who continued on from Liam. 'The Disarming Act banned the wearing of tartans, the pipes, and the Gaelic language – people's culture, in other words. The act was eventually repealed, but the damage was done. Piping only survived because it was integral to Highland regiments, and they were essential to England's wars. No wonder the "Ceol Mòr" – the "Great Music" – is so full of sadness and lament; properly played out of doors, it's heartbreakingly beautiful.'

There was a little silence that Louise chose to break. 'You're right, and I really shouldn't argue, especially when there's a Gaelic scholar here; but am I allowed to say that the clan system was dismantled with *some* justification? Betrayal, treachery and bloody warfare were the order of the day, not just against the English – fair game, the Scots would say – but among the clans themselves. Perhaps the act did set out to destroy a culture, but that was allied to the chaotic lawlessness of the Highlands in the eighteenth century.'

She'd spoken too vehemently – knew it from the sudden silence in the room, and felt obliged to apologize. 'Sorry – much too much heat! But the English are always made out to be the only villains, and I find it unfair.'

It was an argument she'd had before with Iain Macrae, of course, and she feared that her bombardment had been aimed at him. Now he and Elspeth would be able to laugh together over her Little Englander outburst, and wonder how she could expect to settle on Skye. And there was the root of her distress – Iain with Elspeth Mackintosh. For a moment or two she was adrift, desperately trying to go on sitting there with the world spinning all round her. Why now, dear God, to realize what was the matter with her – why be afraid to look at Iain Macrae in case he understood her trouble?

She tried to focus on her father instead, and he, seeing the strained smile she gave him, smiled back and came to her rescue. 'My dear, you were quite right,' he said gently. 'Of course there was another side to the coin of English "brutality" and we shouldn't be allowed to forget it.'

He looked a question at her and then at the piano, but when she shook her head he returned the conversation to their guests; she could safely duck her head for a moment and pull herself together. It was easy after that – pouring more coffee, laughing at her mother's theatre stories, joining in the argument about whether the bridge should have been built or not; she could be merry and bright with the rest of them. But she offered up a silent thanks to heaven when Drusilla herself said that she was ready to be escorted back to her comfortable room at the Toravaig House Hotel. She was promised a family send-off in the morning, and then driven away by Andrew while Iain and Liam went as they had come, across the field paths to the croft.

Janet needed little persuading to retire to bed and Louise was left mercifully alone to clear up after the party. She'd just turned off the kitchen light when her father came back.

'The dishwasher's busy,' she said, smiling at him. 'The rest I'm going to leave until tomorrow. I hope Drusilla said that she enjoyed herself.'

'Much more than she expected to – I don't think she'd realized that civilised life exists on Skye!' He stared at Louise's face for a moment, then went on in a different tone of voice. 'Are you all right, my dear? I'm afraid that seeing your mother again has made you remember all the things you miss by living up here,'

'I'm fine,' she answered firmly. 'Seeing her only made me realize how fond we've grown of each other – it wasn't always so, and it's all the nicer that it should be happening now.' She reached up to kiss her father's cheek. 'I don't think you've ever stopped loving her, though.'

'And never shall,' he agreed simply. 'Janet couldn't understand that, I'm afraid, but this evening helped, and at least the ordeal is over!'

She nodded and said goodnight; the ordeal hadn't been the one he imagined, and it wouldn't be over unless she could recover from loving Iain Macrae. But what she'd said to her mother so confidently remained true: all that counted was how experience and self-knowledge were used. It would have been easier if she liked him more and loved him less, but Drusilla's gods only arranged things for their own entertainment, not for the poor mortals concerned.

They all went to the hotel the next morning – Macgregor only excluded, Jaime explained to him, for lack of room in the car. Drusilla was waiting outside, ready to leave. She had no wish to linger on Skye, but the little group that had come to wave her off were all the family she had, and leaving them made her unexpectedly tearful. Perhaps that was the reason for Janet's surprising invitation.

'Scots don't make much of Christmas as a rule, but we must now for the bairns' sake. You'd be welcome to join us – weather permitting, of course.' She spoke more diffidently than usual, expecting a polite excuse, but Drusilla's sad face brightened.

'I'd like that – I'll come whatever the weather.' Then she kissed them goodbye, and got into her car, en route for Glasgow and a flight back to London.

They waited until she was out of sight, all of them aware that, although the sun was still shining, the morning had gone dull; Drusilla had somehow taken warmth and gaiety away with her. She might not be a continual joy to live with, her daughter reflected, but they would miss her as an enchanting guest.

Jamie was the first to speak, squeezed into the back of the car with his sister and Louise. 'Granny didn't hear me play my mouth organ, or see Fee's shells.'

'Your playing and Fee's collection will both be even better by Christmas – let's look at it like that,' Louise suggested. But the expression on his face told her that she'd sounded curt. 'It was a very quick visit, love – we'll persuade Granny to stay longer next time.'

A smile suddenly chased away his hurt. 'I can sleep in the porch with Macgregor; then she can have my bed. Let's look at it like that!'

The repetition of her own words made her smile – at last he was becoming properly cheeky like any other small boy.

'We'll see when the time comes who sleeps where. Right now I'll leave the rest of you to go home – I've got some practising to do in church.'

Deposited at the gate, she went inside aware, as she always was, that peace really did come 'dropping slow' within its walls; she needed that more than ever now, and would sorely miss its comfort. The hymns chosen for the final service were familiar favourites – not much rehearsal required there; but the voluntary she'd decided to close the service with was a different matter. She went over parts of it again and again until she was satisfied; it still wouldn't sound as it should – she needed a grand pipe organ for that – but at least the congregation would file out for the last time with the kirk's colours flying.

She stopped playing, and felt the silence close round her again. What would it be like to live in this prayer-haunted place? Churches, she'd read, were like power-houses, generating currents of communication with Almighty God through prayer. Might that not be difficult to live with? The thought inevitably brought Iain Macrae to mind; and just as inevitably, it seemed, he was suddenly there himself, standing in the open doorway – time enough to get her heartbeat and voice under control before he reached her. As usual, he went directly to what he wanted to say.

'I distressed you last night without meaning to; a Canadian has no right at all to pass judgement on the English for past sins against the Scots.'

She managed to smile at him. 'Well, if it means you're beginning to feel that you belong here, that's all to the good. I'm afraid I shall remain obstinately English however long I stay.' Her thin hand swept a circle of the sunlit building. 'It's hard to believe that this church dies after tomorrow's service. But Liam says you hope to live here – I was just wondering how that would seem and there you were, appearing in person like a genie out of a bottle!' She was talking too much, she thought, made nervous because he was looking at her so intently.

'I may not be allowed to buy it,' he answered. 'But I'm relying on Tom Hepburn, whose friends seem to occupy usefully high places! I draw up mental plans in the night watches of how I think it should be converted. Elspeth can't quite rid herself of the idea that it would be sacrilegious, and probably Janet Maitland will feel that way, too.'

Unable to contemplate him living there with Elspeth, she changed the subject again. 'Liam's told me about Kate MacNeish, and wanting to settle here. Can he go on working for you?'

'For as long as he likes – there's more than enough work for two of us, and he feels like someone I've known all my life. Your mother has that same gift of immediate friendship – and so do you with everyone except me. Why is that, I wonder?'

It was wickedly unfair, she thought, to slip the question in like that. She stared down at her hands still resting on the organ keys; miraculously they didn't tremble. 'Incompatible?' she finally managed to suggest. 'I'd think it was that, wouldn't you?'

If she started to play again would he go away or bang the organ cover down on her hands to make her stop?

'What I think,' he said slowly, 'is that you still believe Brett Macdonald's marriage won't last. Either Ellie will get sick of playing second-fiddle to your ghost or Brett will leave and come looking for you because he can't bear not to. It won't happen, Louise, despite what Liam seemed to say last night.'

At least it made her angry enough to be able to look at him. 'I don't care what you think. Yes, I miss Brett – as any friend would do. No, I do *not* expect him to turn up on the manse doorstep. Liam also says, and I believe him, that his brother and Ellie are happy together – together for good. If that makes things clear perhaps I can get on with what I came to do.'

Without conscious direction her fingers returned to what she'd played before, but he reached over the keyboard and gripped her hands.

'Listen to me, please. I want you to be happy, but you never will be unless you can forget about Brett.'

She could have convinced him of the truth then, but Elspeth stood in the way; so she spoke the truth in a way he wouldn't believe. She even managed a fleeting smile. 'I shall continue to remember Brett as our dear friend, but I intend to be *very* happy in my new career as music teacher at Kilchrist School. I don't think we have anything else to say to each other so perhaps I can now finish practising for tomorrow.'

She thought it hung in the balance for a moment whether or not he dragged her off the organ-bench and shook her; but at last his hands released hers and she gripped them in her lap to stop them trembling. He looked at her down-bent face, and then his fingers gently traced the line of her cheekbone and the hollow beneath it.

'I'd give a great deal to be able to make you free of what you want; since I can't do that I can't help you at all.'

She didn't see, only sensed, the moment when he admitted defeat; his footsteps sounded on the flagstone floor, and then she heard his car drive off. The tears beginning to trickle down her face finally put an end to the rehearsal; she closed and locked the organ, smeared away her tears, and walked slowly home – no, the ordeal certainly wasn't over yet.

Twenty-Five

The church was full the following morning and communal sadness was in the air. The minister, clearly unwell, performed his part bravely, but was seen to be in tears as the service drew to a close. Janet, sitting in the front row with Andrew and the children, kept grief at bay with anger at the impious age they lived in. That churches should have to close for lack of men or women to lead them was a sign, to her at least, that humanity didn't deserve the redemption won for it on the Cross. It remembered little, now, of what Scripture taught and learned even less.

Louise acknowledged her family but looked no further than the front row. She must concentrate only on the music and play it well enough to lift the spirits of a disheartened congregation. Purcell's glorious 'Voluntary' at the end certainly did that and no one moved to go for as long as it lasted. Then people began to file out but, saying goodbye to the minister with her father and Janet, she could only return Liam's wave as he left with Iain, Elspeth, and the MacNeish family.

With the morning came another traumatic event – Fiona's first day at school and Louise's initiation as a music teacher. The new pupil was only slightly more nervous than she was, the new teacher thought.

She'd agreed with Elspeth that she would begin with the most senior children, and had planned the lesson accordingly. They'd learn the notes that made up the ascending musical scale, sing what they heard her play, and listen to the way several notes sounded together could make either unpleasant discord or lovely harmony. Interested because they were involved, the children looked disappointed when the lesson came to an end.

Elspeth was waiting to ask how it had gone. 'Well – was it as bad as you feared?'

Louise shook her head. 'Five minutes into the lesson I was beginning to enjoy myself, and I can tell you this, Elspeth – those children love to sing. I think we should try to start a choir!'

She expected her friend's usual eager response, but when Elspeth replied she sounded unenthusiastic to the point of indifference.

'I suppose we could, but there'd be all the bother of asking their parents to let them stay on late at school.'

'Let's ask the children first,' Louise suggested, 'they might say no.'

Elspeth nodded, still seeming so preoccupied that Louise decided to risk a blunt question. 'Tired? – you sound it. I suppose the start of a new school year is always stressful.'

'Too long a walk yesterday is more likely the reason,' Elspeth admitted. 'After church Iain and I went up Sgurrr Thearlaich. It's a stiff climb and, because the weather changed, we had a race to get down.'

Louise was puzzled now, as well as disappointed over the reaction to her choir idea. What Elspeth had just described was the sort of challenge she would normally have loved. But instead of saying that, it seemed time to risk a different question.

'Liam mentioned that Iain Macrae might try to convert the kirk into a house – not to everyone's liking perhaps. What do *you* think?'

Elspeth's shoulders lifted in a little shrug. 'I can see nothing wrong with the croft myself – it's a dear wee house, and Iain likes it too. But I know what he's thinking: if he were to move out, Liam and Kate could move in. It's time he thought about his own needs, not theirs.'

Louise heard in the sad comment what her friend hadn't said – that it would be nice if he were considering not only his own needs but hers as well. But Elspeth feared that she'd sounded forlorn, and forced herself to smile.

'Take no notice of me – I'm missing him already. He's away to Edinburgh today to talk to people about the kirk, and then to Inverness – it's crofting business there, I think. He'll finish up representing all the Skye crofters before long.'

'If you mean he can't resist taking charge, I expect you're right.' But even lightly said, it wasn't something Elspeth could accept.

'You don't understand him,' she said earnestly. 'It's only that he can't help leaving other people behind, even when they're trying to keep up.'

Louise smiled with affection at the girl beside her. 'I *was* teasing, just to see you rush to his defence! If it makes you happier, I'll admit that this corner of Skye will probably bless the day he decided to buy Donald's croft, and we've certainly good reasons to be grateful to him. Now, I must tackle my next class – Fee among them. I expect she'll insist on explaining loud and clear that I'm not their teacher at all, just her and Jamie's Lou-Lou!'

They parted company with Elspeth smiling again, having recommended a weekend walk together if Iain wasn't back.

When Saturday came she arrived early at the manse, suggesting that Louise should be ready for a longer walk than usual. Her pupil agreed, wishing she could say that the day seemed too sultry and windless for any energetic exercise at all. Starting off from Sligachan as usual, Elspeth buoyantly explained that the higher they could get, the better they'd feel; up on the hill the air would be fresh and invigorating.

'And also nearer to Almighty God?' Louise queried with a smile. 'Perhaps that's why the Greeks built their monasteries on the Holy Mountain – almost inaccessible without angels' wings or the nerve and lung-power of Everest climbers!'

They went in silence after that, each of them content to follow some train of thought of their own, until Elspeth finally called a halt and said that it was time for a rest before they started down again. Munching the raisins and chocolate she was offered, Louise realized that they had indeed climbed higher than usual without her minding or feeling nervous; perhaps she was making mountaineering progress. She could certainly begin to understand the sort of rapture that climbers achieved, poised between heaven and earth.

She broke the silence to comment on the panorama spread out below them – the heather turning purple on the hillsides, the green and gold of the valley fields; beyond that Skye landscape the sister island of Raasay floated in the distance, and on the horizon the mainland mountains made a mauve backdrop against the sky.

'All just put there this minute by the Creator's hand,' Louise suggested. 'That's what it looks like to me.'

Elspeth turned to smile at her but made a different comment. 'I'm sorry I took such a scunner to the choir idea; I shouldn't have, but I wasn't feeling quite myself at the time.'

'That sounds like heart trouble; was it?' Louise asked gently.

Elspeth nodded. 'I give myself away too easily. I couldn't help pointing out that Iain would be lonely when Liam left to get married . . . I suppose I wanted him to know that I'd always be there.'

'What happened then?'

'He said there were worse things than loneliness – you could get used to that, but not to being with the wrong person. He was warning me very gently that I wouldn't do! To soften the blow he explained that he'd asked someone to marry him; she'd turned him down – imagine any woman being so stupid! – but he couldn't put anyone else in her place.'

Louise could have found nothing to say, but it didn't matter because Elspeth hadn't quite finished. 'At the time I thought he'd referred to something that happened a long time ago, and if I waited long enough he'd get over it.

Now I don't think he will – I shan't stop loving him, but
he won't change his mind; he's not that sort of man. I
shall have to make do with other people's children!' she
ended up sadly.

'Perhaps not, Elspeth.' Louise said with difficulty.
'Someone else might make you change your mind – I hope
so; you deserve to be happy.'

They both fell silent again, and only then did Louise
realize that the mountains she'd been staring at across
the Sound were no longer visible. Raasay, too, had disappeared, and a thick, grey cloud was rolling across
the landscape towards them. It was her first experience
of the alarming speed with which mountain weather could
change. Elspeth, so much more experienced than herself,
would surely have noticed the alteration sooner had she
not been so deeply absorbed in thinking about Iain
Macrae.

But she was suddenly alive to the danger now. 'Weather's
changed – we must go at once. If we can't get down in
time we'll have to stop. Put your jacket on, Louise – it
will suddenly get cold when we're in the mist.'

They'd gone no more than a hundred yards when the
outlying streamers of cloud reached them; a minute or two
later they were in the thick of a swirling grey fog that
obscured the markers along the path and soon even the
path itself, completely disorientating them.

'It's no good – we must stop now,' Elspeth's disem-
bodied voice said. Then almost as she ceased speaking
she bit off a sudden sharp exclamation of pain; the next
moment Louise realized that the shadowy figure beside
her was no longer there.

Too terrified to move, she could only try to call out.
'Elspeth . . . answer, please . . . oh God, where are you?'

At last there came a faint response that she could barely
hear.

'Don't step sideways – we were too near the edge of
the track. I've slipped down on to a sort of ledge; I can't
see anything beyond it.'

Louise knelt down in the vague direction of her voice. 'Listen, Elspeth – if we can grip hands you must try to scramble up as I haul myself backwards. You won't slip because I'll be holding you and I'll be lying with my weight flat on the ground.' She inched forward carefully. 'Now I'm at the edge – reach up if you can.'

'I can't . . . I can't move; I've hurt my ankle; broken it, I think. I trod on a stone that tipped up – that's why I fell. You *must* stay where you are until the mist clears.' She tried to hide the tremor in her voice, but Louise knew that she was not only hurt but afraid.

'We'll sit it out together if there's room on the ledge for two. I'm coming down. When I swing my legs over, guide my feet if you can, because now I can't see the ledge at all.'

'Do my best,' Elspeth answered unsteadily.

Louise swallowed the sickness in her mouth, prayed to God that she wouldn't faint with sheer fright, and eased her legs over the edge. It was a mercy in a way not to be able to see what lay below them – presumably nothing but the hillside falling away towards the valley bottom. But at last Elspeth's hand touched her boots, and she knew she was being guided on to the ledge. For what it was worth, at least they were together. She wedged herself between the backdrop of rock and the injured girl and put both arms round her for warmth and comfort.

'Ankle hurting?' she asked when she could manage to say anything at all.

'A bit . . . better after I'd got my boot off.' Elspeth's grip on her hands tightened. 'I'm so sorry, Louise . . . all my fault. We went too far, and I wasn't even paying attention – Iain won't forgive me; this is what novices do.'

'I don't see why you should take all the blame – I was there too, remember? We're still in one piece, and either someone will come looking for us, or I'll go in search of help when the mist clears.' She managed to sound cheerful but Elspeth had more bad news.

'My mobile isn't working,' she said dismally. 'It must

have got damaged when I fell. No one will know which track we're on, even when they can set out to look for us.'

Louise peered at her watch by holding it under her nose – nearly five o'clock. Her father would soon be expecting them back, but how long would he wait before deciding to raise an alarm?

'Well, for the moment we must put up with just sitting here getting cold and damp,' she said as calmly as she could. 'No point in "troubling deaf Heaven with our bootless cries!" My father maintains that Will Shakespeare provides the perfect phrase for every occasion – I never guessed how apt *that* one would turn out to be!'

Elspeth gave a little laugh that turned into a sob, and then relapsed into silence. Louise was mentally reviewing the rest of the Bard's output to keep her mind off their situation when Elspeth suddenly spoke again.

'It was *you*, wasn't it?'

'What was?' Louise had to ask.

'Iain proposed to you, not someone in Canada.' It was a statement now, not a question. 'I don't know why I didn't realize that straightaway.'

What else, Louise wondered numbly, did this dreadful afternoon have in store? How to answer now – lie, deny the truth, pretend that a hurt girl was light-headed with shock and pain? But Elspeth's mind wasn't wandering, and already there'd been too long a delay in giving her an answer.

'Yes,' she finally admitted. 'It was me, but I wasn't the right person either. She was someone he knew in Canada – he referred to her once, I remember. But he's a quixotic man underneath that careless exterior, and he seems to think the Maitlands can't manage without him, but that's mostly because of Jamie – Iain was able to get through to him when the rest of us couldn't. But a proposal inspired by concern for one's nephew doesn't seem enough to marry on.'

Elspeth considered this for a moment. 'So there was no

need for Iain to think he ought to wait in case you changed your mind?'

'None at all,' Louise agreed, willing her voice not to tremble. The conversation was becoming almost unbearable, but if Elspeth needed to talk about Iain Macrae she must somehow go on without giving herself away. 'We've had this discussion before, I seem to remember. Iain has been self-sufficient for too long to change now – he doesn't need other people in the way that the rest of us do. It's . . . it's hard on the impressionable females who cross his path, but there it is!'

'Not hard on you, though,' Elspeth pointed out after a moment. 'Iain hasn't enchanted you.'

'Certainly not!' but it didn't sound quite convincing enough. 'We first met by accident on the train from London to Edinburgh – mutual dislike at first sight! Things have improved a little since then, that's all.' More than that, she prayed, wouldn't be asked of her, and mercifully Elspeth seemed content to give a little sigh and slip into some kind of doze.

Slowly the time dragged by while Louise tried to decide whether she only imagined that the blanket of greyness around them was beginning to thin. No . . . surely she'd just felt a breath of air move across her face. Please God let it strengthen enough to blow the mist away. When she looked at her watch again she could see its face more clearly – nearly six o'clock. Darkness came late, but even so she couldn't afford to wait any longer before setting off to get the help that Elspeth needed.

She roused the other girl and explained that it was time to leave. She helped Elspeth to prop herself against the rocky side of the hill, and cushioned her with the jacket she'd taken off. 'Visibility is improving, so maybe I'll meet the rescue team already on its way. All you have to do is tell me how to get off this ledge when I'm not, alas, a bird!'

'There, I think,' Elspeth said, pointing to the right. 'You won't manage it here; there's too much overhang.' She tried to smile, but her mouth trembled. 'I don't like your going – Louise, be very careful – it's such loose treacherous scree out on the hill.'

'I shall walk like Agag, whoever he was,' Louise agreed, trying to sound calm. Then, with another hug for her friend, she crawled off the comparative safety of the ledge on to a hillside that fell away into the still-invisible valley below. There was no question of walking, of course; she crawled painfully upwards on hands and knees, sometimes slid back and then made a desperate grab at any vegetation that came to hand; but at last she could heave herself back on to the path they seemed to have left hours ago.

She left her rucksack to mark where Elspeth was and then set off downhill; her knees were still trembling from the strain of climbing up to the path, but at least it was now visible for several yards ahead. Did mist sink down as it cleared, or float upwards? On that depended when the searchers could set out. Her tired mind wrestled with the problem rather than acknowledge the pain of her torn hands and the effort to keep moving; more than anything in the world she just wanted to sit down and weep. But she told herself that sooner or later she *must* suddenly walk into the arms of some large and competent rescuer coming the other way.

Then, almost between one moment and the next, it happened – she seemed to step through a curtain of grey gauze into a brightly-coloured world again. And there on the path below were men with ropes and lanterns, moving at the steady pace of climbers who knew exactly how to behave on mountains. She stopped now, overcome with relief, waiting for them to reach her. Afterwards she remembered trying to explain where Elspeth was, but the rest of the journey down was lost in a haze of fatigue. She was driven to the hospital in Broadford and found her father already there, face drawn with the anxiety of waiting for news. Her hands were painfully cleaned and dressed, and then he was told that she could be taken home. Elspeth, the men with them said, had been safely found and was now being brought to the hospital.

Late as it was when they got back to the manse, Janet Maitland was still waiting, with hot soup ready for both of them. She sounded brusque as usual, almost angry with two feckless women who should have known better than to be out risking their lives, but she couldn't stem the tears that trickled down her face when Louise enfolded her in a hug. Whatever they disagreed about in future, they were kin now and always, and both of them at last realized it.

'I kept thinking of the bairns,' Janet said, dabbing her wet cheeks. 'I didn't know how we could ever tell them that they'd lost you as well . . .' Her voice trembled and broke, but such weakness had to be overcome, and she managed to sound cross again. 'It's good soup . . . drink it, Louise . . . and you too, Andrew. The pair of you look like ghosts.'

They did as they were told to please her, and then Louise climbed the stairs expecting to spend the rest of the night reliving the day's ordeal. But she fell into a pit of sleep at once, and woke the following morning to find Jamie and Fee beside her bed, watching her – forbidden by their great-aunt to disturb her, but determined not to move until she opened her eyes and smiled at them, confirming that life was still secure.

Twenty-Six

Getting showered could be managed once her bandaged hands were protected by the rubber gloves that Jamie fetched from the kitchen. But she abandoned the struggle with hooks and buttons involved in putting on clothes, and went down to breakfast in dressing gown and slippers. Andrew had already rung the hospital and was able to report that, with her ankle now set and plastered, Elspeth was quite comfortable. They must go to church, as planned in Broadford, Louise insisted; she'd be happy left at home.

But when they'd driven away, the reaction she hadn't bargained for set in. Life now matched the early autumn sadness already seeming to lie over the gardens; the year's dying fall had begun, and ahead lay the long dark winter. Disgusted with this pathetic melancholy she was relieved to hear a sudden ring at the door, but when she went to answer it she found herself staring at Iain Macrae.

'You're supposed to be somewhere else – Inverness,' she managed to sound merely cross, rather like Aunt Janet, she thought; but a pitiful little show of anger was her only defence against a longing to burst into tears.

'I *was* in Inverness; now I'm here,' he confirmed, brief and to the point as usual. 'May I come in?'

She clung to the door, not holding it open. 'I'm not dressed for morning calls, and everyone else has gone to church.'

'I didn't come to see everyone else and I don't care how you're dressed. Now may I come in?'

She gave up the struggle and led him into the kitchen; not invited to sit down, he would surely soon go away.

'Liam rang me,' he said next. 'I can see that you hurt your hands; apart from that are you all right?'

'I'm fine,' she insisted firmly, 'but Elspeth isn't, I'm afraid.'

'I know I called at the hospital on my way through early this morning.'

It explained the tiredness she saw in his face – he must have been up half the night to have got back from Inverness so soon. It seemed all wrong to drive him away when she'd have given anything for the relief of weeping in his arms, but pride led her to what would irritate him most.

'I hope you didn't berate Elspeth for what happened yesterday – I was equally to blame for not noticing the change in the weather.'

It made him angry, as she'd known it would. 'I don't berate a damaged girl who is blaming herself quite enough already. What makes you think I would?'

Colour stained her pale face and she felt obliged to apologize. 'Sorry – I'm not thinking straight this morning. I'll start again, and hope your mainland trip was successful.' But the clutch at polite small talk did nothing to remove his frown; he was still recovering from the shock of Liam's telephone call, and the knowledge that she might easily have been killed yesterday.

'My trip went well, thank you, but that's not what I came to say. I just want you to promise to let me know when you next feel inclined to wander the Cuillins in a blanket of mist.'

She took a deep breath and tried not to shout. 'We weren't that mindless – there was *no* mist when we set out. But I can safely promise to leave mountains alone in future; I should have known I'd never make a climber.'

His strained expression still didn't change. 'According to Elspeth you did rather well for a non-climber; but you could have got yourself killed trying to fetch help.'

She hid her hands in the pockets of her robe, unnerved by the unexpected tribute that seemed to be included in what he'd just said. It was still more unnerving to have him there at all, and she strove to say something that would bring the visit to an end.

'We were an awful nuisance to everybody yesterday, and I don't think I remembered to thank the rescue team properly. I'd be grateful if you'd do that for me.'

He nodded, searching her face for some small sign that she would like him to stay. But the guard she was keeping on herself still held, and at last he was defeated by it.

'I'll let myself out,' he said curtly and turned towards the door. There, he turned to face her again. 'In case you're interested, I did manage to persuade the authorities to let me take over the kirk. I can do what I like with it provided I don't change its outward appearance.'

Louise's face broke into a genuine smile at last. 'I'm glad – an unwanted building is always sad.' She nearly said that Elspeth would get used to the idea of living there, but remembered just in time that apparently he didn't propose to share it with her. Lacking the unknown 'right' woman, he preferred to be there alone.

'I'm sure your great-great-grandfather's ghost will make you welcome,' she said instead, then stood waiting for him to leave. He hesitated, still reluctant to go but so clearly unwelcome to stay that at last, with a brief nod of farewell, he turned and walked away.

Now she could weep if she wanted to; but why, she asked herself, why not thank God instead that she and Elspeth were still alive? Their shared misfortune now was simply to love a man who could manage very well without them but unrequited love didn't last; that was a well-known fact. Two lovesick women would surely reach the point where they could laugh at themselves for being such fools; then they'd know that they were cured. But not just yet, though; for the moment it hurt enough to send hot tears trickling down her cheeks after all.

A week later, hands almost healed, she went back to school and, with Liam's Kate helping her at home and a walking-plaster on her ankle, Elspeth returned as well; life was back to normal again, except that Iain no longer visited the manse. Jamie went to the croft still, after school, and Andrew came back with news of the great progress that was being made; but whenever Liam and Kate came to supper there was always some good reason why Iain had to remain at home.

Meanwhile the autumn days moved slowly towards winter. Flowering heather purpled the hillsides, the long hours of daylight steadily shortened, and the waters of the Sound were now more often steel-grey than blue. Summer had become a memory. But there was something to look forward to – Liam and Kate's wedding, now planned for the end of November. At the manse one evening, he announced that not only his best man – Brett of course – but also his parents and his grandmother were planning to make the journey to Skye.

'Gran's on the wrong side of eighty,' he said with pride, 'but you'd think she was planning a hop down to Sydney! Ellie can't make it because she's heavily pregnant, but my sister and brother-in-law are there to take care of her.'

'You'll have a church ceremony I trust?' Janet said, not making a question of it. 'It should have been in Kilchrist Kirk, of course, not Broadford.'

'It will be,' he corrected with a grin. 'Iain's fixed it – even found a minister to tie the knot – and Kate's planning on fifteen bridesmaids; her entire class, with Fee among them of course. She says she can't have one without the others, and they're all to wear what they like. Should be interesting!'

Fee's dress, as the wedding day approached, was sketched, decided on, and changed a dozen times; but at last, cut out of pale-blue taffeta and sewn by Janet's expert hand, it was something for Fee to stroke each night before she went to sleep, so beautiful did she know it to be.

A spell of wild weather caused anxiety, but it blew itself

out over the mainland, and by the time Liam's family arrived some soft, calm days were forecast – the best they could hope for at the tag-end of November.

The next day, the eve of the wedding, Louise went down-stairs early as usual to give Macgregor his first morning dash round the garden. She was startled to find someone there – a slightly older, leaner version of Liam, but with a smile all his own.

'G'day, my dear,' said Brett's remembered voice. 'I can't tell you how good it feels to be back here.' He held out his hands and she hurried forward to kiss him.

'It's lovely to see you,' she said, 'but I thought you'd still be sound asleep after that journey.'

'I wanted to look at Jamie's vegetables, and to stretch my legs – I hate aeroplanes!' His hands rested gently on her shoulders. 'How have you been? We love your letters, but reckon you leave out all the bad bits.'

'There aren't any bad bits now,' she insisted. 'We're fine. And we love having Liam here. You must be sad at losing him to Skye.'

Brett shook his head. 'I wanted him to stay – just so one of us could be here.' His hands moved down to grasp hers. 'He told us about the scare on the moun-tain.'

'All forgotten now. I want news of Ellie. It's sad not to have her here, but she's got the best of reasons for being at home.'

'She thinks so too.' Brett hesitated, choosing words more carefully than usual. 'We're happy together – I mention it in case you're afraid we might not be. Marriage suits us both very well.'

'I'm glad,' Louise said with conviction, 'that's all I need to know.'

His eyes examined her face – thinner than he remem-bered, something sad about its expression when she forgot to school it into serenity? No bad bits, she'd said; he doubted that it was true. But she sounded cheerful enough when she spoke again.

'I hope Liam explained that you're all dining here tonight? Even Iain is coming for once – he doesn't normally visit us now.'

'Why's that?' Brett wanted to know. 'I reckoned he was part of the family.'

'My fault probably,' she had to admit. 'I can't help feeling that we owe him too much . . . that he wouldn't be here at all if it weren't for us. But my father and Jamie go to the croft – they say that Iain and Liam are transforming it.'

'That's true,' Brett agreed. 'I sneaked over there last night . . . wanted to make sure I'd done the right thing in sending Iain my little brother.'

She smiled at the adjective, but asked a serious question. 'Are you sure now?'

'Couldn't be more sure. Skye's changed Liam – made him grow up. Kate's had something to do with that, of course, but it's mainly the way Iain handles him; they make a good team.'

Louise merely nodded. 'Are you coming indoors for breakfast?'

'Love to, but I ought to get back – we're all going to meet Kate's family this morning. We'll see you this evening instead. You'll like my mother. Dad's not quite so easy, and Gran, well – she's what the Scots call a "mettlesome piece"!'

He saluted and walked away down the drive, leaving her grateful for the unexpected visit; they would meet simply as friends now, and not even Iain Macrae's watchful eye would see anything to take exception to.

With Elspeth, invited to complete the party, all the guests arrived on time that evening. Brett and Liam's mother was, as expected, kind and easy to like. Her husband, John, a sunburnt giant of a man, was slightly ill at ease with Andrew Maitland to begin with, but scholar and sheepman gradually discovered that they could talk to one another. The only surprise was the 'mettlesome piece', breeder of a tribe of tall men, who turned out to be all of five feet high, and obviously in the habit of ruling her family by force of character rather than by size.

She was introduced to Janet and Andrew, and then inspected Louise. 'So you're the "grey-eyed witch" I've heard so much about.' There was a hint of deliberate provocation in the remark that its victim decided to ignore.

'Broomstick not required tonight,' she answered with a smile. 'I'm only here as the chef, Mrs Macdonald.' But she added as an afterthought. 'I've heard a lot about you, too.'

Gran shot a suspicious look at her grandsons, both now smiling at the ceiling, then returned her fire to Louise. 'You don't have to believe all you hear from a couple of villains like these two.'

'They spoke of you with great affection,' Louise answered truthfully. 'Now, if you'll excuse me, it's time the chef returned to the kitchen.'

'Nice girl,' Gran remarked of no one in particular, and Andrew smilingly agreed.

The evening went smoothly after that, with Iain exerting himself to keep their elderly guest in order and so well entertained that, by the time dinner was over, she confided that she'd taken quite a fancy to him.

'You'll miss Liam, troublesome though I'll bet you good money he is. It's high time you got married yourself – a confirmed bachelor's a sad old thing.' The comment fell into the ill-timed silence that sometimes occurs among a group of people, but Mrs Macdonald smiled at their nervous faces. 'I'm giving Iain the benefit of an old woman's advice – you don't have to listen.'

She had age on her side, Louise thought, and his natural good manners – enough, perhaps to save her from being demolished. But he even smiled at her instead.

'I did try to marry,' he confessed calmly, 'but the girl I chose turned me down. What do you recommend next?'

In the electric silence that followed Gran thought about this for a moment. 'If she's the right girl, ask her again – you probably botched it first time round.'

Iain's glance skimmed Louise's downbent face and then returned to the small lady on his right, now watching him with the expectant eyes of an inquisitive robin.

'I expect you're right,' he agreed at last. 'I shall have to do better.'

Then, to the relief of everyone except Gran, who was greatly enjoying herself, Janet announced firmly that it was time to return to the drawing room. There, once coffee had been passed around, Brett took out his mouth organ and smiled at Louise. She nodded and went to the piano – the saving grace of music would somehow see this odd party to a harmonious end.

It was the simplest and nicest of weddings the following day. The church organ had already been removed, but the pews were still in place, and, since no one minded where they sat, as many people were crammed in behind the bridegroom and his family as there were on the other side of the aisle.

Kate, serious and beautiful in a long, white dress, was led in by an enchanting, rainbow coloured flock of small bridesmaids who parted in front of the minister to allow her to stand beside Liam. Louise did her best to concentrate on the solemn words of the marriage service, and to smile at Fee, who occasionally forgot the importance of the occasion enough to turn round and wave at her aunt. But as often as she commanded herself to forget the previous evening, her mind returned to it again. It had meant nothing at all – a courteous man indulging a tiresome old lady; or perhaps it had meant that Iain Macrae's 'right' woman, in Canada or wherever she might be, still hadn't been forgotten; or . . . but that was as far as the unholy turmoil in her mind would take her. And now Kate and Liam turned to face the congregation as man and wife, and began to move towards the church door, to the music of the pipers waiting outside. The service which she'd largely failed to register was over.

A splendid ceilidh at the Clan Donald Centre that evening rounded off the festivities. Then Liam and Kate drove up to Uig the following morning to catch the ferry to Lewis for a brief honeymoon, and the Macdonalds said goodbye to the family at the manse. It was time for life to return to its normal, peaceful routine.

Twenty-Seven

Wintry weather was setting in early; the Cuillins' high peaks were already capped with snow as Christmas approached, and even Elspeth had to admit that the hill-walking season was over. She never talked about Iain – living alone again at the croft now that Liam and Kate occupied a cottage near by – and Louise taught herself to accept that it was exactly how he wanted his life to be. He'd listened politely to an old woman's misguided advice, but that was all . . . end of story. What she had to do herself was bury heartache deep enough, smile cheerfully enough, and wait for unwanted, unrequited love to die of sheer neglect. It couldn't feed for ever, could it, on the scraps of news that Jamie brought back from the croft? The dark afternoons curtailed his daily visits, but there were still the weekends. He loved the animals – cows now replacing sheep in his affections – and seemed very drawn to the trees that Iain was planting.

'I shall make a forest when I grow up,' he announced to Louise one day, 'and then I'll live in the middle of it with Macgregor . . . but you and Fee and Gramps and Aunt Janet can visit me, of course.'

She thanked him gravely, but he hadn't quite finished with the subject. 'Did you know that Skye once had lots and lots of trees that stupid people cut down? Iain says that when his ancestors arrived in Canada they called it "Tir nan craobh", the land of the tree, 'cos they weren't used to seeing them by then.'

'Iain says' were how many of Jamie's conversations began, but for news that didn't relate to the farm she had to rely on her father or Liam and Kate. Iain, it seemed, was already deeply involved in the island's farming industry, and becoming a spokesman for his crofting friends. Work on converting the kirk had already begun and, in short, said Liam, there weren't enough hours in the day for all that had to be done. In short, Andrew thought, but didn't say, Iain Macrae seemed to be a man driven by the need to fill some terrible emptiness in his life. But it was Janet who pointed out one day that the same determination never to have time to stand and stare filled his daughter as well.

Andrew stared at her, afraid that she might be right. 'I know she's very busy always but . . . unhappy would you say?'

Janet nodded. 'Missing her old life,' she said briefly, 'but I don't know what we can do about it; the time to send her back to London was months ago. It's too late now.'

'Shall I . . . tackle her?' he asked hesitantly.

'She'll smile and say she's got to go and coach her choir – Kilchrist is to hear Christmas carols sung as they should be this year by pure children's voices.'

'I could talk to Drusilla when she comes,' Andrew suggested as a last resort.

'*If* she comes; I doubt that she will myself,' his sister maintained in the voice of one who was rarely wrong.

But she was wrong this time; the day before Christmas Eve her ex-sister-in-law reached Mallaig by train, and Louise took the children on a cold ferry trip across the Sound to meet her and bring her back to the manse.

'Worth every minute of that appalling journey,' Drusilla announced with her lovely smile as she walked in. 'My dears, I'm so glad to be here.' Her charm worked, Louise reflected, because she always meant what she said.

Andrew, knowing it too, held out both hands in welcome. 'We've had the nativity play and Louise's carol concert – both lovely, I have to say – but now it really feels like Christmas!'

Jamie also agreed, having achieved with his grandmother's arrival his ambition to sleep with Macgregor in
the back porch, but his cup of happiness overflowed when
he woke in the morning to find the garden white with snow.
He broke the news at once to Macgregor that their help
would be needed to bring Iain's sheep down to food and
shelter, and, barely waiting to finish the bowl of porridge
Louise insisted on, he and the dog were out of the house
before the others came downstairs. She watched them run
across the fields to the croft where happiness lay, and with
all her heart she longed to be running with them; but what
she had to do instead was lay the breakfast table; the
common round, the daily routine – that was what kept
heartache under bearable control.

That evening they were bidden to introduce Drusilla
to Kate's family – Iain would be there too, Liam had
reported – but Louise had been firm about not leaving
the children alone in the house. She waved the others
off, settled the excited children in their beds, and then
sat down, thankful to be alone – for an hour or so there
was no one she need smile at or talk to. But the doorbell rang almost at once and she went to answer it,
wondering what her father had forgotten to take with him
apart from his latch-key.

It was Iain Macrae who stood there, but she hadn't
conjured him up out of a fevered imagination; he was real
with fresh snow falling on his dark hair, and brightly-
wrapped parcels sheltered beneath his coat.

'Jamie went off without these so I'm playing Father
Christmas; I took the chance that that might make me
welcome.'

She could still manage to smile after all. 'It's kind of
you, but aren't you expected at the MacNeish's party?'

Iain shook his head. 'I cried off, I'm afraid. If you don't
invite me in I must return to my lonely hearth – doesn't
that move you to pity?'

She wasn't prepared with an excuse to send him away,
and something in his voice hinted that loneliness might

be real; perhaps even a man who normally embraced solitude might be regretting for once that he was on his own.

'It's Christmas Eve,' she conceded. 'I could offer you
a dram of my father's whisky, before your hearth beckons
again.'

Led into the firelit drawing room that smelled of beeswax
polish and pine cones, he glanced round appreciatively.
'Nice,' he murmured, 'just as Christmas used to be long
ago.'

He accepted the glass she offered him and then spoke
in a different tone of voice. 'Jamie didn't leave the presents behind – I wanted an excuse to come when the others
wouldn't be here. Andrew's worried about you – Janet,
too, I think. They reckon you miss your London life.'

'They're wrong,' she insisted quietly. 'I scarcely
remember it now. If I'm not merry as a grig the whole
time it doesn't mean that I'm not content to be here. Nor
does it mean that I'm pining like some Victorian damsel
for Brett Macdonald. I know you find it hard to believe,
but I'm truly glad that he and Ellie are happy together.'

He accepted the reproach this time. 'I know that now.
Forgive me, please.'

She risked a glance at his face and saw entreaty there
and humility. Confused by that discovery as she was, one
thing was certain: the detached observer of other people's
follies had somehow become just as vulnerable as she was
herself to hurt and loss, and even no longer minded that
she knew it.

'Louise, listen to me, please,' he insisted gently. 'When
my mother died I vowed never to trust happiness again –
try to keep it, I decided, and it would disappear. I would
become a self-sufficient man, no attachments needed. You
destroyed that comforting little illusion, but I couldn't bring
myself to admit it, even when I asked you to marry me.
Mrs Macdonald was right – I almost made sure you'd turn
me down, so as *not* to have to admit it.'

Louise shook her head. 'She's an opinionated old lady
much too prone to give advice – all her family say so!'

'But the advice was good all the same. I nearly took it then and there but I was afraid you'd think that I was simply embarrassing you in front of the others. If I ask now and put the truth into words this time – that the need is all mine, not yours – will you try not to turn me down?'

She closed her eyes for a moment, dazzled by a glimpse of happiness that shone like a will o'the wisp far ahead, beautiful but deceptive and surely unreal. If she reached out for it wouldn't that brightness disappear as well?

'You spoke to Elspeth once about the wrong woman being worse than no one at all,' she said gravely. 'I understood what that meant; you'd referred once to someone in Canada whom I guessed you couldn't ever replace. It seemed to explain why you were now willing to take us – the Maitlands – on; at least you could be of help, especially to Jamie, and your life wouldn't be all waste. I've been deeply grateful for that but it didn't seem enough to marry on, and still doesn't.'

Iain got up and came to kneel by her chair. 'Dear heart, there never was anyone in Canada; the woman I talked about was my disapproving stepmother! I only know now what you imagined to be the truth because Elspeth has been generous enough to tell me about your conversation up on the hill that day – she called it her Christmas present to us both. She thought you were right until the night the Macdonalds were here; then she saw me look at you and guessed the truth – there'd never been, never would be any woman but you.'

Her eyes searched his face and understanding was clear at last. 'So all these months I've been wilfully blind and stupid, grateful for your help but resenting it because I was afraid it was born of professional habit, instead of love.'

'Blind, I'll allow; stupid not,' he said gently. 'I've been the fool, refusing to admit that I followed you out of Fort William that morning because my heart, at least, knew that where you went I'd have to go too.' Then his fingers tilted up her chin. 'You haven't given me an answer – is that any way to treat a desperate man?'

She still hesitated, even now not quite sure. 'Iain, is the man desperate enough to take on Jamie and Fee as well? You might feel that they should stay here, but I couldn't leave them behind . . .'

He laid gentle fingers on her mouth, interrupting what else she might say. 'My love, I can't imagine your life without them – of course they'd come. I'll even take Macgregor as well! *Now* could you bring yourself to say yes?'

She did her best to look solemn. 'Well, let me see . . . I suppose I must, because you might never ask me again, and how else would I get to live in that lovely . . . ?'

His arms pulled her close, and what else she might have said was lost against his mouth. Released at last, she smiled unsteadily. 'I thought I'd lied about you very convincingly to Elspeth, but obviously not! In a perfect world everyone would be happy, but I'm being given my heart's desire and she is not; it seems very unfair when she deserves happiness so much.'

Iain gently smoothed her ruffled hair. 'My dear, she's had time enough to learn that life *isn't* fair. What we *can* do, we will – offer her always our friendship and affection.'

Louise nodded, knowing how futile it was to say that she felt guilty about a sadness she could do nothing to change. Instead, she returned to the easier subject of themselves. 'The family will be back soon . . . shall we not announce anything just yet? I need time to get used to my rather dismal prospects being so dramatically changed!'

'We won't say a word, my dearest, if that's what you want, but you mustn't smile like that if we're to keep them in the dark!'

The sound of car doors shutting outside brought him to his feet, and when the others walked in they were sitting with the decorous width of the hearth between them. It was Janet who took the time to stare at them and then broke the silence first.

'Andrew, I think we should telephone Australia in the morning,' she announced briskly.

He looked surprised but willing. 'To wish the Macdonalds a happy Christmas you mean?'

'Well yes, of course; but Mrs Macdonald will want to know that Iain has taken her advice.'

Mystified by the reference to someone she didn't know, Drusilla waited for Andrew to explain. It took him a moment to recall an old lady's Delphic oracle perform-ance at their pre-wedding dinner party; and then under-standing dawned, and he held out his hands to Louise and Iain.

'My dears, I'm so very glad,' he said simply, then turned to smile at Drusilla. 'Come and congratulate your daughter and your future son-in-law!'

She was doing just that when a small tousle-haired, pyjama-clad figure wandered in from the porch. 'You're making a lot of noise,' he said plaintively, 'and why are you all kissing each other?'

Louise did her best to explain. 'It's nearly Christmas Day,'

'And your aunt has just agreed to marry me,' Iain said to make matters clear.

Jaime stared at Louise with suddenly anxious eyes. 'Does that mean you'll go to live at the croft, or the kirk when it's ready?' She nodded, unable to prevent what she knew he'd say next 'Would . . . would there be room for Fee and me as well?'

'If Grandpa and Aunt Janet can spare you, all the room in the world,' she agreed gently.

He gave her his brief, rare grin but went to stand beside Janet Maitland, and gently touched her hand. 'It's just that Macgregor's more used to living on a farm, Aunt Janet; otherwise we *could* stay here.'

Louise found that she was holding her breath, but after a moment her aunt answered as gravely as Jamie had spoken.

'You're right,' she said. 'We have to think of Macgregor; there's no doubt he'll be happier at the croft. But you'll come and visit us, won't you?'

'Every day I 'spect,' Jamie said, 'just to make sure you and Grandpa are all right.' Then, as the long case clock in the hall struck midnight, he looked again at Louise. 'Listen, now it *is* Christmas Day.'

'So it is,' she agreed unsteadily, 'and "joy cometh in the morning" just as the angels foretold.'